XENO'S PARAGON

MISSION 3

BLACK OCEAN: PASSAGE OF TIME

J.S. MORIN

Magical Scrivener Press
www.magicalscrivener.com

Publisher's Note: This is a work of fiction. Names, characters, places, and incidents are a product of the author's imagination. Locales and public names are sometimes used for atmospheric purposes. Any resemblance to actual people, living or dead, or to businesses, companies, events, institutions, or locales is completely coincidental.

Ordering Information: Special discounts are available on quantity purchases by corporations, associations, and others. For details, contact the publisher at the address above.

J.S. Morin — First Edition

ISBN: 978-1-64355-995-7

Printed in the United States of America

XENO'S PARAGON
MISSION 3

THE WALLS GLEAMED white and clean and gave the impression that Jessie Ramsey was somewhere that cared about doing things the right way. She sat with hands folded in her lap atop freshly laundered pants. All of her felt refreshed, from her undergarments to the properly knitted bones and teeth and ligaments that no longer ached as a background sensation to her every motion. Only a nagging worry of waiting for the gotcha to sneak up and ambush her kept Jessie from truly relaxing.

"You should be receiving an invoice from Planetary Medical Services. Don't be alarmed. Just ignore it. Once your asylum application is approved, all your medical expenses will be taken care of." The laaku on the far side of the pristine plasticized steel desk gave a wide, reassuring smile. The nameplate read Klaree of Kethlet, and it sat between a stationary holo depicting a family of five and a propped-up plaque identifying the owner as Employee of the Year 2590 for the Ministry of Immigration and Refugee Processing, Kethlet location.

"What are my odds?" Jessie inquired. She didn't want to

get her hopes up. It wasn't as if she'd needed organ replacement, just a basic overhaul of shoddy, first-aid-grade care and a replacement hormone regulator. Yet any expense was going to put her into debt at this point.

"Of what?" Klaree asked. "Oh, you mean of your asylum application being accepted. Don't worry. Seriously. Don't. An Earth Navy vessel literally broadcasted a demand for your surrender over an open comm channel. You'll be getting top-listed as soon as I finish filling out the forms."

Klaree tapped on a datapad as she breezed through basic questions that ranged from personal history to job skills to political affiliations.

"Logged more hours in astral as a kid than most long-haul freighter captains."

"Planet I spent the most time on? Dunno. Earth, I guess. Basic training was the longest I ever spent in one place."

"Never did the politics thing. Yeah. No, really. I enlisted without ever registering to vote."

"I know my military record is classified, but I was—"

"Oh, we have your records," Klaree cut in. Jessie blinked. "How is this surprising? Until the Dissolution, we had full access to covert ops personnel."

Jessie leaned forward, trying to surreptitiously peer at the laaku's datapad. "How much you got in—?"

"Everything. Right up to the court martial in absentia after your magi-temporal incident."

At hearing that, Jessie cringed. She waggled a tentative finger toward the datapad. "Mind if I see?"

The ministry agent shrugged and turned the pad 180 degrees as she slid it across the desk. Jessie gave a cursory glance over the details. By the end, swiping down quickly as she skimmed, she found herself shaking her head and muttering, "Those assholes."

Klaree retrieved the device when Jessie lifted her gaze. "Not my place to judge, but I tend to agree. They made it sound like you volunteered for a risky magical experiment."

"It was *not* by choice."

"Of course." Klaree tapped away on her pad.

"What're you writing?"

"Oh. Nothing to concern yourself with. Internal ministry datawork. Sorry." She looked up and cleared her throat. "So, a few basics. Once your application is approved, you'll be assigned standard housing in the refugee district. Clothing and meals are provided at no charge within the zone. Security is for your protection; you're welcome to leave and re-enter freely, but for a high-profile case such as yourself, it's highly advised that you remain within the secure zone."

Jessie smirked. It was almost sweet of them. "I can look after myself."

Klaree tapped the datapad with the backs of her fingers. "Hey, it's boilerplate. Same spiel for youth pastors, journalists, and covert operations specialists. Bear with me. Where was I... Oh. Here we go. Um, clothing. You can wear anything you like, but blue and red are generally considered political colors these days, especially when worn on shirts, hats, and prominent accessories."

"I was just on Echo Niner. The local Mars-leaning warlord was big on blue."

Klaree set down the datapad, laced the fingers of her upper hands, and gave Jessie the Disapproving Mom look. "We're talking intragalactic politics here, not a game of Parcheesi with blasters. Wear whatever you like, but be prepared for fistfights and nights in protective lockup if you parade around in red track suits."

Jessie scoffed. "Like I'd go red."

"Or blue. Look, I'm just here to help you through the process."

"Sorry." Jessie was too used to picking at the edges of rules and systems.

Klaree flashed a tight-lipped smile. "Very well. As implied, you don't need to work while you're here. Your basic needs will be provided for. The refugee zone includes a community center, theaters, museums, vocational training, and plenty of outdoor space. But if you like, you can find work and plan for a future beyond the zone."

"Vocational training?"

"With your background, corporate security or consulting could put you in high demand. However, given your current status, you may prefer something with less exposure."

"Maybe...."

"Well, that's about it. The rest you can find on the local omni or stop by to ask anyone in the ministry for assistance." Klaree opened a desk drawer, pulled out another datapad, and slid it over to Jessie.

Jessie turned the datapad over in her hands. She wasn't one to drool over A-tech toys, but this was beyond top-of-the-line from five years ago. "JaighTech? Wow."

"They're a sponsor. Consider it a present for one of the birthdays you missed."

Jessie snickered without glancing away from the screen as she flew through the baseline setup and personalization script.

"Any questions?"

Jessie blinked and left the datapad to wonder about her musical tastes. "Um. Yeah. Actually. Why you guys still operating all in English? I get it having a human-speaker interviewing me, but all the signs the whole way here are still in my species' language."

Klaree sighed. "You wouldn't believe the number of

humans who don't even know laaku have languages of our own. But the answer to your question is twofold. We're still part of a multi-species alliance, and English is by far the most commonly spoken among all the member races of LoIP. But worse, I don't think most of *us* had realized how many laaku didn't speak even Kejathi."

"Wow. And I felt like a slacker barely knowing how to buy breakfast in Kejathi."

"There's a committee to develop a true galactic language. Pronounceable by all species. No inherent biases or cultural underpinnings."

"Nice," Jessie replied, not knowing how else to respond. She cleared her throat. "Um. When should I expect to hear about my asylum approval?"

Klaree grinned. "I'd been trying to stall you on that question. Usually, it takes—" The laaku social worker's datapad dinged. "Aha."

"Aha, what?"

"I told you I was top-listing you." She stood and offered a handshake across the desk. Jessie shook, still slightly confused. "Congratulations. You're officially a Phabian resident under the protection of the League of Independent Planets."

Jessie stood, unsure what to do. She had plans for how to survive until her application had been bounced around enough to find someone with the authority and courage to take a chance on sheltering her from Earth's predations. "You... you couldn't have finished that application fifteen minutes ago."

"Welcome to a new way of doing business. This is Phabian. We're done fucking around."

As Eric entered the interview room, he noticed several things. For one, the room was exceptionally clean. Shiny, white walls looked freshly built just to greet him. The runes scrawled in long lines all around the room's perimeter caught his eye next. In the middle of the rather small office was a desk with a friendly-looking laaku waiting for him. But the final thing Eric noted was the presence of two ssentuadi flanking the door just inside the room.

Eric stuck out his tongue and waggled it at each of the door guards, then hissed a polite greeting. Both guards inclined their heads in acknowledgment.

"Didn't know you spoke the language," his interviewer commented as Eric sat down in the only chair available for him.

"I kept it brief. My pronunciation is a little horrific."

"Wizard Eric, do you understand what we're doing here today?"

"It's not *wizard*, actually. Just Eric is fine."

The interviewer fiddled with a datapad a moment. "My mistake, Mr. Ramsey."

"Eric. Like rice with the 'e' at the front but pronounced differently."

"As you prefer. Eric, do you know why you're here?"

Eric looked all around for clues but didn't spot anything that altered his initial impressions. "Well, based on the runes, I'd imagine you're worried I might break all the tech in a ten-block radius."

"A precaution. We don't have so many wizards come through here that we have gradations of interview room."

Eric nodded along. "Well, I wasn't planning to do any magic, so it shouldn't matter how pompous the runes look."

"As a general rule, we don't try to use technology to ID the magically proficient. So, we're going to run through a few quick questions."

"OK." This sounded easier than he'd been led to believe the asylum process would be. Figgy was going to get an earful for making him worry.

"Full name?"

He hadn't inflected his voice upward, which called into question the legitimacy of the query. Eric banked on this not being the kind of quiz with tricks like that and answered the implied "what is your" as if it had been tacked onto the beginning. "Eric Clapton Ramsey."

"Date of birth?"

"January 3rd."

"Year."

Eric huffed a sigh. "I was hoping you weren't going to ask that."

"It's a straightforward question."

"Yeah, but I traveled five years forward in time. I'm twenty-two years old. I think. But if that's true, did I drag my birth date forward with me? It was a clean five-year jump, so the date should have stayed put. But did I move the year?" He noticed the laaku tapping on his datapad. "What are you writing down?"

"It's basic math."

"Basic? My timeline has an aneurysm in it. I consulted a licensed philosopher and couldn't get a solid answer on what year I was born."

"We're calling it '64. On my authority."

A sigh left Eric sagging in his seat. "Thank you. I can't tell you how much of a relief that is."

"Indeed. ANYWAY, let's move on. Do you believe yourself to be the same Eric Ramsey sought by Earth's Convocation?"

Well, if that wasn't a nesting doll of a question... "How many of us are there?"

The interviewer—oh, there was a nametag on his desk; his

name was Gunthi—tapped away. "I'm jotting down a yes. Do you fear for your safety if you return to Earth?"

"I can't really say what they'll do to me."

"But you're afraid of it."

"I try not to be unduly biased against the unknown."

"But you fled your homeworld—"

"I've only lived on Earth for school."

"You fled your *species' ancestral homeworld* rather than find out."

Eric shrugged an indifferent affirmative. "I guess so. When you put it like that."

Gunthi stood and walked to the far wall of the room, taking his datapad with him. "Very well. It's all a formality anyway. Your request was pre-approved; I just needed to verify your identity." He touched a spot on the wall, and a previously invisible seam appeared as a panel opened. Gunthi tucked the datapad inside and shut it. "Now we're just going to perform a basic magical assessment."

"A test?"

"There's no pass or failure. More of a measurement."

The two ssentuadi approached. Gunthi reached into his desk and pulled out a fist-sized cube—his fist, not Gunthi's—upon which someone had carved a rune into each face.

"Alphabet blocks in Sanskrit?"

"Eric, these runes each represent a different level of influence. Try to see how many of them you can light. These two proctors will attempt to thwart your efforts."

"When do we start?"

"Any time you like."

Phabian, as a whole, was a wet wipe of a planet when it came to magic. It was soaked in science, spongy, resistant. Every arcane effort felt like you needed to rinse your brain afterward. Nevertheless, Eric lifted the cube and studied the faces. It was gibberish. Like trying to find literary merit in an eye chart. One of the runes, it seemed, was practically trying to light itself.

"Does speed matter?" He hadn't tried anything yet. He hoped his ssentuadi proctors knew that.

"No. Just light as many as you can."

"Do they get in trouble if I win?"

Gunthi shook his head. "This is just an assessment."

He said that, but Eric wondered if that was just for the sake of getting an accurate result. After all, if Gunthi admitted these two poor working wizards were one bad performance away from getting fired, maybe Eric would go easy on them. Or, maybe, because a lot of Convocation wizards hated the ssentuadi, Gunthi didn't want to rouse any latent bloodlust that might skew the results.

After a moment's debate where Eric tried to look puzzled by the cube, he finally just gave in and decided to let supernature take its course.

Just light them all. Not too bright; just enough to tell they're lit.

Gunthi gasped. The proctors hissed their surprise.

"What?" Eric asked as he set the cube down to balance precariously on one point. He gave a gentle twist to set it spinning, letting everyone see all six sides as it revolved. Then he noticed that Gunthi wasn't paying attention to the cube at all. Turning in his chair, he followed the gaze of the ssentuadi as well.

All the runes around the room were glowing.

"Dammit!" Eric exclaimed. "Sorry!"

Not those! Turn those off.

The runes in the wall went dark. A pop and crackle sounded from the far wall. Smoke leaked from the hidden panel, outlining the edges.

In a panic, Gunthi leapt into motion. He opened the hiding place and coughed as a billow of smoke escaped. When he pulled out the datapad, he held it between thumb and forefinger, scorched and blackened.

"Give it a minute," Eric said with a cringe. "Maybe it'll be OK."

Gunthi set the ruined device on his desk. "It happens. We're practically made of datapads around here."

Eric brightened. "Really?"

"No. Not really. But I'll requisition another and fill in your file from memory, along with the results of this assessment. You're free to go."

"Super!"

"However, there are some reporters who'd like to speak to you. Is that all right?"

"I'm all asylumed up, right?"

"Yes."

"Sure, then. Sounds like the least I can do."

The two proctors escorted him out a side door as Eric tugged the wrinkles from his shirt.

⬚

The interview room was a peculiar combination of cozy and huge. Eric's ssentuadi escorts guided him to a pair of plush chairs with a low circular table between them. One of the chairs contained a laaku with slicked-back scalp fur and a snazzy business suit. The other, he presumed, was for him. What seemed out of place were the rows upon rows of simpler chairs that rose like a wave ready to crash onto the low theater stage whereupon Eric's and the laaku's chairs rested.

A woman in a pink rhinestone jumpsuit with matching lower gloves bustled out, tapping at her datagoggles. They looked expensive, so Eric tried super hard not to do anything that might fuzzle them. "We're on in two minutes. Relax your instinct to blur the cameras. Sit. You can cross your legs or not, but don't sit with them spread. We're going for an all-ages rating, so anytime you curse, we're going to have to trim it from the galactic feed. Do you have an agent?"

"No."

"Blasty. Pablek, you good?"

"As always," the slick-furred laaku replied with an ease that sounded second nature to him.

As this exchange was going on, doors at the rear of the theater had opened, pouring in an audience comprised mainly of laaku but with a token human or tesud here and there.

"This interview is being filmed before a live studio audience?" Eric asked, suddenly very much aware of being the center of attention.

"No worries, kid," Pablek assured him. "Just focus on me and forget about the cameras."

"If I forget the cameras, they'll forget about me right back."

Pablek patted the air with a lower hand. "Granted, kid. Granted. Just make sure they can see you, and ignore the rest. After the first question or two, you'll get in the slot."

At the side of the stage, the woman in the pink jumpsuit stood on one hand, counting down from fifteen on her fingers. The last finger of the countdown descended like a headman's axe. It severed Eric's privacy in one clean blow.

Behind Eric and the host, a huge holo popped up, spelling out PABLEK in three-meter-tall letters.

"Welcome, Phabian and points beyond, to *Pablek Tonight*. I'm your host, Pablek of Everywhere. My guest tonight is a magical refugee from Earth and Mars. Caught between sides in the human civil war, he finds himself, like so many of his kind, coming to Phabian as his port in a storm.

Please give a warm, Pablek Tonight welcome to ERIC RAMSEY!"

The audience supplied the thunderous applause. Eric waggled a shy hand in response.

"Eric, tell us about your journey here. Trapped aboard a little-known space station. Blockaded by an Earth Navy destroyer. What was that like?"

Eric paused a moment, unsure how he was expected to answer. He was on a holovid show. Was he meant to be entertaining? "Like an off-campus kegger at Oxford when the police show up," Eric quipped.

There were a few nervous titters in the audience.

Pablek smiled. "I'm sure it was harrowing. That's why there were reportedly thirty-seven fatalities during the Earth Navy blockade of the station."

Oh, shit. "Really?"

"Official sources have no way to corroborate, but as someone who was there, were you witness to any of the carnage?"

Eric swallowed a lump in his throat. He looked into the audience to judge their reaction. Did they blame him? Was this some kind of gotcha show? Spotlights stung his eyes, and the crowd was little more than glare. "I... uh... there was a lot of chaos. Loads of running and loud noises. That sort of thing."

"And the body that was found in the pilot's seat of a Martian Circle hover, believed to be one of their tech liaisons. Care to comment on that?"

"His name was Damien. He helped us escape," Eric blurted. "He was terrified of what they might do to him, but he helped us anyway."

Presently, Damien owned and tended bar at the beachside tiki lounge where he met his third wife. If there was a time or a place to bring up *that* topic, Eric had yet to think of it.

Pablek leaned forward in his chair. "You have to admit, there's a trail of shattered lives in your wake, not all of which can be conclusively blamed on the forces pursuing you. Care to set the record straight?"

Did he? Accepting an errant premise was a mistake for a rookie debater. While Eric had never been good enough to make the Oxford squad, he wasn't about to lose a classical debate to a holovid presenter. "I don't think that's a fair assessment. A trail implies there was a line that follows one to the next. And while it's possible that ancillary lives might have been *lost*—and attribution for those losses is still an unsettled matter—I don't know that there are grounds for the presumption of shattering."

Pablek stood and strode to the front of the stage. "Let's open this up to the audience." He pointed into the crowd. Eric shaded his eyes with a hand and spotted a laaku woman as one of the show's assistants handed her a portable speaking wand. "You, ma'am. What's your question for Eric here?"

"How can we be sure it's safe to have you on Phabian? Everyplace else you've been is all violenced up."

Eric lowered his hand self-consciously. All eyes were on him. "Um. Maybe your personal safety is an illusion reinforced by the excellent reputation of Phabian Investigative Services. I'm philosophically opposed to violence, so you're probably safer with me here to stop it."

Pablek roved the front of the stage, selecting another questioner without a break. His next selection was a human woman.

"What would you say to the relatives of the victims of the Echo Niner riots?"

What an interesting and accusatory theoretical question. "I suppose, 'Hi, I'm Eric. Nice to meet you.'"

But Pablek didn't move on this time. The woman had a

follow-up, asked through gritted teeth. "My brother was Leffrey Koenig. He was murdered five days ago because *you* wouldn't turn yourself in."

"Any response?" Pablek prodded when Eric didn't say anything.

Eric slunk out of his chair. "I don't think this is what I signed up for." Come to think of it, he hadn't signed up for anything. Everyone around him had just presumed, herded, and coaxed him along like a lost farm animal. Now he was discovering that it was Market Day, and Erics were on the menu.

I rescind permission for pictures. Without any way to tell for sure, Eric figured that the universe was no longer allowing the holovid cameras to capture his likeness.

"Sorry, everyone. Carry on without me." He scurried toward the exit, stage right.

He dodged production crew who didn't dare impede him. Without knowing where he was heading, Eric made his way there with undue haste. Just as he left earshot, he heard Pablek recovering with friction-free aplomb.

"Well, I guess it's time to address the elephant in the room. Without further ado, the guest you've all been waiting to meet..."

Eric spared a glance over his shoulder back at the stage. He saw show crew carrying off the chair he'd used and four laaku carrying another seat easily four times its size out to replace it.

But his suddenly piqued curiosity didn't carry the message to his feet, and Eric rounded a corner, cutting off his view and presenting him with a door to someplace that promised to be quieter and more private. At this point, a starport terminal would have satisfied both qualities.

Right now, all Eric wanted was to find someone official and make sure he never had to do anything like that ever again.

Jessie exited the ministry and sucked in a huge breath of fresh air. Well, Phabian fresh, anyway. While there was technically nothing unhealthy in the air, it still carried a faint sniff of the pollutant neutralizers that counteracted the exhaust from billions of ion engines and outgassing from various industrial concerns planetwide. Nothing hinted at plants or animals or weather of any sort, but medically speaking, there was nothing *bad* in it.

The pedestrian mall felt like a refuge from the omnipresent aerial traffic throughout the planet. Jessie tucked her hands into her pockets and headed toward a multi-tiered fountain surrounded by a low wall. Plenty of other people—a mix of humans and laaku—had already taken up spots along the surrounding edge as seating, and it looked like as good a place as any to wait for Eric to finish up.

"You owe me a starship," a voice startled her from behind. Her hand only flinched a centimeter toward a blaster she wasn't carrying before logic took over and she identified the voice.

"Hey, Figgy. Insurance payout didn't cover everything?"

Her savior from the Echo Niner incident was a pace behind her. Lorenzo lounged casually against a decorative lamppost.

"The difference between a savvy businessman and a prisoner on an eighteen-month insurance fraud sentence is—"

"That asshole registered it before Earth Navy shot it up?"

"Can't claim insurance on a ship I didn't own," Figgy confirmed. "So, until I get a replacement ship, I'll be your new fur coat."

Jessie started walking backwards, heading the direction where her LoIP-issued datapad claimed she'd find her apartment. She could reconnect with Eric in the morning if she had to. "You realize this is more of a moral debt than a legally collectible one, right?"

Figgy followed, and Lorenzo fell in behind him like a bodyguard. "You're going to pull that card on me? After I literally saved your neck?"

"I seem to remember a lot of that plan being my idea. And you're forgetting the extra neck I saved." She hooked a thumb toward Lorenzo.

For the first time, Lorenzo spoke up. "To be fair, I was only in danger because of you."

"Authoritarians are running amok these days," Jessie countered, unwilling to bear full responsibility for Earth Navy's witch hunt. "You either turn into one of them or risk getting amokked on a little. I mean, thanks for not turning out to be some spineless bootlick, but I bailed your ass out. Debt settled."

"His maybe," Figgy said.

Jessie stopped within sight of the Ministry of Immigration and Refugee Processing's front door. If she kept going, she was committing to ditching Eric, possibly kicking off a worry spiral depending on how his interview went. His asylum case was even clearer than hers, and scuttlebutt was that Phabian was eager to bolster their magical resources. But nothing with wizards ever seemed that straightforward.

It was time to cauterize this wound.

"Look. I get it. But I'm in no position to get you a new ship. I've got a skill set better suited to stealing a vessel than buying one. Let's face it, good credit isn't one of my superpowers. But once I get my feet under me, I'll see what I can pull together."

"Seventy-five. Or two-ten in marbits."

Jessie suppressed an "oof" as that figure hit her in the gut. Maybe if she got in contact with Esper, that kind of money might fly. Other than that, she was looking at crime. "How much you get for that old freighter again?"

"A convenience fee," Figgy replied with more steel in his voice than she'd heard before. Jessie hadn't realized how much he'd been betting on his buyer not making the sale official.

"Fine," Jessie snapped. "Now get off my case."

"I'll be on-world as long as you are..." With that, the laaku turned and ambled away in the other direction.

Lorenzo lingered. "You got somewhere to crash? My place is only about twenty minutes from here."

Jessie blinked. "Well, they did set me up with a free apartment. And they harped on the security around here. Feel like an asshole if I ditch the secure zone my first night and— wait, you have your own apartment here?"

"Live here. Since before the war. But I get it."

Blood running hot, Jessie realized she had an opportunity here. "You know, I'm feeling tip-top. Didn't want to get the detox until I knew my expenses were covered, so I can still feel a little buzz lingering from that Reck-it-All. Want to help me get it out of my system?"

"Wow."

"Wow, what?"

"Does that actually work?"

Jessie glanced aside and gave a sheepish shrug. "Yeah? More of a last-call kinda thing. Make you a deal. I may not have starship cash on me, but I've got pocket money. Quote me a number of beers, and I'm buying."

Lorenzo snickered. "Just coming right out and saying you want to get me drunk and take advantage of me?"

"I'll match you, drink for drink."

"Somehow, I think I'd be the one in the detox wing if I matched beers until you were hammered. Besides, beer's not easy to find around here. And we're ten hours off ship time. I'm not really ready to call it a day."

Fuck that transport. Jessie had slept eighteen-hour days to help speed her recovery. Her bio-chrono was all off anyway. Unfortunately, she was out of arguments.

"All right. See you around, then."

"Adios."

Jessie raised a hand in a wave just before Lorenzo turned.

Eric was on his own. Phabian wasn't dumb enough to turn a wizard loose to wander without assistance.

She was going to find her new apartment and find out just how cold the shower ran.

A door slid open, and light poured into the tiny closet in which Eric Ramsey sat with his knees hugged to his chest. He peered up to see a laaku in a security guard uniform and an auburn-haired woman in the Earth-styled robes of a working wizard.

The wizard looked to the guard. "Thanks. I'll take it from here."

"I'm more of a 'he' than an 'it,'" Eric replied glumly. "Unless you're talking about my friend here." He patted the inert automaton that loomed over him. The janitorial robot hadn't made a peep since Eric snuck inside with it, but that didn't mean it wasn't just both patient and polite.

"Eric Ramsey, my name is Hecuba Tennyson." She extended a hand to help him to his feet.

"Like the queen of Troy?" he asked.

She grinned. "Most people ask about the poet." Eric accepted the hand, and she pulled him upright.

"You're not taking me back to the public inquisition, are you? If so, I think I might stay."

"That bad, was it?"

Eric nodded.

"I don't watch Pablek, but I heard they'd set up a special theater for him. He's really popular, but I'm not into that sort of thing."

Eric fell into step beside Hecuba as she led off in a direction he hadn't been yet. "What sort of thing?"

She shrugged. "Popular things, I guess. It's all just so crass and shallow and... and mean-spirited."

Eric looked all around as they strolled through the building, reading names of agencies and services provided by the ministry. "Why would they let him in here, then? Everyone else has seemed pretty nice so far, present company included."

Hecuba blushed slightly. "Well, I mean. Thanks. But he's a big deal. And there's some high-profile xeno who arrived a few weeks ago who's been a big hit. I think you were supposed to be the appetizer or something."

"Warmup act," Eric corrected. "My dad's a musician. That's what they call it when you bring out someone less interesting to give a crowd something to compare you to."

"Your dad was big enough that he had a warmup band?"

"No. He *was* the warmup band. Early Data stuff. They have it in museums on, like, corduroy placemats, but my dad and his friends play it live."

"That sounds fun." Hecuba had a way of smiling with just her voice. Eric didn't need to glance over to know the expression she wore, yet he did anyway just to double-check. The starlight caught her eye as they stepped out the main doors and into the Phabian night.

"It got repetitive. And scratchy. Imagine listening to music that sounds like it can't clear its throat but keeps trying. But it's like holiday songs; they may not be *good* good, but Dad's music sounds like home."

"That's sweet. I grew up on Earth. My family tree has a few tech liaisons, but my older sister was the first one to actually get her degree in magic. I was a terramancer—"

"Wow!" Eric's eyes widened.

"—'s assistant. Until the war broke out. The terramancers on my team defected to Mars, but I couldn't see myself taking either side. So..." She shrugged.

"Phabian's nice. I've never lived here, but I've visited a few times."

They strolled through a promenade paved in artificial stone. Eric dragged his fingers through the pool of a fountain they passed by. Real water. Not science fakery. He flicked droplets from his fingers and wiped his hand dry on his pants.

"Yeah, it's real water," Hecuba confirmed. "Most other stuff around here's fake, from the stone tiles to the lamplight. But more of the amenities are real where we're going."

"Where are we going? You never said."

"Oh. They were supposed to. It's not a secret or anything. We're heading to the Wizards' Quarter. You've got an apartment waiting for you."

"Oh." Eric craned his neck to look back as they left the refugee center behind them. "I'm supposed to be meeting up with my sister."

"It's late. She's probably already found her accommodations. Don't worry. It's Phabian. Nothing bad happens here. Someone will take care of her."

"Oh, I'm not worried about her, per se. I'm worried about her worrying about me. If that makes sense."

"I get that."

They turned at an intersection. Despite the late hour, they were far from the only ones partaking of the night air. "Are there a lot of wizards here?" Eric swept a hand to indicate the varied pedestrians sharing their stroll.

"Here here, or just on Phabian?"

A solid point for clarification. It was so easy talking to wizards, all things considered. "The refugee district."

"Oh, loads. I mean, not on the scale of Boston or Shanghai Prime. But there's plenty of work planetside and not enough laaku wizards to do it."

Eric fought back a laugh at the notion of laaku wizards. It wasn't nice. It was mildly xenoist. But his time at Oxford had really hammered home the species-wide ineptitude of laaku when it came to magic. You hardly saw a laaku on campus unless they were part of the maintenance staff.

"I saw that. Go ahead. Chuckle. But I've met a few who aren't half bad. None of them are candidates for Grand Council—setting politics aside, even—but, oh, wait, here we are!"

Hecuba stopped in front of a short tall building. There was no other description that seemed to fit. On most colonies, it would have numbered among the largest of structures, stretching close to twenty stories, if Eric was counting the floors correctly. Yet on Phabian, even with such close proximity, true skyscrapers loomed over it, glowering down from blocks away with heights in the middling triple digits.

"It looks nice," Eric commented politely as they traversed the soulless, blank-walled entryway and headed for a set of double doors that slid apart to reveal a lift car.

Hecuba stepped into the lift without hesitation, so Eric felt confident in following her in. "We got you a nice tenth-floor unit with a courtyard view."

Eric didn't respond instantly, preoccupied with the dial set into the left wall of the lift car. It was big and clunky but didn't look overly technological. Though the laaku were known to produce cunning facsimiles of many substances, this dial looked like real, polished granite. As soon as the doors closed,

Hecuba twisted the dial from L to 10. Seconds later, the doors opened onto a corridor.

"Wow."

"I know, it's a little different from the technologists' version, but this is—"

"A gravity-alignment lift. They had one at the Order of Hephaistos building near Oxford."

Hecuba made an impressed little grunt as she led them down the corridor. "Forgot you had a fancy education. Still, most people can't tell." She stopped at a door on the left side of the hall, marked 1007. "This is yours."

She stood aside and gestured to the doorknob. Figuring that this would have been an awkward setup for a booby trap, Eric turned the knob and found it unlocked. A tingle in his hand suggested that maybe, to anyone else, it would have been.

Inside, the accommodations were simple, yet cozy looking. There was an easy chair sitting under a pull-chain lamp, an empty bookshelf, and a writing desk.

Hecuba pointed to a side door. "Bedroom's in there. That's a washroom. You've got your own." She indicated the other door on the left wall.

"Nice," Eric commented, peering in and examining both the single-occupant bed and poofy bedspread atop it. Moonlight streamed in through the window, whose curtains were parted.

"And *this* is your balcony." Throwing wide a matching set of full-height curtains in the living room, Hecuba revealed a sliding door, which she proceeded to open. Cool air breezed in. She stepped out into the night, and Eric followed. "Hope you're not afraid of heights."

Eric leaned over the railing, peering straight down at the courtyard they'd crossed on the way here. "Not really." He swept the full spectrum of his view to take a quick inventory.

But upward was a sight that caught his eye and held it. A pale, patchy, white-and-silver orb hung overhead, glinting in reflected light. "Whoa, that's the biggest space station I've ever seen."

"That's no space station. It's the moon."

Eric rubbed his eyes. "Really?"

"Lovingly reassembled and patched and currently home to twenty million. Once it's finished, they're planning to have nearly two billion people living on or in it. The Lunar Reclamation Project has been big news everywhere that's not currently at war."

"Missed a lot these past five years."

Hecuba laid a hand on his shoulder, warm even through his shirt. "Well, you're going to get caught up quick. You'll be working with my division starting tomorrow."

"I have a job?"

"Are you independently wealthy?"

"I'm not even dependently wealthy."

"Then, yes, you have a job. Look, they tell you that everything's provided here, but that's only if all you ever want to do in life is eat, sleep, and wander around doing nothing, buying nothing, owning nothing."

That sounded idyllic, but he didn't want to be rude. Besides, the job might be fun on its own merits.

"OK. When do I start?"

"Tomorrow morning. I'll come pick you up."

"How early? I want to try to find my sister for breakfast."

"Oh. You'll have plenty of time. We work 10 a.m. to 3 p.m. with an hour and a half for lunch. I mean... we're still *wizards*."

Jessie's new apartment was in Human Accommodation Building 06 of the Kethlet Refugee Security Zone. It was, to sum up in a single word: efficient. Her tour started and ended at the opening of the door to the common hallway. From there, she identified the couch that pulled out into a bed, the wall-mounted food processor, and the corner shower stall with the fold-down toilet seat and sink.

"Cozy," she pronounced it. Satisfied, the laaku building superintendent left her to settle in.

When the door shut behind her, Jessie dropped her welcome package on the couch and poked through it. Halfway between a backpack and duffel bag in size, its squoosh was a hint at the contents. To her utter lack of surprise, she found a set of towels and two full sets of clothing that included a t-shirt, sweatpants, socks, undergarments, a zippered light jacket, and slip-on sneakers. Everything worn as an outer layer was a drab light blue, including the sneakers. Her t-shirts, socks, panties, and bras were all stark white. On each individual piece of clothing, a discreet "P-A-L" logo boasted about the largess of Phabian Athletic Leisurewear.

Jessie took that icy cold shower she'd promised herself. Despite being thin enough to stuff into a care package, the towels were soft and absorbent. Rather than tap the button to extend her couch to bed size, Jessie got dressed.

All of it fit like she hadn't stolen it from random strangers.

Studying herself in the large mirror built into the outer wall, she had one intrusive thought. "We'd better not be color coded."

Growing up on starships, Jessie's threshold for claustrophobia took a lot more than a cramped apartment to trigger. But she knew herself to be an outlier. It wasn't like her laaku hosts to overlook that kind of potential issue. Taking a guess, she tapped the mirror.

Instantly, the reflection vanished, and Jessie was looking down at the pedestrian square some eight stories below. "That's more like it."

Behind her, the couch silently reminded her of its duality.

The problem was, Jessie wasn't tired.

On the contrary, she felt *right* for the first time since coming to this future. Security. Food supply. Medical access. Base of operations. Eric was similarly taken care of. Phabian was a sigh of relief, apart and apathetic toward the grievances between Earth and Mars.

Well, maybe apathy wasn't quite right. But LoIP wasn't taking sides in the civil war, wasn't handing over deserters, and wasn't affiliated with the Convocation. That was what mattered.

The shower hadn't cooled the burning inside her.

Jessie was wired. Kethlet and the transport that brought her from Echo Niner were ten hours offset. This felt more like getting off duty early than anything resembling a bedtime.

Before she thought better of it, she zipped up her jacket and set out to explore the refugee nightlife.

Phabian never slept. If she was so inclined, there was a whole planet out there. However, she stuck to her self-promise not to test the limits of LoIP security just yet. Cloying safety could smother her for a few nights at least.

What Jessie needed was a drink.

And some company. Phabian was legendary for its love of tech and gadgetry, but sometimes she just craved human contact.

It took half an hour wandering, not wanting to rely on her datapad for directions, before Jessie stumbled onto a dance club within the refugee zone. It had a Kejathi name in a stylized font she couldn't read and probably wouldn't have understood if she did. But there was music, and it thumped a hypnotic beat that overwhelmed the ear. Synthesized melodies filled the space where conversation might linger. There was no cover charge, and Jessie wandered through dazed, slack-eyed revelers, wondering what chemicals were popular around here.

Seating was hard to come by. Red faux vinyl stuck out like a beacon wherever the muted attire of the partiers didn't block it. Yet travel through the cavernous club was neither quick nor direct, constantly dodging semi-comatose dancers. Four times she spotted a place to park herself and take in the vibe; four times someone got to it first.

Instinct screamed methods to exterminate the opportunists. Those instincts needed to calm the fuck down. She didn't need a checklist of ways to snap a neck, improvise a blade, or drag someone to an unattended lift shaft.

Finally, Jessie caught a break. A seat opened up when she was only a few meters away. Reflexes took over, and she won a game of musical chairs before the omnipresent music even considered stopping.

Taking a breath, she surveyed her surroundings. It was a communal booth with a table scattered with empty drinks. An in-tik waiter breezed by, using one wing to sweep empty glasses into a bin with a clatter.

"You take drink orders?" she asked.

The in-tik squawked back. A vocal converter worn around his neck replied in English, "Yes, ma'am."

"Beer. Full liter. Whatever's on tap is fine."

Even without the translator, she understood the cackling laughter. "No beer. Just fizzies."

Oh.

Shit.

This may have been a corner of their planet devoted to the housing of human refugees, but laaku still ran Phabian. Liquor wasn't legal. Of course, Jessie had gotten her hands on booze plenty of places it wasn't allowed, but this was neither the time nor the place.

"Well. Um. Fuck. Never mind. I'm good." She shooed the waiter away to avoid drawing further attention to herself.

"New to the scene?" a choir-boy voice inquired from next to her. Her previous seatmate had vacated, and the newcomer was a smooth-skinned young specimen, glossy and hairless, wearing a vest that showed off lean, sculpted muscle. His drooping lids showed off dark eye shadow, the color impossible to judge in the kaleidoscopic club lighting. A perfect, white smile showed off dimples.

A quick-firing circuit in Jessie's brain instantly registered a verdict: fuckable.

"What was the clue?" she replied with a smirk. "The donated duds or forgetting that Phabian's dry?"

He shook his head, denying the obvious. "Too awake. You're not hearing the sub-sonics."

Jessie snorted. "You're baked on the notes you can't hear?"

He shrugged. "It's meditative. Tantric. You can lose yourself in it."

"Let me guess. You can teach?" she asked sarcastically.

What was wrong with her? Here was a fisherman handing her a line, and she'd come here trying to get caught. Sure, maybe she was dressed like a high school track coach. And yeah, this wasn't her usual type. Somewhere in the parts of her brain she didn't fully understand, Jessie liked the illusion that, despite her training, a lover could manhandle her a little. She'd been with better-looking guys before—and she had to admit that, while she couldn't pull off the bald look, he was prettier than her.

Her would-be lover for the night slipped an arm around her shoulders. "I'd love to teach you everything I know." His breath was minty fresh.

She could headbutt him. Break his nose. Exposed throat. Easy target. Pin him out of view behind the table, hands on his throat. Moan a little, and people would just assume it was sex.

Jessie blinked.

The club's heat was getting to her.

She finally put a finger on what was bothering her.

Despite days passing, Recitol still lingered in her bloodstream. The two-hour rating on the pills had been for the benefits, not the side-effects. Without the pounding heartbeat and the red creeping in at the edges of her vision, it was easy to forget it was there.

Jessie shoved the young man aside before learning his name. "Buy a hat, asshole."

Better he feel insulted than try to follow her home right now. Jessie was a predator, and he was registering as prey rather than a mate.

All the way through the club, she shouldered dancers out of her way, avoiding eye contact and not making any apologies.

The night air refreshed her but, at the same time, fueled the rising need for violence.

Tomorrow, she promised herself. Tomorrow she'd get that blood detox.

In the meantime, she needed to find an all-night gadget store.

⸻

"Have fun at work," Jessie had bid him as a breakfast farewell. She'd had a rough look but claimed that two hours sleep and a cup of coffee—though she'd actually had three just over breakfast—was plenty to sustain her. Eric had to trust that, with the running-and-getting-shot-at portion of living in the future out of the way, she was correct in her supposition.

Hecuba led the way after a polite, reserved introduction at the cafe. Eric kept up with her brisk pace, trailing half a step behind her and to her left. "I really think you're going to love working on the Lunar Reclamation Project. We're doing such great things."

"Why's it called that? Luna is Earth's moon."

"Linguistic hitch," Hecuba replied, not the least bit stumped. This must have come up every time they brought on someone new, after all. "They named it in English. None of the variations with 'moon' in the name were any better."

"Re-Moon-dling," Eric replied off the top of his head. "New Moon Rising. Moonbase Beta. I mean, did they really even try?"

Hecuba giggled. "Maybe next major project, you can consult on the name."

"My rates are reasonable."

"Here we are. Just up ahead." They arrived at a little tram station that appeared to be just for employees. The car had eight seats, with room for another four to six people standing. Not that there was anyone else aboard right now.

"Are we early or late?" Eric asked.

"Shorthanded, more like. But yes, we're starting a few minutes after most people show up."

"Not a good look on my first day." Eric had never had a *real* job before. Before his first shift, he was already a malingerer.

The tram accelerated with a gentle jerk, whooshing them through the city to an unassuming skyscraper a few blocks away in a matter of seconds. All the scenery passed in a literal blur. The car pulled right into the building before gliding to a halt.

When the doors opened, a wash of industrial fumes wafted over them. Hecuba didn't seem bothered by the smell, so Eric didn't bother trying to breathe around it. He followed on her heels, marveling at the busyness of the place. Even at what appeared to be a simple employee transit station, trams were arriving and departing in all directions.

Without staring or holding hands, he kept a vague awareness of Hecuba's proximity, not allowing himself to get lost while he had an actual guide on hand to prevent just such an occurrence.

"They space out the starting time to keep this place from overcrowding," Hecuba explained.

Just how many people worked here, he wondered. Then he recalled that he didn't have to muse idly. "Just how many people work here, anyway?"

She shrugged on the way through a doorway that led to a more secluded area of the factory—that is to say, one in which people scattered rather than teemed. "I've never asked. We've got twenty-eight in the Magical Services Department. It'll be twenty-nine the moment you clock in."

Eric brightened. "There's a clock?"

"Sorry. Just the figurative kind. No one really tracks our hours. I mean, if someone doesn't show up, there will be questions. But it's more like, *Hey, where's Dracula today?* Oh, his kid had a school thing. *He coming in at all?* After lunch, he said. And that's that. I guess if someone didn't come back, they'd stop paying them. But why would anyone? This is one of the few places on Phabian no one minds us using magic."

They hadn't progressed during Hecuba's babbling. Workers with close-fitted sleeves—mostly laaku—gave the wizards space to become an island in the flow of foot traffic. Seeming to notice this, Hecuba dodged out of the way and found a slipstream to rejoin the trickle.

"This isn't where we work, but it's our changing room." Hecuba led the way through a swinging door. It flapped back and forth, back and forth between them until she caught it and poked her head back outside. "It's co-ed. This isn't Earth."

When he ventured in after her, what Eric found was a drastic shift in scenery. While the factory had presented a standard twenty-sixth-century facade of gray metal and harsh lighting, this wizards' changing room was dark polished wood and lush, deep pile carpeting. Rows of cubicles lined the walls and formed aisles akin to a library for checking humans in and out.

Each cubicle had a name plaque, lovingly etched with the name of the occupant.

Vaclav.

Cassiopeia.

Hector-Luiz.

None of the names were people he knew. There had been a Hector-Luis in his Introduction to Runes class, but he'd spelled it differently. Hecuba waited patiently, expectantly even, by his side.

Then he saw a cubicle that caught his attention and held it.

Eric.

They'd given him a dressing room of his very own. Eric ran his fingers down the red velvet drape before daring to pull it aside, sliding on a series of brass rings along a rod that ran well above head height.

Inside, a similarly upholstered bench awaited him in front of a wooden set of cubbies and a closet rod hung with baggy-sleeved waistcoats.

Hecuba drew the curtain, isolating him to get ready for his first day of a new job.

The fabric was silky, but not silk. Not here. Laaku didn't like natural fabrics. Real wood seemed to be where they drew the line at expensive touches of luxury for their magical workforce.

A few minutes later, Eric followed Hecuba through a short stretch of factory, both tucking their hands in their sleeves.

"Welcome, Wizard Eric," a laaku in loose sleeves greeted him as they entered a spacious room with conveyor belts running in and out through the walls. "I'm Doonah of Urpoth." He stuck out a hand, and Eric shook it.

"Just Eric, actually. Never got the official title."

Doonah cocked his head and narrowed one eye. "According to whom?"

Eric blinked. "I see your point. But if we don't acknowledge Convocation authority, who's to say who is a wizard or not?"

"You any good at magic?" Doonah asked. Quietly, Hecuba snickered.

"I'm all right."

"In my book, you're a wizard. Come on. It's not like we do science around here. Grab Kipper's old spot on the line and get to it. Hecuba's going to show you what we do."

"Kipper?" Eric echoed softly once Doonah had wandered off to whatever supervisory duties required him.

"He retired a week ago. Otherwise, we might have lost you to another department." Hecuba shrugged and gave a sly smile. "Lucky us."

The two of them took up positions standing to either side of a conveyor belt just wide enough that they couldn't reach across without leaning on it. Machinery grumbled. The conveyor advanced. A slab of steel emerged from the next room and continued until it stopped between them.

"OK. Do you know what this is?"

Eric considered. "A sled?"

"A window."

"Shitty window," Eric blurted. "Oh. Sorry. No, it's a very nice window, I'm sure, despite being completely opaque and a dingy shade of gray."

But Hecuba, far from offended, was giggling.

"What?"

"It's a window-to-be. It's not transparent yet, but this glassteel is still just steel. We're here to glass it."

"Ooh, fun!"

"I know, right?" Hecuba replied, matching the grin that had sprung onto Eric's face. "Once we're done here, these get shipped up to the moon to go into greenhouses, restaurants, luxury surface and super-surface housing. Some get to be interior windows, but I like to think that people are going to stargaze through them. But before that, we have to—" She stumbled over her sentence. "What was that? I felt something."

"All done."

"Huh? Wait. Where's the window?" She looked all around.

Eric knocked just above the conveyor belt, producing a deep, guttural clang, like a gong that someone hadn't tuned.

"You turned it invisible."

Eric nodded confirmation. "That's glassteel for you. Invisible."

"No, that's invisible steel. People are going to freak out. You need a touch of glare, a hint of refraction, for people to accept that it's real glass. No one wants invisible steel."

Rather than protest that he'd have been fine with it, Eric remembered an old colonial teacher—something of a retrovert—who mentioned the difficulties that birds had with regular windows. Crashing into them. Getting hurt. He wondered if that little glint of reflection was what kept humans from banging into them.

"Sorry. Here."

Eric shut his eyes for a second.

My bad. Glassy-looking, not invisible.

"OK. Well, it *looks* right now. But the way we do it is a

permanent change. There's a ritual. Chanting. We hold hands over the piece. It's a two-person job to do it properly."

Eric thought she sounded pretty excited about the whole operation.

"It's all right. Magic's not a science. We can fix it. Let me just undo your spell, and we'll... and we'll... Hold on a minute. Let me grab Doonah, and we'll get this piece reset."

Hecuba headed off. Meanwhile, Eric watched what his new coworkers were up to. Spaced out around the room, they monitored other conveyor belts scattered at various heights around the room and accessed by an Escher's worth of metal stairways. All of them appeared to be performing the ritual Hecuba had briefly outlined.

"What seems to be the trouble?" Doonah inquired in the manner of a professor who knew damn well but wanted to be sure his students comprehended their mistake before stepping in to fix it.

"Quickie magic. Looks like glassteel, but we don't know for how long."

"Ah."

"I couldn't unravel it."

Doonah nodded appraisingly. "Indeed. Well, can't be cutting corners. Can we?"

Eric, who'd been brought up to believe that all magic was an exercise in corner-cutting, kept meekly silent. His life had so many cut corners that it must have been a circle by now.

Moments passed. Doonah's expression evolved from contemplative to concentrating to consternated. At long last, he huffed a sigh of frustration. The glassteel window remained unchanged. He turned to Hecuba. "I thought they said he'd been kicked out of Oxford."

Eric cleared his throat and raised a finger. "It wasn't for being bad at magic."

A nozzle rose from the center of the table, angled toward Jessie's cup, and refilled it with a pre-measured mixture of steviol glycosides, soy milk, chai, and of course coffee. The liquid steamed, and she blew across the top before taking a sip. Without glancing down at the drink in her hand, she watched Eric and his new coworker depart.

Jessie shook her head and let out a long sigh.

What a weird world Phabian was. Jessie was unemployed for the first time since being appointed the band's sound technician at age fourteen. It had been a bullshit excuse to wring some labor out of her in exchange for the terras she was always begging for. Eric, on the other hand, had been useless ever since deciding he wanted to study magic.

Now, Eric was off to work while Jessie lingered at an outdoor cafe, in no hurry to arrive at her only appointment of the day.

In fact, Jessie passed hours lost in her own thoughts, refilling her cup time and again. While food and basic drinks were free at the cafeteria a block away, that hadn't felt right for a celebratory breakfast with her little brother. Besides, it hadn't been expensive, and the coffee was complimentary with a meal —despite finishing so long ago she was growing hungry again.

Eventually, the caffeine jitters told Jessie it was time to move along.

Museums.

The park.

One of the fitness centers.

It was one thing to be bored between duty shifts or between assignments. But there was always an "until" that provided a terminus to the tedium. Jessie's outdoor cafe seat had allowed her to watch the comings and goings of hundreds of strangers.

While, statistically, there might have been someone more useless in that bunch than her, it didn't feel that way.

Setting down her cup for the final time, Jessie got up and left the cafe.

Eric had picked the numbered laaku breakfast facility for the novelty of outdoor dining on a core world. But Jessie would have preferred a restaurant that didn't have an unobstructed view of the Refugee Employment Center. Crossing the paved square in between took a few minutes, the building growing the whole way.

That girl...

She and Eric had headed off to work together, him trailing her like a puppy. Her floating on clouds. Before she'd come to claim him, Jessie had imagined a plastic mannequin for all the lack of detail in his description of her. But upon seeing her, Jessie had realized a time bomb in the waiting. Bird-boned and mousy, with big green eyes and cute in a "never heard of cosmo" kind of way, she was clearly smitten with her oblivious brother.

Jessie had retired from tending the hurt feelings of potential girlfriends. Eric had a sensitive, vulnerable air that attracted a certain sort of girl that was a bull's-eye for this Hecuba. Someday, Eric was either going to succumb to a late puberty or he was going to learn to identify the symptoms himself and stop leading them on by accident.

Arriving at the employment center came with both relief at a diversion from worrying about her brother's love life and dread at the humiliating conversation to come.

Clear signage.

Easy directions.

A quick queue.

Her name called.

Jessie entered a tiny office just big enough for the two

chairs with a desk between them. She sat in hers. Across the desk, Kippi; it said so on the name plate. Kippi was a laaku in her late forties, if Jessie was any judge, wearing a pair of semi-decorative light datalenses. She peered at Jessie over the latter after tapping for a silent moment on her console.

"Good afternoon, Miss Ramsey."

Jessie bit her tongue, stopping herself from insisting that she was either Lieutenant Ramsey or just Jessie. She was sure as fuck no "miss." But antagonizing Kippi didn't seem like a great foot to get off on. Besides, the Lieutenant part probably wasn't even true anymore.

"Hi, Kippi. I'm new at this, so bear with me."

"Everyone's new at this. Takes a real stretch of cosmic bad luck to end up a refugee twice."

"I suppose."

"If you don't mind a personal observation..."

Jessie shrugged. What did she care? Not like she was a delicate flower. Kippi was just a job kiosk with extra steps.

"Are you sure you're ready for the workforce? Maybe a counselor might be a better first step in your life journey."

"There are comets with fewer kilometers on them," Jessie replied. "I'm 'journeying' just fine. I don't do well with nothing to do, and I'd rather what I do be something productive and lucrative."

"Well, we can certainly look for an opportunity that matches your skill landscape. I've had a quick look over your file, and there are a number of missing areas I was hoping we could fill in together."

"My military record," Jessie concluded. "Thought you people had access to all that."

"'Us people' aren't all cleared to view those records. While the specifics of your service in the ARGO Combined Forces may be classified, maybe we can come up with some economic multiplier factors that you can furnish a prospective job-creator."

It was a whole other fucking language built out of English words. "Sure. I guess. I'm a great pilot."

Kippi looked constipated. "Yeah... you have a note in your file that we shouldn't place you anywhere that takes you outside the secure zone."

"Thought I was free to leave whenever." She made it clear by her glare that if she discovered otherwise, there was going to be a problem.

"You are. But we're not supposed to encourage it. Don't worry. Plenty of employers either offer security-verified transport from the zone or operate within it. Have you ever waitressed? We have several live-service restaurants that cater to human clientele."

"I have a 99 firing range rating."

"Hospitality?"

"I'm a certified hand-to-hand combat trainer."

"Do you sing or dance?"

"Is there a job on Phabian for a human woman that isn't about making someone else happy? My training *really* leans into making the wrong people *unhappy*."

Kippi sat back in her seat. "We might have some office jobs available. Let's have you take an assessment exam. See what kind of a piece you are and what puzzle may be missing a perfect fit." Some humans might have been fooled by the forced smile that followed, but Jessie had grown up around laaku, and Aunt Shoni had a smile just like that; it got dragged out for approving of horrible art projects, pitching sub-standard dinner options, and listing the amenities available on backwater colonies.

"Yeah. Great." Jessie didn't even pretend to be excited at the prospect.

Two hours later, Jessie breathed free air again. Her tapping finger was sore from the screen in the test center. She felt like a remedial exchange student at a laaku high school. How many office jobs needed calculus or dealt with quantum mechanics? Why was an alien species quizzing her on her native language? Why did she have the sneaking suspicion that—despite the "we're just assessing here"—she'd failed the test?

With nowhere pressing to go, Jessie stood a moment, watching the aerial traffic high overhead. All *those* people had somewhere to be. Jobs. Families. Responsibilities.

Then, one of the hovers broke from the orderly flow of traffic. It descended and headed straight for the square where Jessie was standing.

No.

It wasn't heading for the square she was standing at the edge of. It came straight toward her.

The lower level of the refugee zone was pedestrian only. Her urge to take cover gave way before the surety that anyone getting away with violating that regulation on Phabian had permission to do so.

Long, black, with tinted windows on all sides including the front, the hover pulled up right alongside her. The door nearest her opened. A laaku in a suit and dark shader lenses leaned out. "Jessica Ramsey, please come with us."

"Uh uh. Not without a little more than that. This may be Phabian, but I'm not that easy."

In her head, she imagined the armaments that the laaku might be packing, how many he might have with him, her odds of making it to cover back inside the employment center.

"I'm with Section 74. I think we might have a job for you."

"Section 74?" Jessie echoed with a smirk. "Sorry. I had clearance to know better. There's no such thing."

"What if I told you that your information is five years out of date, that our previous status was intentionally covert, that we're currently recruiting individuals with uncommon skills, and your service record suggests you'd do well working for us?"

"I'd ask for proof."

"You want proof. You got it." The laaku jerked his head. "Get in."

Jessie didn't budge.

"Or you get to take the logistics job Kippi's lining up for you based on that shitshow of a placement test. Between you and me, it's a waste of your talent operating a grav sled. But I guess food crates don't unload themselves..."

What did she have to lose, really? Eric was safe enough. If these fuckers killed her, at least she wouldn't die of boredom.

———

The black hover shot through Kethlet like a rail gun slug. Jessie couldn't help tensing up as a nondescript skyscraper rushed toward them with no sign of deceleration. They rocketed through an opening with less than a meter to spare on all sides of them. Inside, blackness.

Seconds later, the door opened.

A laaku, wearing what looked like a store-bought costume with no insignia, was holding it open for them. Jessie stepped out at a nod from her as-yet-unnamed escort. The latter followed her out of the vehicle and took the lead. By the pop of her ears, Jessie imagined that she'd dropped below the planet's surface during her unseen trip through the building.

"Nice gravity stone," Jessie commented offhandedly. "How far down are we?"

"Ten stories. Not bad. Most first-time visitors never pick up on the elevation change." They boarded a moving walkway that led straight to a door that opened just as they approached and shut just as quickly behind them. The corridor beyond seemed mostly made to give the walkway someplace to lie. "If you don't mind me asking, what was your plan if I turned out to be lying? Syndicates or something?"

He peered back and up at her, but Jessie didn't make eye contact.

"I'd have killed you with the blaster you pulled on me."

"And if the rear compartment was blaster-shielded? (Which it is.)"

This sounded like an unofficial test from someone with power outside the strictest rules of his hierarchy. Jessie only had a gut reaction to go by, but this felt like a prelude to figuring out whether she wanted to spy for Phabian. If this was some Section 74 spymaster, A) he looked great if he was old enough to earn that kind of a position, B) he'd have discretion to bend or break any rule he damn felt like if he liked the cut of her jib.

"Unless you were packing a granny blaster, there's enough juice in one of those to blow out the engines of a mid-sized hover. Hard to direct the blast on a quickie IED, but I'd do my best. Worst case, I'd take out at least you and the pilot for fucking with me."

Her escort shook his head. "Humans..."

Well, if that didn't sound like a failing grade, Jessie didn't know what did. "Hey, you asked. I wasn't a spook. I was field ops for high-leverage forward insertions. But you knew that because Phabian had access to ARGO-classified military personnel records."

The walkway was part of a system with hubs and intersections. Jessie stepped from one to the next, following her escort as, presumably, he tried to confound her internal compass. She half expected the casual interrogation to continue on an indefinite moving walkway ride. Instead, her escort stepped off at a bare stretch of wall that looked more like an emergency service lane for exhausted passengers than a destination of any sort.

Then that wall opened.

"Interrogation room?" Jessie made it sound like a joke in case it wasn't true.

Her escort walked in. "My office."

True enough. Beyond the door, it was almost homey inside —for a laaku definition, at least. The desk had holos of a family. Awards and certifications adorned the walls, including a medal that Jessie was pretty sure Phabian Navy gave out during the Third Eyndar War.

"Ex-Navy?" Jessie inquired as she took the seat her escort offered with a lazy lower-hand gesture as he circled to his own chair.

"No one comes up straight into Section 74. We need people with a variety of skills. You, for instance, pose an interesting opportunity."

"Haven't been called that in a while," Jessie responded sarcastically.

In studying the laaku's desk, she spotted his name on the commendations. Banlee of Jinka. He'd graduated the Phabian Naval Academy in '44, which suggested a birthday in 2522 or '23, putting him just shy of 70 years old. He looked to be in great shape, so he must have kept up an exercise regimen. Now that she looked closer, the fur was a common tint color—a couple shades darker than what Aunt Shoni used, but the same product line.

Leave her in this office long enough, she'd figure out his golf handicap.

"Your official records suggested a streak of borderline insubordination. Nice to see our files are accurate."

"Borderline? Shit. Someone writing those reports must have liked me."

"We like independent thinkers, but we need to know that people can take an assignment and do it."

Jessie snorted in amusement. "Really? Only reason I'm not at least a lieutenant commander by now is this whole shit that happened with my brother. But you probably know all about that, too."

"Magic's not my department. For all I care, you got cryo'ed for five years. What matters to *me* is where you stand in the Earth/Mars war."

"You should update the forms at refugee processing; ask flat out instead of nagging about voting history and shit. Or, hell, the employment exam. Wouldn't have been any weirder a question than the one where I had to mediate a theoretical lawsuit between a fox and the family of the chicken he ate."

Banlee snickered. "Yeah. Those employment people are a slapper, huh? Tell you what."

He paused.

"What?" Jessie answered once it became clear that this was a bit. Dad pulled this crap, too. Had to feel clever by coaxing her into playing along.

"You tell me what my wife's name is, based on the information you have at hand, and you've got the job."

"What job?" Jessie demanded, exasperated. "You haven't even said."

"It's polite to wait to be told certain information that seems like it's about to be revealed. I was curious how long you'd remain polite."

Jessie glowered.

"Intelligence analyst. I'm interested in your brain, not your trigger finger."

Jessie blinked. "You... want me doing datawork?"

"Can't have you in the field. And until your loyalties are clear, there's only so much I can give you. But you have potential. I think. Find out my wife's name, and I'll know for sure. There's no guideline, but I *am* watching the time."

"I assume beating it out of you is off the table?"

The subtle smirk in reply wasn't enough information for Jessie to risk it on. When Banlee glanced down at the chrono on his datapad, she knew she needed to get thinking.

Not content to crane her neck and swivel in her chair for clues, Jessie stood and prowled the room. She scanned the wall for documents with the wife's name on them. But no one gave an award or a professional accreditation that acknowledged a spouse.

A formal coat hung on a peg by the door; Jessie rifled through the pockets.

Tchotchkes from a dozen worlds lined a display shelf, but none had been personalized.

She tried the desk drawers, but they were locked, and she could feel the bio-scanner pad just under the edge. Without warning him first, Jessie grabbed one of Banlee's upper hands and maneuvered a finger to be scanned.

Thunk.

The drawers unlocked. Jessie slid them open one by one, pillaging the contents and spilling them across the desktop. Nothing jumped out as listing the spymaster's wife's name.

Still leaning over the pile, she shot Banlee an accusing look. "You even married?"

"Fifty-seven years next month." If he was offended by her rough handling, his mild response, tinged with amusement, didn't betray any anger.

Jessie scanned the holo displays. Two kids. She could see the *image* of a wife, but she wasn't wearing a nametag. Only the two kiddos had their names on their individual emitter pads.

Bansalk, age 8.

Powlee, a little girl age 4.

"They're all grown now. Those are just my favorite memories of them."

Jessie heard a hint being given, but she'd already heard a scratching of an idea trying to claw its way out of her skull.

Bansalk, Powlee.

Ban - salk. Pow - lee.

She swapped syllables around.

Ban - lee. Pow - salk.

Roddy and Shoni hadn't gone that route, but she seemed to remember it being a common method of naming children in certain laaku cultures. Two-syllable names worked perfectly for it, especially given an adherence to one of the old syllabic languages.

"Powsalk."

"Of?" Banlee asked, letting his eyelids droop.

Shit. Given name wasn't going to be enough. Clues... Clues...

Wait. Assuming Banlee wasn't lying earlier, he mentioned they'd been married fifty-seven years. Shit. If her age estimate on him was right, that meant he was married before age twenty. Which suggested a high-school sweetheart, not someone he met in college or later. Military career. Made sense. Sort of. Committing to a lifetime at that age struck a weird chord in her head.

This wasn't a time to judge life choices. It was time for logic. Powsalk hadn't been a point-blank shot, either. It was an educated guess. She was going to assume that Banlee hadn't been a galaxy-trotting ladies' man as a teenager.

"Powsalk. Of Jinka. Same as you."

Banlee smiled and offered a handshake. "Welcome to Section 74."

"Thanks. When do I start?"

"Immediately. Your first assignment is to clean up the mess you made of my desk."

━━━

Eric munched on french fries that had never met a potato. He'd already finished his cow-free hamburger and dairyless milkshake. None of it was half bad so long as you accepted the premise that imitation food still filled a belly. Across the wide table from him, Jessie scraped the bottom of her ice cream bowl and sucked the fake, soppy mess from her finger.

"I can't picture you working an office job," Eric commented while chewing, shaking his head at his attempts to conjure the image. He pantomimed tapping at a console with both index fingers and made a poor imitation of her voice. "*Yes, sir. Right away, sir. I'll make two graphs and a holo show tout de suite.*" He laughed at his own jest. "But seriously, congratulations on becoming a productive citizen again."

"How's life as a factory worker?"

Eric paused. How best to describe it? "This is the greatest experience of my life."

Jessie perked up. "Oh?"

"Yeah. They called me Wizard Eric like I actually finished my degree. I have a personalized changing cubby with velvet drapes. And I'm making pieces of a moon!"

Jessie raised an eyebrow like she didn't believe him.

"No. Honest!"

"Drapes. They got you with upholstery."

Eric scowled. She was trying to ruin this for him, but he wasn't going to let her. "The cubbies are real wood. *Real wood.* On Phabian, no less. Commercial lumbering isn't allowed in this whole system—they mentioned that a couple times, as I recall."

"This mood wouldn't have anything to do with a particular wizard—what was her name? Heckuva?"

"Hecuba. And it has everything to do with her."

"Well, she was a heckuva looker."

Eric ignored the rude comment about what—to her—was a stranger's appearance. "She's shown me around, taught me the ins and outs."

"Given you the lay of the land?" Jessie suggested, perhaps to highlight Eric's overuse of workplace clichés. He couldn't let her get away with needling him. Not without a fight, anyway.

"At least I'm not coordinating waste reclaim cleaning schedules."

"At least I'm not singing campfire songs to slabs of steel."

Oh, so it was going to be this kind of meal, was it?

"At least I don't work in a tiny box."

"At least I don't brag about the upholstery of my tiny box."

"At least I earn more than civic baseline."

Jessie winced visibly. "Fine. You win. But you really have been gushing about your new work friend."

"What's not to gush about?" Eric asked as he stood, gathering his tray to return it to the tray-eating machine by the door. "She's great. I don't know what I'd be doing right now without her. Crashing on the floor at your place, I suppose. By the way, there's a symposium tonight. Bunch of people from the factory are going. How offended would you be if I took a weather-delay on dinner tonight?"

Jessie dumped her tray in the machine as soon as Eric's had finished being devoured. She fixed him with such a look. He couldn't categorize it, though it fell somewhere under the general umbrella of puzzled. "Are you asking me permission to hang out with your new friends?"

Eric cowered a little. "Yes?"

"Go. Have fun. Or whatever you have at symposiums—or symposia. Whatever."

"Both are correct. And it should be a hoot. There's this newly contacted species that looks like bipedal elephants. Their ambassador is speaking."

"I hadn't heard." There was a tiny hitch in her voice, a flatness that her typical banter lacked, that suggested his sister was lying. Rather than spill the beans, he allowed her deception to simply fail to trick him.

"Well. I plan to have a grand time. Maybe I'll start picking up a 38th language."

With a smirk on his face, Eric parted ways with his sister and headed back for the afternoon shift at the glassteel factory.

Eric wiped sweat from his brow with one baggy sleeve as he made his way out of the glassteel enchanting room. It wasn't that the magic was taxing—far from it. But the chant had gotten boring, so he'd set it to music so it could be sung. The song had caught on, and once a catchy song was loose in the wild, a little dance was inevitable. There wasn't much *to* the dance, given that it had to be performed within the constraints of two people holding hands across a conveyor belt. But there was hip-waggling and shoulder shimmies, and that added up to a workout over time.

Doonah had even ordered up a two-piece band to accompany them, since the up-tempo version of the song had sped up production markedly. So, as he made his way to the boss's office, Eric felt reasonably confident that he wasn't getting fired.

A quick whispered thought, and the perspiration dried from his clothes, his skin, the cloud of rank air that followed him. The eldritch glow that lit the administrative wing of the magic department didn't blink. Most of the staff here weren't wizards but some kind of support personnel akin to the Convocation's tech liaisons. It hadn't yet been a full week, and he was making progress learning everyone's names.

Eric lifted a hand in a static wave. "Hi, Keith."

He poked his head into an office with just a brief hitch in his stride. "The brownies were great, Andrea. Thanks."

"Missed you at the holos last night, Lupok."

"Sure, Clea. I'll put in a good word with him."

Finally, Eric reached Doonah's office and gave a quick knock before stepping through the open door.

"Eric! Come on in, my boy. Shut the door. Have a seat."

Despite being a sliding door, it was non-mechanical, gliding along a well-oiled track in the floor. Eric made sure it didn't slam and settled himself into the plush upholstered chair on the guest side of the voluminous wooden desk.

"Hi."

"Eric, have you thought much about your future?"

"If you'd like to get technical, I think I'm constantly living five years in my own future. I'd have to think back well into your past to even mull my present."

Doonah snickered. "Not like that. But I see your point. More specifically, have you considered your career?"

"I'm pretty sure being a wizard is for me. Out of curiosity, what were you thinking to suggest?"

Unlike so many non-wizards out there, Doonah didn't get flummoxed by following the simple logic of a conversation. "Still a wizard. But maybe more of one. Look, glassteel is a journeyman department. It's harder work than maintaining star-drives but easier than building them."

Eric scowled. "You want me to make star-drives."

Doonah sighed. "No. Frankly, that seems like a waste of your considerable talents."

None of this sounded good. Eric was just getting used to his new job making glassteel. It was easy and fun, and his coworkers were great. "I'm really not that talented."

"We both know that's not true. And I only know this because it's patently obvious. In a twist of logic, I can't *hear* the truth behind your words, which proves those particular words true. The universe wouldn't keep your secrets if you didn't impress it."

Eric swallowed. "It's not something I *do*. It just happens."

Doonah leaned back in his chair and spread all four hands. He had nice leather walking gloves on. "Look. I'm not criticizing. We don't get a lot of wizards opting out of the Earth/Mars conflict. We can't be choosy. And we see vanishingly few of your caliber. You can do a lot more for us than churning out glassteel, no matter how much you've done toward getting us back on schedule."

"I don't understand. I thought that was a good thing."

"It is. It is. But there are other departments in even more dire need of the type of assistance you can offer."

Eric's eyes widened. "You can't. I just got here."

"You've brought unprecedented productivity to the glassteel department. The majority of future lunar residents don't want to live with the ambient one-sixth gravity Moon Version Two will provide. There's an oppressive demand for gravity stones, and I think with your influence with the universe, you could—"

"But I'm happy making glassteel!"

"You could do so much more."

"Why?"

"Because you can. Because the pay is better."

"I don't care about the pay."

"That's a minority opinion. Most change their tune when they hear *how much* more money we're talking about. I'm talking about a serious bump from your current salary."

It was Eric's turn to spread his hands. "I haven't even figured out how much I'm making."

"Eighteen hundred credits a week. Initially, we tied the Phabian Credit to the terra, but since we started letting the valuation float—"

"That's not the point. I can eat. I have a nice place to live. I'm making friends."

"You can make new friends."

"They're not disposable."

"For eleven thousand credits a month, I think your new friends would understand."

Eric shook his head as he got up to pace. "None of this is making any sense. If I wanted to make more money, I could."

"Then why wouldn't you?"

"Because I'm happy."

"Hypothetically, wouldn't that be possible being more productive and earning more money?"

Eric was growing cross. "Hypothetically, I could keep my friends and take whatever I wanted if I wanted to be rich." He swallowed and noted that Doonah was looking skeptically at him. "Hypothetically, that is. Without breaking laws, I don't see a way to do whatever I like and have lots of money. I just want a nice, quiet life, meeting interesting people."

"You could be so much more productive..."

Eric huffed and sat back down. "Then can we have a conversation about how much *less* productive I'd have to be at making glassteel to keep my job?"

―

Jessie yawned. She moved to stifle it, but behind the encryption mask she wore, it hardly mattered. The sleek black device fit snugly over her nose and mouth and sealed airtight, canceling out all sound generated within. Only someone keyed to the same channel would be able to hear a word she said. Currently, that list was limited to her supervisor, Futhrek of Vendrey.

Her office wasn't what Eric apparently envisioned. Instead of a low-walled box open on one side, her workspace was a black-walled cell with a hand-scan lock that required security clearance. The only amenity was a shockingly comfortable reclining chair that took up most of the available space. If it might have finally been enough for her to feel claustrophobic, the datagoggles took care of that.

By the magic of laaku technology, the glossy black walls were merely backdrop to an infinite simulated datascape. Her first three days on the job, Jessie had done little more than run through system tutorials and set up the interface to make intuitive sense to her. The goggles responded to hand gestures, allowing her to manipulate files with the flick of her finger.

The three days since that, she'd been familiarizing herself with the data she'd been assigned to pore over and working her way through the backlog that built up as she struggled through the learning curve.

Her preferences setting displayed the giant, automated comm-sifting and decryption system as an old-timey, overcomplicated steam-powered cartoon factory. It churned and chugged and occasionally spat out comms that the laaku-programmed algorithms felt needed a second look.

J-L-R-1095: COMM FROM ID-44A7F109 TO ID-CB415J9M

Having us a Phabian party. Y'all bringing the bananas?

Jessie had learned that part of the expertise she was being asked to draw from was a personal understanding of human vernacular conversation. But it didn't take a human to peel back the nuance on this one.

She flagged the comm sender as xenoist and the recipient as a "maybe," then moved on to the next.

This one had been tagged for follow-up by a colleague with the analyst ID sanitized to prevent bias.

J-L-R-1096: COMM FROM ID-19GTBWLG TO ID-UKUZ9VR4

Got a 12 going into Kethlet. Your 5 on stand firm or surrender.

On the one hand, she could see the vaguely threatening terminology in reference to the very district in which the intelligence center operated. On the other, for fuck's sake, had none of these laaku spooks ever heard of *Planetary Patrol?* Reaching into the deep omni, she flicked through a quick search and packed a playable copy of the game into her report.

These were her days, sifting through harmless communications that the laaku computers couldn't rule out as nefarious doublespeak and debunking her fellow analysts' lack of the finer understanding of a human culture that—quite frankly—they were as much a part of as she was.

Phabian had a higher English-literacy rate than Orion. They had archbishops in the One Church. Why couldn't they figure this shit out on their own?

Jessie purposely set up her rig to keep the chrono out of convenient view. Allowing herself to lose track of time until reminders pinged kept her days from dragging—or at least they didn't drag as much. But comfortable as her workstation might have been, she'd been lying there long enough to grow stiff. It had to have been hours since lunch.

Soon.

She'd shut down the virtual interface, scan her hand to unlock the office door, and file through the black maze of corridors alongside her fellow analysts, mainly laaku with a scattering of humans mixed in for species diversity, all wearing encryption masks.

Conversation might have been buzzing all around, but Jessie had no way to tell. To her, the processions were all silence except for footsteps and fabric rustling.

Then, she'd arrive in the locker room, peel off her mask and set both it and her goggles in the sanitizer to be clean and sweet-smelling the following morning. Her jumpsuit, slip-on shoes, and undergarments would all go down a chute. She'd step into one of the many showers where, alongside an automated cleaning and blow-dry, she'd be scanned to the sub-cellular level before exiting out the far side. There, she'd retrieve her civilian clothes and stumble exhaustedly out into the real world.

All the security was soul-numbing. She supposed that once the numbness set in fully, she'd stop caring. Humans could get used to just about anything. There were mood-stabilizing programs built into the interface, but she'd shied away from trying any of them... in case they actually worked.

Lifting her goggles, Jessie took a moment to rub her eyes. Dry eyeballs and lazy eyelids coordinated their own recovery efforts with a series of blinks. When her vision cleared, the walls seemed to close in. The vast expanses and her new duties beckoned, so Jessie slipped the goggles back on and wriggled her facial muscles until they settled into their proper fit.

With no biomechanical idea how they did it, neither the mask nor goggles left marks that lingered through a shower.

The high-sec omni rushed up to surround her once more.

She was just in time for the cartoony factory to spit out her next snippet.

J-L-R-1097: COMM FROM ID-M8EY1HRT TO ID-9T9VJY3S

Elephants stomping traitors? Sounds like justice to me. Set something in motion.

For the first time in her short tenure, Jessie couldn't see how this was harmless banter. While the basic messages were stripped down, Jessie had sufficient clearance to view the time and date stamps on the missive.

She cross-referenced.

She compared broadcasts.

She even went so far as to view the full interview from *Pablek Tonight*. She'd made a point of avoiding the show since Eric's treatment by the host, but she'd had to watch the follow-up guest as a professional matter. Now, she had to go back to review it.

Tiny in the goggles' view, Pablek's guest towered over him from the chair next to him. Haathee, people were calling them. Thick-limbed and barrel-torsoed, their ambassador would have made a stuunji look like a runt. With floppy ears, a trunk, and tusks that had to have measured a meter and a half apiece, he'd have cut a truly terrifying figure if he wasn't at the same time so utterly charming.

Something about interspecies differences made emotions harder to read, but even beneath the trunk, it was impossible to misunderstand the smile that seemed almost permanently fixed in place. It only disappeared often enough to mark a contrast.

"How is it out in your arm of the galaxy, Grosstet, old boy?" Pablek asked. *"War? Peace? Your people out there conquering star systems, and if so, how long until your fleet arrives?"*

Even as a tiny holograph, Jessie wanted to strangle the asshole.

Whether his understanding of the local language was lacking or he really was just that sanguine, the question didn't faze the ambassador. He was a public address system with facial expressions.

"WE ARE THE PEOPLE OF PEACE. NO WAR'AE WITH OURSELF. NO HUNTING THE ANIMAL'AE. NOT UNTIL THE STAR'AE DID WE FIGHT. WHEN WE MUST. ONLY MUST. YOU SMALL SPECIES'AE. SO MUCH WAR. SO SILLY. NO GAIN. YOU HAVE SUCH THE GOOD FOOD'AE. SUCH THE GOOD SONG'AE. SHARE, SAY ME."

To his credit, Pablek didn't let the elephant bury the lede. *"So your people have enemies. Spill. What're they like? We've all seen the Gallery of Life listings. Who's out there? Tarantulas? Polar bears? What do the mighty haathee fear?"*

The haathee laughed from his belly and leaned aside in his chair. Reaching out with his trunk, he ruffled the fur on Pablek's head. In the privacy of both her cell and her encryption mask, Jessie burst out laughing. The little laaku instigator wasn't such a firebrand with someone who looked like he could casually turn him into a meatball.

"WE STEP ON THEM, THE SPECIES'AE WHO TRY TO HURT US. THE SQUISH IS DONE. PEACE. HAPPY. I COME VISIT TO MEET NEW FRIEND'AE."

Jessie double-checked the timestamps. The missive came a few minutes after the *Pablek Tonight* interview. Why had the algorithm taken so long to regurgitate this one for review?

She opened a channel to Futhrek of Vendrey. He appeared in avatar form in her virtual comm interface.

"Sir, I think I may have found something."

"Excellent. Categorize it for further review."

"Sir. If you don't mind. I think this one might be a little more urgent." She shared the missive and linked the interview, using the system's native software tools to highlight and compare the phrases and times.

"Hmm. What's your hypothesis?"

Jesus fucking Christ. Was he being deliberately obtuse, or

was he really not seeing this? "My hypothesis is that whoever sent that is interested in forming a military alliance with the haathee. Given the reference to traitors, I'd suppose a civil conflict, and given the political circumstances in the galaxy at the moment... I mean, without clearance to view the participants, I have to strongly suspect either an Earthling or Martian military officer and a subordinate."

Futhrek's fingers twitched. The veil of secrecy lifted as he authorized her to view the de-anonymized version of the comm.

Sender: Rear Admiral Marsha Beams, MARS Navy

Recipient: Tamara Muncie, Director of Martian Intelligence Services

"Oh. Shit."

"You may feel free to omit that commentary from your official report. I'll attach a priority flag. Please complete this before any other task."

"Yes, sir."

Jessie knew, deep down, that "other tasks" included ending her shift and getting dinner.

It was a relief arriving back at the little nook of the giant factory where magic took place.

There were other magical alcoves, Eric knew, but the glassteel shop was his haven. All his life, one thing or another had set him apart. Well, as far back as his earliest memories, leastwise. Maybe when he was a baby, he was normal. Fit in with the other babies. Didn't make people feel weird just being himself.

He'd wanted to be a wizard as far back as he could remember. That alone made people act differently around him if they knew. He'd *thought* it was all going to be better once he got to Oxford. But rather than magic setting him apart, it was economics. There were, in theory, cheap wizards' schools out there. But few attended Oxford without parents who could afford the tuition without blinking. He'd made friends, but even in his clique, he was the one with lower-class tastes and wasn't bothered by doing his own chores around the dorms.

Glassteel.

He'd never have thought. But seeing the smiles and waves as wizards briefly interrupted their work to greet his return warmed an ember in Eric's heart that had gone so cold he'd been surprised it *could* be rekindled.

"Hey, bud!"

"Breaktime's over. Back to work, ya slacker."

"What'd Doonie want? Your socks not match or something?"

Hecuba set down a sketchbook and charcoal pencil. "Well, enough dillydallying, I suppose. Let's make some magic."

Eric had yet to peek inside to see what Hecuba drew. She always left the cover closed and had yet to offer him a look. He had yet to ask. Now wasn't the time. "Right. Back to it." He clapped his hands and rubbed them together, then reached across and took Hecuba's.

They sang and shimmied. Steel turned to glass. Conveyors grumbled. The two-piece band played.

It was, in short, a perpetual party that churned out space station windows as a byproduct.

Between songs, as new pieces were dragged into the enchanting room, they chatted.

"It's quaint, in a way."

"What is?" Eric asked. There wasn't a lot on Phabian that counted as quaint, and if he were missing out, he wanted to know about it.

"Not taking the promotion. Staying someplace you like.

Leaving the money on the table, so to speak." She brushed a lock of hair over her ear. Since the work required looking down, it kept falling out of place.

"You wouldn't have?"

"Doubt it," Hecuba replied breezily. "They already got me once. I was working in star-drives over in Pellan, and they said I was too talented to—how did they word it?—'squander my chance to make a difference.' That's how I ended up here."

It occurred to Eric that there was a stair-stepping social construct here that threatened to separate the two of them. He'd been started out in glassteel and offered a promotion mere days later. If he had to be honest with himself, gravity stones sounded pretty easy, too. How long would they let him work *there* if they realized? What next? Personal security details? Terraforming? Maintaining the glyphs that defend the galaxy from ancient evils from beyond the inflection point?

Eric's academic adviser had informed him, in no uncertain terms, that the latter job didn't exist. A shame, too, since it almost sounded like fun work. Important work.

Would Phabian want Eric as a librarian for their very own Plundered Tomes repository? Aunt Tiffany said that retrieving and guarding dangerous books was important work, but he knew she acquired those books almost exclusively through murder. He'd had that on better authority than she'd have imagined.

"Eric? ERIC?" Fingers snapped in front of his face. Eric blinked. "You zoned out again. That's fine, but we've got another window ready."

Eric glanced down and found that Hecuba was correct. A two-hundred-kilo steel slab had snuck up on him unnoticed. "Sorry." He took her hands in his. "My mind wanders off if I don't keep a tight leash on it."

"Where were you just then?"

"Pondering the myriad career choices pulling us through life. It's like swimming against a riptide to do your own thing. Everyone acts like being self-directed is lazy, but it's a lot of work."

They sang another piece of glassteel into existence. Without letting go of his hands, Hecuba struck up a new conversation once the conveyor hauled it away. "Hey. Um. What would you think of having dinner tonight?"

"I was planning on it. I don't always, but I've got a good situation for developing some healthy habits. Pliny and Jin were—"

Hecuba shook her head. Another aspiring window rolled toward them, a trickle of sand through the glass of their social interlude. She blurted out, "I mean you and me. *Just* you and me."

Well, he'd planned an evening loosely around the snooker table in the back room of O'Mallory's Pub. They kept it around almost exclusively for wizards' use, and Eric looked forward to playing without magic.

"Sure," he replied instead. He hadn't even hesitated.

Hecuba shared a coy smile with him, and they started the enchanting song anew.

⊏⊐

Jessie cut into her steak, marveling at how impossible it would have been to tell it wasn't the real thing. Food processors had gotten a lot better in the last five years. Ice cream for every meal had gotten boring quicker than she'd predicted, but ice cream had been easy to replicate. This steak was a sign that maybe she wouldn't be eating all desserts for however long she was on Phabian.

The booth was empty except for her and her plate. Somber

faux-wood decor, low lighting, and glossy red upholstery gave the place an Old Earth feel. Light conversation buzzed at the surrounding booths. The jazz wasn't live, and the volume kept it from being either intrusive or so faint that it led to inadvertent eavesdropping. Jessie had the clink and scrape of dinnerware for company.

Eric hadn't exactly stood her up. They hadn't agreed to eat all their meals together outside work hours. But it was always nice catching up with him. Weird as he was around everyone else, he felt normal to be around. He understood her on an axis that no one else saw.

But her brother had his own life.

On a logical level, she knew that he'd been out on his own at Oxford. Making friends. Attending classes. Managing to feed himself, even if it was only at on-campus eateries. But she'd never been second fiddle to him before. Eric was the one who got lost in large shopping centers, who didn't answer his shouted name in deep forests because he was fascinated by a mushroom, who didn't hit back when he got in a fight. She'd always looked out for him. He'd always needed her to.

He didn't owe her anything. That's what family was about, after all. It just gnawed at her a little that he was out having fun with new friends while she was eating an admittedly delicious steak alone in a human-themed laaku restaurant.

At long last, her plate was empty. Three hundred forty grams of factory-fresh imitation meat now rested in her belly. Now she had to decide whether to chase it down with a dessert that was—nutritionally speaking—virtually identical to the steak or wash it down with beer that was—alcoholically speaking—not beer.

"Mind if I join you?" a smooth laaku voice inquired.

Jessie glanced up. She'd heard the light, plastic slap of walking gloves approaching from her blind side, but the greeting came as a surprise. He was dressed smartly in a black suit and tie, with unobtrusive datagoggles that hinted at function over form. "Sorry. Just decompressing after work."

"Nothing to be sorry about," the laaku replied. He slipped into the far side of the booth.

Without letting her guest out of her peripheral vision, Jessie scanned the restaurant. "Plenty of open seating. I came here for the quiet."

"After all day in a little closet they call an office?" The laaku clucked his tongue. "I'd recommend a walk by the riverside. There's a cultural festival everySunday night. Music, manual boat rides—"

"Who are you?" Jessie snapped, fighting to keep her voice down.

"A patriot. Like you."

She scoffed. "Fuck off. You don't know what you're talking about. Earth and Mars both want me dead or in prison. I don't even know who wants which."

The interloper seemed nonplussed. He wagged a finger. "You and I actually share a loyalty. To ARGO."

"There is no ARGO." Even as she said that, she wondered if there was a layer here she was missing. All this was destined to end up in a report in the morning. She tried to commit exact wordings to mind in case someone with a better cultural vocabulary could pick out details she missed. "It died when Mars declared independence."

A hovering cart arrived, dropping off a drink that she hadn't seen her guest order. It was impossible to judge the contents except by elimination. The liquid was clear, very likely wasn't alcoholic, and could have tasted like anything. He took a sip immediately. "Lotta people think that way. But ARGO wasn't just a military alliance. It was an idea, a mixing of cultures. Cultures I think we can both appreciate. You grew up with laaku friends. You understand that, over the centuries, our two species have become inextricably intertwined."

Jessie motioned back and forth between them. "What is *this*? Who are you, really? This some sort of test? Hazing?"

"All you have to do to find out is nothing."

"Nothing?" Jessie echoed incredulously. She paused. "Done. Now, how about some answers?"

Her guest threw back the remainder of his drink in a single motion, leaving the empty glass on the table as he stood. "Tomorrow. Monday shift. You have all day to decide whether our conversation warrants an entry in your daily log. I become someone else's problem. But if you want to know what's being done to reunite ARGO, just wait. My colleagues and I respect patience. And discretion. Especially discretion."

"That why we're talking in the open?" It felt like a gotcha that would invalidate his whole line of logic.

"Oh, you wandered a block outside the refugee security perimeter. Defiantly, if I might make a personal observation. We don't have surveillance here. You're on your own. Own life. Own decisions. Own future ahead of you."

Jessie snickered. "This is the safest planet in the galaxy. I could eat a blaster barrel here and wake up in the hospital with a headache."

"Safest for some. Most, even. Not for people like you and me." The laaku gave her a solemn nod as an equal. "Good evening, Lieutenant."

Jessie watched him disappear out the restaurant door. He'd left her with a lot to think about but not his name.

The candles weren't real fire, but they looked pretty close. With the uncommonly dim lighting in Chez Gorpek, all Eric could make out clearly were the white tablecloth, the two place settings, the tuxedo-clad waiter when he came by, and Hecuba's smiling face.

Eric was glad she seemed to be enjoying the ambiance. This was fancier than he preferred for mealtimes.

"Have you decided?" their laaku waiter asked on his next visit to the tableside.

"What's the *poisson du jour?*" Hecuba asked as if it were the most natural question on the planet.

The waiter found nothing weird about this question, either. "We have *sole meunière*, fresh from our very own farm in the Zamik Ocean."

"Sounds lovely."

"And for you, sir?"

Eric hadn't found anything to his liking on the menu. Luckily, this place operated on a fairly simple ancient language, so he improvised. "*Nuggets de poulet avec moutarde au miel*, if you please."

The waiter narrowed his eyes almost imperceptibly. "Very well, sir. I'm sure we can accommodate you."

Eric raised a finger to forestall the waiter's departure. "And sparkling white wine."

"For two," Hecuba added.

"Of course..."

Hecuba sighed when they were alone again. "I've always wondered what it would be like to go back to the days before technology saturated everything. Be able to dine by actual candles. Eat food prepared by master chefs who studied for years to perfect the culinary arts." She had a wistful look in her eyes. Then she refocused and tried to look Eric in the eye.

He glanced subtly aside. Plenty of experienced wizards could look one another in the eye safely. He doubted Hecuba had the willpower to hold steady if Eric grew distracted while they locked gazes. Trying to avoid offending her, he played along. "We aren't going to be eating handmade food?"

"Real food is hard enough to find around here. They wouldn't trust expensive ingredients like live fish or chicken to anything but a computer."

"I'm sure we won't be able to taste the difference."

Moonlight crept through the many-paned window, giving a blurry and slightly distorted view of the street outside. Pedestrians passed in both directions. Those passing right to left were barely recognizable as humans and laaku; the ones traveling left to right came right up to the windows and were merely hazy mannequins walking past.

Eric fought back against the distraction of imagining in the details of the people outside. He made small talk. He exchanged stories about his family for those of Hecuba's much more interesting relatives. She had a sister who taught pre-collegiate magic on Orion and an uncle who'd fought in the Zheen War. Her mother was a painter, and her father was treasurer of a non-profit charity that helped stranded colonists.

"How often do colonies even fail?" he asked.

"Apparently, it's not that uncommon. People try to live some weird places without terraforming them first. It's scary to think of living on a colony with a 4-person shuttle as the only transportation when two hundred people live there."

Eric shrugged and remembered to swallow his chicken nugget before commenting. "I was a spacer kid. My home 'colony' was one ship, and it fit exactly everyone who lived on it."

"Must have been tough."

Eric's final nugget had just gone into his mouth, but he couldn't let that statement stand for the duration of proper chewing. "No way. It was great." He hastily swallowed. "My dad was a musician, and we traveled with his band. Whole big, extended family. It was a fun way to grow up. I must have seen, oh... 137 planets, depending what you call a planet these days."

"Wow. I can't picture living that way." She sounded more intrigued than pitying, which had been the reaction of most of his Oxford classmates.

"Dessert?" their waiter asked, slipping up to the table as soon as they'd both finished their meals.

"Mind if I pick something for both of us?" Hecuba asked.

Eric shrugged. "OK."

"We'd like *Tour des Pyrénées* cheese platter."

Eric's eyes widened. "Ooh. What's in that?"

"Cheeses, sir. Several cheeses." Their waiter departed.

Hecuba leaned forward and lowered her voice conspiratorially. "There are also crackers. Good ones, too."

"I didn't realize you'd been here before."

"Oh. Um. I came with my parents, once. They came to see me after I was settled."

"That was nice of them, I—"

Eric stopped mid-sentence. Something caught his eye from the window. One of the moving blurs had stopped. No, two of them had. He glanced over for a better look. Two heads. Four eyes. One figure taller and wider than the other.

No.

It couldn't be.

Could it?

He had to know.

"Excuse me," Eric blurted. He dabbed the corners of his mouth with the napkin from his lap and left the white cloth square behind as he rushed from the table.

"Are you sick?" Hecuba called after him.

"I just need to check something!"

Eric raced past the lectern, where a human woman in a demure black dress took names, and burst through the door.

Out on the street, night had fallen. Streetlamps fought back the towering gloom that stretched all the way to the stars. Panting for breath, Eric ran to the middle of the road for a better vantage.

He spotted two figures about the right sizes, their backs turned to him, scurrying through the pedestrian crowd ahead of the general flow.

Shutting his eyes briefly, Eric tried to feel for disturbances in the laws of science.

But this was Phabian. It was like listening to classical music in a machine shop, hoping to pick out one off-key note.

Or, in this case, two.

He got nowhere.

Opening his eyes, Eric set off at a jog.

Whatever they were doing here, Eric wasn't afraid of them. He was in the right, this time. The Phabian government had granted him asylum. He was protected by law. If anything, they were the criminals this time.

If Eric was correct.

And Eric wasn't going to know for sure whether he was right about this unless he caught them red-handed.

But as he quickened his pace and his lungs were burning, Eric faced one domineering question.

What are Snow and Slater doing on Phabian?

⊏⊐

Since the queue was mostly laaku, Jessie had a clear view of just how long it might be before she got a chance to enter the banquet hall. Everyone was smartly dressed, but not quite tuxedos and evening gowns. She wore a black blazer and slacks, matching flats, and a white blouse. Her hair, which she'd started to let grow out, was slicked back; she still hadn't gotten used to the little flyaway hairs tickling her temples or getting in her field of vision.

Twisting to see behind her, Jessie checked the time. Across the way, atop the advertised listings of current offerings, the holotheater displayed the time.

6:12 p.m.

The event had officially kicked off twelve minutes ago, and she was still stuck in line. Her invitation had come out of nowhere. A quick local omni search suggested that tickets were tough to come by but non-transferable; otherwise, she'd have hawked hers for the spare cash in a heartbeat. And if she weren't curious about who'd hooked her up, this line at the door would have had her making alternate plans for the evening.

A shift. Jessie shuffled forward one space as everyone waiting advanced.

She fought the temptation to check her datapad, mostly because she'd had to leave it back at her apartment. Security dictated no recordings of the event or its participants. No recordings meant no recording devices—a low-tech evening. Out in the borderlands, it was still possible to find datapads that only had basic comm functions and a few omni apps, but good luck convincing anyone local that you were operating what amounted to little more than an abacus. By Phabian standards, tonight's guests were already roughing it.

The waddling, shuffling, fidgeting line eventually allowed Jessie up to the security station, where a phalanx of armed laaku security guards manned a scanner booth. Jessie stepped inside without hesitation. Translucent blue walls surrounded her like the shower stall of a cheap starliner. Digital writing snapped into view in front of her, listing biographical and biological data.

A muffled voice from outside the booth asked, "To the best of your knowledge, is all information presented correctly?"

Jessie gave everything a skim. "Yeah."

With a *bloop*, the far door of the booth opened, finally allowing Jessie into the venue. She stepped into the airy, vaulted ballroom of the Chapodie of Abnek Center for the Performing Arts. This wasn't the theater, of course, but a formal gathering hall that would have better fit on a human-built world. Ionic columns rose to support the chamber in an utterly decorative fashion; Jessie would have bet her back teeth that the whole place would have stood up fine without a single one of them. But, they broke up the room and lent a borrowed air of charm and dignity that laaku had ascribed to ancient humans for centuries.

Right as she entered, a waiter swung past with a silver platter, and Jessie plucked a champagne glass bearing a pale pink liquid that turned out to be a fruit concoction devoid of alcohol. Tasty, if mildly disappointing.

Jessie minced her steps and navigated the crowd where few of the other attendees came as high as her chest. Those few numbered mainly fellow humans but also included scattered tesuds, azrin, in-tik, and a surprising number of stuunji. Presumably, members of shorter races were in attendance as well but hadn't been visible as she got her bearings.

The crowd, however, had not spread evenly throughout the ballroom. It was hard to overlook a distinct gathering a few dozen meters away, pressing into the entryway of one of the side rooms off the main ballroom. Drawn as if by social gravity, Jessie found curiosity leading her to the outer reaches of the cluster.

It became immediately clear what the attraction was.

"OH. YES. VERY MUCH. I HAVE THE STORY TO TELL YOU ABOUT THAT. WAIT. FIRST, WHAT IS THAT FOOD YOU HAVE? MAY I? OH, DELIGHTFUL. THANK YOU."

The voice, permanently set to bellow, carried like a public address speaker even from the next room and over the buzz of the crowd. Despite a clear unfamiliarity with the language, the English was clear and passable. Careful not to trample her laaku hosts, Jessie shuffled forward to get a better look. Luckily for her, size played to her advantage. Polite, safety-conscious partygoers made way as she impinged on their personal space. Soon enough, she reached the doorway—far taller than the average laaku construction, she realized. The whole place actually showed signs of recent renovations to accommodate the visiting alien dignitary.

Jessie caught sight of the haathee and blinked in utter shock.

She'd heard Mom and Dad's stories about Poltid, Kubu, and the whole munching giant race. But she'd never met one in person; not since she was old enough to remember, anyway. That left Ambassador Grosstet as the largest sentient creature she'd ever seen. Easily over three meters tall, he reclined on a throne-like chair as eager laaku pressed in on all sides, carrying on a conversation where only one side was audible throughout the whole room.

Grosstet was dressed in a loose garb that mixed elements of toga, kilt, and kimono if Jessie had to cobble it together from human clothing. His long tusks bore rings from which tassels dangled, and he gestured with a thick, three-fingered hand as he spoke. His comment about the food was evidently in reference to the cart that was now being maneuvered from the wall over to his seat. When it came within reach, the elephant-like trunk reached out and delicately plucked a pastry and popped it into the ambassador's mouth.

"I TASTE A SMALL RED FRUIT. WHAT IS THE NAME?" A besuited laaku climbed onto the armrest of the chair and cupped his upper hands to Grosstet's massive, flappy ear. "STRAW BERRY? VERY GOOD. WE HAVE THEM ON MY WORLD. SMALL FRUIT. BIG FLAVOR. WHO IS THAT?"

A finger the size of a cucumber leveled across the room. Jessie glanced self-consciously around her, scooting aside to avoid confusion as the haathee indicated someone in her vicinity. But the finger tracked her diligently even as its owner browsed the pastry cart with his trunk, sniffing around before selecting another croissant.

"HOW CAN YOU NOT KNOW? THIS IS YOUR PARTY. I ASKED FOR HUMAN'AE. THAT IS A HUMAN. I HAVE SEEN PICTURE'AE. I KNOW IT IS." The laaku, who was clearly acting as Grosstet's handler for the event, spoke something Jessie couldn't overhear. Even across language and cultural barriers as yet unplumbed between human and haathee species, she could read the exasperation in the spread hands and incredulity in the look in all directions around the ceiling. The ambassador beckoned with his trunk, nodding with what she imagined was reassurance. "COME HUMAN. BE KNOWN TO GROSSTET, ENVOY OF THE HAATHEE."

Jessie had come to this meet-and-greet with the intention of being as discreet as a human among laaku could be. Now, she found herself the center of attention. This couldn't have been what her mysterious benefactor had in mind.

Could it?

Fuck him, whoever he was.

Jessie had been raised a spacer. She knew more non-humans than the majority of her kind had seen in a lifetime. If this ambassador wanted to meet a human, she'd embarrass the species less than most.

"Hi," she called out, raising a hand as the crowd allowed her to advance. Like a distant mountain, the haathee ambassador grew larger and larger the closer she got. One hand lifted in a non-threatening wave.

Dumbass, Jessie chided herself. *What's this guy got to worry about from me? Looks like he could step into traffic and be more a hazard to passing hovers than the other way around.*

"COME CLOSE." Grosstet beckoned with one hand, mouth agape in what she supposed to be a smile. "I DO NOT EAT MEAT."

Jessie tried not to let it show that putting that notion in her head rattled her just a hair. She didn't break stride as she walked up to the custom-built chair. "If you wanted to kill me, I'm not sure I'd care what became of me after."

Grosstet laughed, guttural and hearty. He slapped a hand down on his armrest, and Jessie felt the jolt through her feet. "VERY SMART. ARE ALL HUMAN'AE?"

"Nope," Jessie replied casually. "I'm pretty average, but we have some real idiots in my species."

The ambassador leaned down, careful to keep his tusks clear of her, and reached out with a hand, one finger extended. When Jessie hesitated, he asked, "IS THIS NOT YOUR CUSTOM?"

Oh, shit. This was a handshake? Shaking off her confusion, Jessie gripped the finger with all her might and gave a firm shake. The haathee skin felt like tree bark, and his handshake was like bending a branch. Any motion at all was his doing, though it was clear he was being dainty about the interaction. "Pleasure to meet you. I'm Jessica Ramsey."

"OF?"

He'd clearly been talking to too many laaku. "We humans don't typically do an 'of' like the laaku. First name. Family name. Sometimes the other way around, but not in my case. There can be middle names to clear up confusion or honor someone."

"DO YOU HAVE ONE?"

"Judith. After my grandmother."

Grosstet nodded along. "PLEASURE TO MEET YOU, JESSICA JUDITH RAMSEY OF THE HUMAN'AE. I AM GROSSTET, GREAT EXPLORER OF THE HAATHEE. CAPTAIN OF MY SHIP. SINGER. DANCER. POET. LOVER. FIGHTER WHEN I MUST. CONNOISSEUR WHEN I CAN. A FRIEND TO FRIEND'AE AND ENEMY TO FOOL'AE. AND YOU?"

Wow. Despite being awkward and a little stilted, someone had fed this guy a load of vocabulary in a short period of time. And she couldn't help being amused that when he said his own name, the first syllable came from his trunk in a weird sort of stereo.

"I'm a guest of the laaku people right now. My people are in the middle of a war, and I got caught between sides."

"I HEAR SO MUCH OF THE MIGHTY HUMAN'AE. SO FEARLESS OF THE RACE'AE THAT THEY CAN FIGHT A WAR WITH TWO SIDE'AE. FOR ONE MONTH—ALMOST—I HAVE ASKED. TODAY, I FINALLY MEET A HUMAN!"

Grosstet raised his trunk and let loose a deafening trumpet.

The next day at work, Jessie took her lunch at the Section 74 cafeteria. The chairs were low, lower than strictly comfortable, but within the General Ergonomic Accommodation for human use. Tables spread apart in varying sizes, making inefficient use of the space but allowing for room to breathe after a morning spent cooped up in a tiny dwelling. Anechoic walls ate the clatter of flatware and kept eavesdropping to a bare minimum. Jessie picked out an unoccupied three-seater and sat down with her tray laden with falsie beer and nutrient-dense chocolate bars.

Just being away from the interface was relaxing. Even customized to her every whim, the flood of data to absorb and process was daunting. Here, familiar flavors and a few minutes to think her own thoughts were the respite she needed to get through the rest of the day.

Remembering the suggested decompression techniques from her orientation, Jessie tried to keep her breaths long and slow, mindful of her body's needs. The mind would look after itself if the body calmed.

"Mind if I join you?"

Jessie instantly scowled at the interloper. Then, she recognized the mysterious visitor from the restaurant the other night and froze.

"I'll take that as a yes." The laaku wore an outfit like hers as he slid into one of the empty seats at the table.

"I'm waiting for two people," Jessie chastised him.

"Funny. I'll have to remember that one. How was the gala?"

"No work talk," she reminded him.

The laaku shrugged and dug a spoon into his banana split. "What's work? You got to see the circus last night. Toughest ticket in town to snag. Can't buy them with anything but pull."

"Your doing?"

"Me? Who am I? I'm wondering myself just who got you invited."

Jessie let one raised eyebrow convey her opinion of that claim.

"He stand up to the rumors? Heard he speaks better English than half the League."

Jessie bit off a chunk of her chocolate and chewed. "Surprisingly good. Little weird, but considering he just got here... yeah. The One Way Expedition met his people on an exploration mission of their own."

"He talk about his ship or crew at all?"

Jessie wagged a half-eaten bar in admonition. "Now *that* is starting to tread on work."

To be fair, Grosstet had been cagey about his journey to ARGO space. All she'd been able to get out of him was confirmation of facts available on Phabian newsfeeds. He had a massive ship orbiting the planet that defied all attempts to scan the interior and had come to the surface in a shuttle that had thwarted polite attempts at state-sanctioned burglary.

Oh, the ambassador had brushed off the idea of being offended that Phabian Investigative Services had tried to pop his security locks to snoop inside. But if Jessie knew the common mannerisms that crossed species barriers, she suspected that he was actually smug about it. Aside from that subjective and possibly erroneous observation, he hadn't given any intel worth putting into an official report.

"Maybe you've got some less-than-professional thoughts you wouldn't mind sharing, say, over dinner tonight?"

Jessie narrowed her eyes.

"What?"

"You've read my psych records, haven't you?"

"What're you implying?"

She wasn't letting him off so easy. "You just go around asking human women on dates all the time, huh?"

"Dinner isn't a proposition."

"But it could have been, if I'd said yes?" She shook her head. "Just because I've had a couple non-human boyfriends—"

"Whoa." He held up his upper hands. "Look, if you want to get promoted out of data analysis, you've got to handle these situations better. Yeah. I've read your file. *Our* file on you, that is. You've got buttons, and it's not hard to press them. Want some career advice?" He didn't wait for Jessie to answer. "Figure out those buttons and disconnect them."

"So, you think I should have just said 'yes' to advance my career."

Her mystery companion shook his head as he finished a bit of his dessert. "On the contrary, a real ace would have shot me down in flames before I got off a shot. Point is, you got defensive, anti-social, confrontational. If you wanted information out of me—and I know you do—you should have used my intentions to manipulate me to your advantage."

"Look, I only have one lunch break a day. Mind if I actually relax before I get back to ensuring the safety of Phabian's population?"

The laaku enigma chuckled. "Dinner at eight."

If he wanted a sparring partner, fine. Jessie could play that game. "Holotheater at nine. And I want your name now, or you can just get a new chew toy."

"Bernek of Fenzel," he replied without hesitation. "But you can call me Bernie."

―――――

Eric was right on time for work, which was easy because he showed up two hours early and waited. As soon as Doonah arrived with the ornate key that allowed access to the magic-shielded work room, Eric raced inside.

Not that he should have expected Hecuba to already be inside; that would have been implausible. Still, when one needs to make an apology badly enough, no amount of wishful thinking seems excessive.

He took his station, shifting weight from one foot to the other as she continued not showing up for work. Other wizards went so far as to start up their conveyors and begin their chants.

There was no music, since the band didn't typically show up this early—something about needing sleep after a nightclub job.

Doonah ambled over and raised a hand to catch Eric's attention over the noise of machinery and arcane entreaties. "Change of plans this morning."

Oh, no.

Plans were welcome to change. They were welcome to not exist at all, frankly. But something about the way Doonah said it, there wasn't going to be a welcome continuation of the laaku wizard's line of reasoning.

"Hecuba and Elroy are out today. You'll be paired up with Shin."

Eric cleared his throat. "Um. I'd much rather work with Hecuba."

"It's just for today."

"But where is she?"

Doonah offered a perfunctory shrug. "I don't ask. Not my business. If she didn't tell you, it's not yours, either."

Wow. That hit like a fist to the stomach.

Eric did as he was told.

Shin was a serviceable partner for the day. He had soft hands and used a moisturizer that smelled of lilac. He could also sing on key in a practiced tenor. But he didn't make the work fun, nor did he know the little dance moves that Hecuba and he had worked out together.

As soon as the workday ended, Eric headed out to find her.

Leaving in the middle of dinner was rude. That much he knew. Whether leaving during the dessert process exacerbated the offense, he couldn't say. Skipping out before discussing payment for the meal was *certainly* a social faux pas. No. It was worse. It was taking advantage.

Eric desperately needed to apologize.

If she'd skipped work because he'd embarrassed her or

saddened her, he needed to reassure her that he was the one in the wrong. She'd done nothing worth being treated so shabbily. Even if he had to admit that his tormentors had managed to chase him across time, space, and lines on a political map, he'd do it.

But where to find her?

The most obvious place to look was the wizards' dormitories. He didn't know her apartment number, but that didn't deter him.

"Do you know where Hecuba lives?" he asked a worker fixing one of the swinging doors in the lobby.

"Who?" Eric conjured a smiling image of her. "Sorry. Don't know her."

Eric got similar reactions as he wandered the halls. Wizards around here, it seemed, kept their own counsel, not getting involved in one another's personal lives. But eventually, someone did know.

"Hecuba? Wow. That's a rewind. Pretty sure she stacked ions months ago."

Eric shook his head. "I had dinner with her last night."

The young human wizard with the science slang shook his head emphatically. "Naw. I mean she moved out. Got her own place with that factory money she slurps."

"Do you know where she lives now?"

The helpful wizard put up his hands. "Hey, brother. Kind words: if she didn't *tell* you where she lives, she probably doesn't *want* you to know. Take the hint."

"It's just an oversight. She missed work inexplicably today, and I'm more than a little worried."

"Brother, unspool it. Get to one of the wet clubs and quaff a few. You'll feel better."

This was getting nowhere. Eric skipped dinner and headed out into the city.

He'd seen his holos. He knew the private-eye routine. With a conjured image at his literal fingertips, Eric wore down the soles of his shoes in a labor-intensive effort to track her down.

Fewer than one person in fifty so much as recognized her. Most of those who did hadn't seen her recently.

But a street-corner Seekers preacher had seen her just that morning. Eric engaged the man in a brief chat that left him with complicated questions about his own faith, but during a brief eye contact, he leafed through the conversation the pair had in passing.

"*Have you considered your soul, miss?*"

"*It's in good hands.*" In the preacher's memory, Hecuba untucked her hands from her sleeves just long enough to flash a quick image of the One Church roman numeral one in the same way that the students at Oxford flashed a Convocation sigil to gain quick entry to an off-campus bar. She didn't even break stride. It barely met the minimum standard for a social interaction.

It had been enough.

Eric glanced around to orient the memory to his surroundings. The preacher had been on the same street corner, so there wasn't much trick to it.

"Thanks."

He left the preacher befuddled and headed off in the direction Hecuba had been going.

"Where were you going?" Eric asked under his breath as he marched his way down a canyon of towering, shining, laaku-constructed buildings.

He didn't know the city. Barely knew a fraction of the planet. Had only started getting to know Hecuba.

Quitter talk, he warned himself. He'd upset her, and now she was missing. This was his fault. He had to make it right.

Eric walked through the city, through the night, through

hurt and confusion.

For his trouble, Eric got sore feet, a gnawing hunger in his gut, hundreds of unhelpful responses from locals, several inquiries after his state of wellness, and a weirdly beautiful view of the dawn as it glinted down from the tops of the silvery towers.

Thoroughly lost, he had to ask for directions back to the Wizards' Quarter, where he collapsed from exhaustion on a park bench a few blocks from his apartment.

⬛▭

The lights were just dim enough that Jessie could still make out the steps and rows of chairs in the bowl-shaped chamber of the holotheater. She wasn't terribly early, but there were plenty of seats throughout. Scanning for potential privacy, she found a spot in the upper ring on the far side, just offset enough that she'd have a clear view of the main entrance as the giant central holo-projector lit and blocked the middle of the chamber with previews of upcoming features.

There wasn't a soul within ten seats of her in any direction. She settled in with her bucket of popcorn and liter-sized cup of peach soda like this was any other evening out on the town. Most of the patrons waiting along with her were human. After all, this was still inside the refugee zone. Laaku were allowed, but the theater specialized in comfort food holos from back in human-controlled space.

"*Blaster From the Past*, kind of on the nose, isn't it?" Bernek commented wryly as he took a seat on her right, plugging a canister of Froze Goo into his cupholder.

"Hey, I don't name them. I couldn't resist trying to figure out how Lucille Cray turned *Weekend on Luna* into an action heroine career."

Bernek pulled off his walking gloves and popped a handful of Pucker Dots into his mouth with a lower hand. "You should check the blackmail archive. Fascinating stuff. Explains the entertainment industry way better than the tabloid newsfeeds."

"You seen this one?"

"Nah. I pass on most of them. Too busy."

"Should I feel honored?"

"Subtlety, Jess. Fuck's sake. You're lucky we have an advancement path that fits your... talents."

Jessie fought back a scowl that belonged on her face after that comment. He was baiting her. If Bernek wanted to play that game, she knew the rules. She stared vacantly toward the spot where their holo would be starting any moment. "Just looking to get my feet under me. You know, catch up on five years of missing culture."

Bernek leaned away from her and dug in a pocket, withdrawing a slender device that clicked when he thumbed a switch on the side. "Now that we've got a little privacy, what didn't you report about that haathee ambassador?"

"How illegal are those?" she asked, inclining her chin toward the audio dampener.

"Moderately. Less than the blaster I'm packing. And before you ask, it's not that I'm worried about *you*. On the contrary, if I thought you were a danger, I wouldn't feel much better armed. Just tools of the trade."

"How long before I can get a permit?"

Bernek shrugged. "Start the datawork before your shift tomorrow, if you want. Frankly, I doubt you'll get much pushback. Flip side of the same coin, really. You're not that much more of a threat to public safety if you go rogue, blaster permit or not. Considering your hand-to-hand rating, urban survival training, and explosives knowledge, a blaster's pretty much a status symbol."

"If this is your idea of foreplay..." Jessie warned playfully. He was clearly basting her in preparation for some big ask, but stroking her ego was working.

"Right. Fine. Holo's starting soon. I'll be blunt."

"Please."

"I want to put you in harm's way."

Awkward way to put that, but other than the delivery, not the least bit unexpected. "You and the immigration ministry sure aren't singing the same tune."

"They have their directives. I have mine."

"What's yours?"

"They want you safe. I want Phabian safe. Let's face it, you're going to hate feeling safe."

"Already do," she admitted. Just then, the holo-projector fired up, filling the center of the theater with a 5-meter 3D field showing the sprouting silver skyscraper letters of the Phabian Holographic Productions logo. The sound check momentarily drowned out all hope of verbal communication, leaving a faint ringing in Jessie's ears as it finished.

"It's right in your wheelhouse," Bernek promised. "Your background makes you perfect for this assignment."

"Stop sugarcoating it. I'm getting a toothache."

"What do you think of the haathee? Personal opinion. Off-the-record version."

Jessie suspected that Bernek's part of Section 74 didn't keep a lot of things on the record. "He's personable as fuck. Casually intimidating, and it's not just his size. Knows English way better than he should."

"Little suspicious, don't you think?"

"Maybe." Paranoia was such a well-known pitfall in the intelligence community that she didn't feel a need to point it out to Bernek.

"But also, maybe not, right?" he asked. Jessie gave a slight nod. "That's what I want from you. I need to know if this species sent a fraternity president out into the galaxy to represent them or if it's just a facade to throw us off."

"Anything in particular in mind?" Jessie asked, pausing as a hovercycle chase in one of the previews roared through the holo field.

"Befriend him. By all accounts, he took a liking to you."

"How could anyone tell?"

Bernek chuckled during what appeared to be a heartbreaking moment in the preview Jessie wasn't really watching. No one so much as flinched, so she assumed their privacy protection was working. "You might be surprised to learn that, despite his grasp of the language, he's a passive-aggressive motherfucker. Good enough that no one can really call him on it. You need to gain his confidence and figure out what he's really about."

"What if I end up liking him better than you?" Jessie deadpanned.

Bernek aimed a finger at her. "Better. I like it. But in seriousness, we need to know how he's regarded among his people. How high is he in their government? What kind of political pull does he have? What's the crew complement of that ship we've got in orbit? How open is he to technological exchange?"

"Their shit really that good?"

"We can't scan it. So, yes. But we don't know *how* yes. Because either this guy's balls are as big figuratively as they are literally, or that ship outguns anything we have."

Jessie swallowed past a lump in her throat. ARGO had always held a technological edge over the eyndar and zheen. Never a large one, but it was a comfort going into the various wars against them throughout history. With the alliance split, Earth was now the regional military technological powerhouse,

Mars was the leader in automation, industrial production, and mineral extraction, and Phabian the leader in personal technology and computing infrastructure.

The balance of power might shift around the haathee and his willingness to barter.

"What's the plan?"

Neither Jessie nor Bernek would later be able to give a detailed synopsis of *Blaster From the Past*, but she left the theater with a working outline of a plan to make a friend.

And betray a friend.

———

Eric floated along on a raft fashioned from loose logs tied together with bits of stray rope. The surface had been rubbed smooth, pleasant against bare skin, and he laced his fingers behind his head which he pillowed atop a bundled coat. He clenched a bit of straw in his teeth, more out of a commitment to the ambiance than any particular enjoyment he took in the act. Languid water carried him along, bobbing the raft gently along an endless river as lazy clouds watched from below a cheery sun.

Of course, the clouds and sun weren't the only things up there. Gigantic, tumbling, clearly labeled household objects and artifacts of modern technology remained a constant reminder of The Outside.

Nor was Eric the only one floating on this particular river at this particular moment. A whole flotilla, ranging from inner tubes to paddle steamers, dinghies to royal barges, surrounded him on all sides. But if he kept his eyes skyward, they remained respectfully outside his field of vision.

"Eric, would you be so kind as to increase the rainfall in the Destrin Plains? My realm needs more food by the year."

"Sure thing." Absently, Eric swooshed a hand in the air. He didn't need to. It was all show. But High Agrimancer Nepetunia would have a little story to bring back to her followers, and everyone would know that he was done making the requested alteration.

Another voice chimed in after a suitable pause for a shift in which vessels floated closest to the raft. "Magical attempts to join Old Tembria and the New Tembria Colonies continue to elude us. Our fastest ships take over a month to cross the Katamic Sea."

Eric sighed. "You said you wanted fresh continents to explore."

"Please, Eric. The Age of Exploration has passed. Either aid our magi or allow us to develop flying machines."

"No!" Eric snapped. They didn't know it, but flight would ruin their world. Trivialize it. Technologize it. "Fine. I'll gift you a book on how to connect two points on different continents." He snapped his fingers, causing the promised volume to appear in Ulrich's hands and ending the audience. The requirements would be grueling, only possible during certain celestial events, one of which would be coming up shortly but wouldn't recur for decades.

"Merciful Eric, if you would grace us with—"

The next petitioner's words were lost as the river heaved. Eric sat up, clutching tight to the logs of his raft as it bucked. All around him, ships tossed and captains panicked.

"Eric, save us!" voices cried.

He rolled his eyes. Scary though he supposed it may have been, no one would be hurt here. In their own realms, maybe, but not in this place. Not in his presence.

This was a sign, as much an omen as the Village of Eternity ever received.

"I must go. Return to your realms and look after them until I next return."

Over the protestations and wailing entreaties, Eric shut his eyes.

When he opened them again, Eric discovered the source of the jostling that had translated to his mental realm. A uniformed laaku security officer was shaking him by the shoulder. "No public sleeping. Move along. You have quarters, Wizard Eric. If you must sleep away the morning, I suggest you do so there."

Confusion always accompanied an unscheduled awakening. Eric blinked, struggling to fathom how this strange laaku knew his name. Then he caught sight of his own sketched portrait on the screen of the guard's datapad, along with his name, job, and local address.

"Sorry about that. Long night."

"Pleasant sleep, Wizard Eric," the guard replied with a nod that suggested he'd been dismissed.

As the guard turned to walk away, Eric scrambled off his park bench and followed. "If you don't mind me asking, what time is it?"

The guard pointed out the nearest civic chrono. It read 8:41 a.m.

Eric wasn't even late for work yet.

He didn't feel like working.

Last night came rushing back, along with the crushing disappointment of being unable to find Hecuba anywhere in Kethlet. In fairness, the district had something like a billion people living in it, and he hadn't talked to even a tiny fraction of them.

Sick in his heart, Eric knew what he had to do.

Back in his apartment, he found supplies of ink and paper, along with a selection of quills. He scribbled a quick note.

Wizard Doonah,

I am in no fit state for work today. Please accept my apology and promise that I will return to work when feasible.

Eric

No point getting overly formal or detailed. Haste was called for if he was going to deliver the message before he was docked for being late. Without knowing how he was paid in the first place, he didn't know what the penalty might be; it just had to be worse if he didn't provide adequate notice.

Seven quick folds and some Peractorum origami turned the paper into a model air glider. From his balcony, Eric took aim, squeezing shut one eye and sticking out his tongue as he judged the distance, the wind, and several other inconsequential factors before tossing the glider to fly on magic's wings to the factory and Doonah's office inside it.

With that taken care of, Eric huffed a sigh.

Now what?

He had a day off, and Hecuba could go back to work without having to see him.

What now?

From the balcony, Eric could look across the courtyard and see a wide swath of the refugee district, but that was only a slice of the whole region. He watched people heading on foot in every direction, each one a story captured at a snap-holo in time, stretching off for decades in every direction. Millions of years of personal history traveled in parallel, unknown to one another except in snippets.

"Time to go meet the locals, I guess."

Stick around people. That was the plan. If he was lucky, next time he spotted Snow or Slater, there would be witnesses.

There was an azrin-town in the refugee district. Not caring for the food options available within the confines, Eric walked over with a three-scoop cone of pistachio ice cream made with natural ingredients. It was a race against time as the real McCoy lacked the sciencey bits that kept it from melting in the daytime heat. And it was hard to concentrate on licking around the perimeter to head off dripping rivulets of melting green cream when the entertainment was this good.

Out in the street, an orange-furred azrin, barefoot and wearing a loose black pants and vest combo, was performing a traditional azrin art. Meat juggling, while not appetizing to him personally, was nonetheless fascinating.

What animal had died to provide the bone-in haunches that twirled expertly through the air, Eric couldn't say. Something good sized. The fur had been removed and most, but not all, of the blood. Four bonfires cordoned off the performance area. From the gasps of the crowd every time one of the haunches nearly fell into the flames before being deftly caught and returned to the air, keeping the meat raw was part of the act.

By the time Eric was crunching on the bland-yet-slightly-ice-cream-soaked cone, he'd judged what the gathered azrin seated around the square liked about this show. Time and again, throughout the performance, the juggler would snap his jaws, narrowly missing taking a bite from one of the spinning morsels. Diving, rolling, twisting, always as if his own hands betrayed him, keeping the kinetic feast out of reach.

The crowd slavered.

This was a culinary striptease.

When the show ended, the spectators pelted the juggler's feet with coins. High bidders caught the well-traveled meats the street performer threw them. Eric merely applauded. The ice cream was plenty for him.

"There you are!"

Eric nearly jumped out of his shoes. "Hecuba!"

She lingered at the edge of the crowd. Eric wove his way through the bloodhungry azrin to join her. "What happened? Did you quit?"

"Doonah sent me to track you down."

"Did he not get my note?"

Hecuba produced a creased piece of paper. "This note? This ominous, cryptic message that doesn't say when you'll be back or what your problem might be? He was worried."

"You disappeared yesterday. I thought it was common practice. I didn't want to be the reason you couldn't work. After all, I—"

Hecuba took him by the shoulders. "Eric. Stop. I was with my brother and his wife. I spent most of the day at the Immigration and Refugee Processing, providing moral support and helping with the datawork. They just arrived on Phabian."

"You didn't mention that to Doonah?"

"He didn't ask. And I was going to tell *you* during dessert. But... Yeah, what happened there?"

Eric looked at his feet. Hecuba hooked an arm through his, and he watched two pairs of feet as they walked away from the azrin-town. "Sorry about that."

"Well, sorry's a start. But why? Was it something I said?"

"No. I just..."

"Just what?"

How was he going to explain this? He could sneak into the Eternal Village. Uriela would know how to wordsmith this. Maybe he could bring her there. Maybe she'd understand, then.

"I saw a couple guys."

"You... what? Went to hang out with some friends?"

"Not friends!" Eric objected, looking up before she got the wrong idea. "You're the only friend I have here. Actually, I don't know if that's entirely true, but that's not the point. I wasn't going to see friends. I thought I saw a pair of wizards that used to be assigned as my parole officers on Earth before the war."

Hecuba squeezed his arm. She was a warm, comforting presence, reassuring in ways that decades in his own head could never be. "That was a long time ago. With the war, there's no way that they can—"

"They've already done it twice. On Mars. Again on Echo Niner. They're like bloodhounds with a star-drive. I don't know how they do it, but they keep finding me. I just can't get away from them."

Azrin didn't crowd their sub-district. Low numbers and cultural inclinations favored giving everyone space to roam. The sight of two humans who were obviously wizards created an even wider berth around the pair as they continued on their way unimpeded.

Hecuba knit her brow. "Are you *sure* you saw them? This might be one of those cases where a bad experience can make you *think* you see something when it's not really there."

"Jessie saw them. On Mars, anyway. She beat them up. They're probably really mad at her. Crap. I haven't even told her they're here on Phabian. I was so busy looking for *you* when I—"

"Wait. You went looking for me?"

"Yeah. After work yesterday. All night. I found your apartment, but you weren't home. So I headed out into Kethlet, looking for clues. I lost the trail, but I kept looking until dawn or so."

"I walked to the starport in the morning, spent all day at the immigration center with my brother, and went to dinner with him and Cassie. They were exhausted after a long interstellar trip. I was home by like seven."

Eric blinked. "You mean... I missed you by like half an hour at your apartment."

"Sounds like it." In the middle of foot traffic in the streets, she stopped and drew Eric into a hug. "Maybe next time, you'll tell me where you're going when you run off at dinnertime."

"I'm still really sorry about that," Eric replied, hugging back, feeling the tension ease from his soul.

"Well, you can make it up to me at the dance tonight."

"Dance?" Eric asked. Then, before he risked making things awkward again, he followed up with a quick, "Sure."

<hr />

This was an assignment, not a proper social gathering, Jessie reminded herself. When Bernek had gotten her on the guest list for the Interspecies Cultural Dance Exchange, she'd volunteered her knowledge of Rave Trance and Slip-Hop; she'd snuck off to clubs for that sort of thing in her teenage years when she was still learning her limits for various chemical mood enhancers.

No.

That wasn't the vibe these laaku party organizers were after. Earth got to have three dances represented, which she got the impression was already a concession they'd made with reluctance. The organizers had chosen ballet, which, to their credit, they knew better than to try asking her about. They'd also included a haka, which looked like a lot of fun, but there was a whole team who'd been practicing together for years.

Alas, Jessie *looked* like she'd grown up in North America, so they stuck her with the third and final human dance: the square dance.

Jessie was no historian, but she'd seen her share of holovids. Her getup was straight out of a comedy or a farce. The gaudy, overly tooled, overly fringed leather and cotton attire was all white and rawhide except for a few accents in brilliant red. She had boots that came halfway up her shins and a skirt that didn't quite come down to meet it. She had a red cowboy hat with a drawstring that would keep it from falling off during the dancing. A wig with pigtails had been supplied for the occasion, along with a gun belt containing replica six-shooters.

The guns weren't loaded, since anyone asked to dress up like this was liable to be a danger to themselves.

She'd made a token effort to beg off, maybe just attend as an observer. She'd barely been to Earth. Wasn't from there. This wasn't, technically speaking, her cultural dance. Of course, that resulted in them gamely trying to *explain* the square dance to her. After a few minutes of being patronized, she'd relented.

"It's a fucking square dance, not astral cartography. Of course, I know how!"

Thus, she waited. Alongside her mixed group of cowboys and cowgirls, she watched one of the local laaku troupes performing in the center of the ballroom. An announcer had preambled beforehand, calling it the *Niptu Detaka*, which she was struggling to translate without her datapad, which she'd left back in the apartment. But it involved a lot of lateral movement with the lower hands planted and spread, interspersed with hops to reorient the whole squad as they reset in unison and did it all over again.

Someone from the square-dancing crew leaned toward her, voice so low the drumbeats made it hard to hear her. "This is the kiddie version. I saw this team in Antho, and they do stacking sets, ninety-degree rotations, all the crazy shit. Most non-laaku would get hurt even trying."

Jessie nodded. Sure. Cultural dance-along. Made sense. Nothing *she* was going to be doing was the least bit complicated. Bumpkin colonists across the borderlands taught it to kids as a rite of passage. She'd been subjected to it on numerous occasions, admittedly with the ulterior motive of using it to pick up guys about her age.

The laaku were fascinating, but ulterior motives prevailed. As Jessie made a pretext of enjoying the other dancers, she kept one eye on the guest of honor. Grosstet was rapt as he observed the spectacle from a cordoned area at the narrow end of the rectangular space left clear for the show. His trunk twitched in time with the beat; he swayed slightly along with the dancers.

Then, it was time.

"Come on in. Spread out. Arms outstretched, you shouldn't be able to touch fingers with anyone in any direction."

Spectators who'd been lingering in the front rows now flooded into the performance arena. They scattered semi-randomly and, with some coaxing from the laaku dance professionals, arrayed themselves into a rough grid.

Jessie remained behind, but Grosstet joined in with gusto. Oh, they left him extra room. Even with medical staff close at hand, a trip and fall could cause unrecoverable injuries. Yet, when the music started up again, the haathee ambassador did as well as any of the non-laaku participants. Sure, maybe he wasn't naturally quadridexterous, his joints didn't bend as far, and his bulk shook even the Phabian-made building a little with each hop, but he mimicked the moves accurately and in keeping with the tempo of the music.

Frankly, it was astonishing seeing him move. Stuunji tended to surprise humans with how fast they were in person. Everyone who'd grown up with Hollyworld holos knew that the larger something got, the slower it moved. It was practically a truism. Yet, while the stuunji made humans reevaluate their odds of standing toe to toe with one in a boxing match, they still gave an impression of lumbering.

Grosstet was no ballerina, but he moved. His hops cleared

him a meter off the ground; even if half that was just lifting his feet. The hand thrusts. The hip waggles. All done at the speed of the other amateurs of the smaller, presumptively nimbler species. What power. What physicality.

The azrin were savages to the core. Even with technology at their disposal, they preferred hand fighting.

Stuunji were evolved pacifists who still used mercenaries for the bulk of their military.

Zheen could tear a human apart, but technology closed the gap when it came to actual warfare.

But by all accounts, Grosstet's people were more advanced technologically, and no one knew by how much. And removing science from the equation, Jessie had no idea how she could fight one.

While her dark thoughts swirled, the dance ended. Event staff cleared the floor.

It was time to do-si-do.

Jessie took her spot from the rehearsal earlier and painted a smile onto her face to match the rest of the troupe. The music started up, and the caller sang the dance. There was no trick to this one. A few moves, announced in advance, executed with feigned enthusiasm.

Jessie promenaded.

She boxed the gnat.

She allemande lefted.

And yes, she do-si-do'ed.

The whole demonstration was practically over before she'd gotten into a groove.

"*All right, now. Dancers, pair off. Anyone can be your partner, just agree who's who.*" Of all the dances, only this one and the ballet seemed to make any differentiation between men and women, and the ballet was one of the few on tonight's agenda that wasn't also a dance-along.

The square dance team interspersed with the crowd, forewarned that it would be their duty to pick up stragglers and solo dancers who couldn't find a partner on their own.

Jessie made sure she grabbed Grosstet. It hadn't exactly been a competition. There was a palpable relief among the rest of her team when she made her selection clear. If any of them had resented her securing him as a partner, they hid it flawlessly.

"HELLO AGAIN, JESSICA RAMSEY."

She gave a flirty curtsy and extended an arm elbow-first for the haathee ambassador to take. This was, quite possibly, the most dangerous assignment of her career, and she secretly prayed that the caller skip the do-si-do, since stepping blindly around Grosstet as he did likewise seemed damn near suicidal, but... it was the do-si-do. If anyone had heard anything about square dancing, that was the call they knew.

The music started up just as she finished her silent entreaty that she be spared death by squishing at a cultural dance festival.

With every bouncing step, the floor trembled. Jessie watched her footing for dear life.

Yet, after the first half dozen calls went off without incident, she realized she was enjoying herself. The spicy addition of danger to the mix turned humdrum old square dancing into an extreme sport. With long limbs, she was able to lock arms with Grosstet from far enough that his feet weren't an imminent threat. The biological geometry never worked out quite right, but they muddled through it just fine.

They bowed to one another at the end of the dance, and Grosstet gave her a little wink. "Thank you for not fearing my might," he whispered. "I liked our dance."

Flush from the exertion already, Jessie felt her cheeks warm further.

Before Jessie got to the point of wishing there were a human-compatible version of this guy, he headed back to his VIP area to dip his trunk in a keg of some beverage the staff had provided. Jessie watched over her shoulder as she cleared out herself, making way for a group of in-tik dancers.

"Heyo! Barely recognized you out there, but then I noticed the guns, and I was all, 'oh, that's Jessie.'"

Jessie whirled and discovered the speaker. All thoughts of her assignment were shunted to standby as a grin broke out on her face. "Trebla!" She crouched and crushed her laaku friend in a hug.

Friend? Trebla was a brother. Maybe more of a cousin. Like her, Trebla had grown up aboard the *Mobius*, subject to the whim of Squadron 33 1/3's gig schedule and whatever planets' educational systems they fell victim to.

"So glad you didn't get flattened by an alien dignitary. I was *not* looking forward to placing that comm."

Jessie smirked, keeping one eye on the in-tik dance routine as she represented her species from the front row. "You wouldn't have had to. I'm sure someone official would have called my parents."

"No. I mean Dek. We started a grid bet on how you'd die when you left for Earth Navy. Neither of us had 'crushed by a dancer while dressed as a rodeo clown.'"

"I AM NOT—" She caught herself and lowered her voice. "I'm not even wearing makeup."

"Really?" Trebla cringed. "Ooh."

"Asshole."

"Nice seeing you, too."

She clapped along as others in the crowd started clapping in time with the beat of the in-tik musicians. Wings flapped and dancers twirled. Hopping. Twisting. Twirling. Diving. "What's got you on Phabian?"

"Huh? I graduated. I got a job. I work a couple hundred kilometers from here. Getting into *this* shindig was the tough part."

"How'd you get in?" Jessie wondered how much trouble her laaku pal had gotten into in the process. For old times' sake, she hoped it was a lot.

"Let's just say I'm all out of favors at work, and I may owe a few I'm not looking forward to paying back."

"Nothing *too* bad, I hope," Jessie teased.

"Nothing that faking my own death or a serendipitous marriage couldn't cure."

Jessie snorted a laugh. "Don't look at me."

"Speaking of looking..." Trebla pointed. Jessie followed the finger as it aimed among the crowd now spilling out to the dance floor to join the in-tik performers.

It was Eric.

And the girl, Hecuba, the one he'd met at work.

The two of them were flailing their arms as a pair, vaguely copying the motions the real dancers were demonstrating.

"You wanna join 'em?"

Jessie considered. She didn't know the dance, and it looked harder than square dancing. She was liable to make a fool of herself. Then again...

What did she have to lose?

She watched her brother making an absolute ass of himself—in front of a girl he clearly liked, no less. Unless his college stories were highly redacted, this would be his first girlfriend, and he didn't care one whit how they looked out there.

Plus, at the far end of the fun-only dancers, Grosstet was again throwing himself into the mix. By taking part without insinuating herself, Jessie kept herself from looking clingy or suspiciously interested in his dealings.

"Sure." Jessie held out an arm for Trebla to take. "Let's do this."

—————

The door slid shut. Eric and Hecuba stumbled through the living room, giggling. The apartment was a color-by-outline of Eric's own, though Hecuba had been busier with her Wax-i-Rods making it homey in her own personal style. Not a bit of it had been left as the laaku had provided. Not a wall without adornment. Not a nook without some piece of furniture or bit of collectible art. Cloth abounded, ranging from plush, overstuffed chairs to throw rugs to small tapestries. Without having kept his haggling eye in shape, Eric suspected most of it was mass-produced or colony made, not Sol-based originals.

But the decor wasn't taking a prime spot in Eric's thoughts just then.

"Did you see the looks on that old laaku couple's faces?" Hecuba asked through a grin.

Eric huffed for breath and collapsed onto the two-seat couch. "Well, they probably didn't know what to think of a pair of wizards square-dancing down the street."

Hecuba flopped down beside him. They were both warm from exertion despite the cool night air, and she positively radiated heat where their thighs and shoulders pressed together. "When did you ever learn to dance like that?"

Eric squirmed a little, but there just wasn't enough space to leave a gap between them. Instead, he draped one arm over the back of the couch. "Colonies. Bunch of them go for the Old West theme."

"Old West of what?"

It hadn't occurred to him that someone with a clearly Earth-centric education wouldn't know it by that description.

"North American Second-Wave Colonial West. They were big on square dancing, and so whenever you get a dusty, lawless colony with a lot of blasters, people bundle it in with the rest of the motif."

Hecuba heaved a theatrical sigh. "You're so galactic."

"Not really. I mean, I traveled a lot. But it was mostly low budget. I didn't see a lot of the big sights. My first trip to Orion IV, we never got to see the Blue Gardens."

"Oh, I always wanted to go there! All those plants that thrive in the blue sunlight..."

"Well, we got two nights hanging out at the Woodstock 600 Music Festival. I was pretty little; had to wear earmuffs because the songs and crowds were too much. Wasn't a lot of fun. Then, the day before we had tickets, there was some sort of argument, and we had to leave the planet in a rush. Dad promised we'd get back at some point, but..." Eric shrugged. He'd still yet to see the Blue Gardens, 22 years later—even though it only *felt* like 17.

"Maybe *we* could go sometime."

"Do we get vacation time? I never asked."

Hecuba narrowed her eyes slyly. "We can get a lot of things if we just ask nicely." She climbed out of the shockingly luxurious grasp of the couch's poofy cushions. "On that note, if you'll excuse me a moment, I'm going to change into something more comfortable."

"Like a bird?"

Hecuba giggled. "I mean clothes. I (ahem) glowed a bit tonight with all that dancing." When Eric didn't object, she darted into her bedroom and shut the door. And why *would* Eric mind? After all, Mom had explained a long time ago that many women denied perspiring. That whole glowing business was more a euphemism for a sheen of sweat than any actual luminescence.

While she was gone, Eric strolled the room's perimeter, admiring the details of the tapestries. It was like a miniature art museum, except there were no docents lurking to bombard the unsuspecting visitor with extraneous facts that demystified masterpieces. Eric preferred his ancient artwork as mystified as possible.

Alas, the minutiae of the local stitchwork didn't make it any more fascinating. Seeing the individual threads just emphasized the artifice at work. He'd liked the scenes better from a distance, when he could choose to believe they were frozen moments from a fairytale.

A pair of hands covered Eric's eyes without forewarning. "Guess who?"

"Hecuba." He turned to make sure he was correct. She grinned up at him. "It was pretty easy to figure out. You were the only other one here, plus I could sense you coming."

"Not *all of us* can do that," Hecuba scolded teasingly. "Sometimes I can tell Doonah's coming, and my professors. You're stronger than any of them; I know it. But you're a ghost. I have to touch you to know you're even real." She put a hand on his chest, right over his heart.

In glancing down at that hand, Eric took in Hecuba's change of attire. There wasn't a lot to inventory. She wore a flimsy red silk nightgown held up by tiny straps. Her hair was loose, too, unbound from whatever clips, ties, and charms she used to tame it; he'd made a point of not inquiring how she achieved her coiffure since it was even odds to give offense.

"I'm about 80 percent sure I'm real," he replied, gently guiding her hand into his and giving it a reassuring squeeze. "And you certainly look a *lot* more comfortable."

"You're welcome to do likewise..."

Eric shook his head emphatically. "I can't pull off a nightgown."

She burst out laughing, and Eric joined in. In custody of one of his hands, Hecuba towed him back to the couch and threw herself onto it.

But Eric didn't topple after her.

His eyes widened.

He was no longer seeing the room around him.

"What? Eric? What's wrong?"

"Do you feel it?" His voice was hollow.

"Feel what? Eric, are you all right?"

Blinking, Eric shook his head to ground himself. "Two wizards. Humans. Here on Phabian."

"There are plenty of us around. And I told you: I don't really notice auras."

"These two you might. They make Doonah look like a streetcorner charlatan hiding a pea under walnut shells."

Hecuba was off the couch in a flash. "Eric, you're scaring me."

Eric put his hands on her shoulders. "Look. I'm sorry. I don't like scaring anyone, least of all you. But these two wizards are bad news."

"Who are they?"

Where to even begin? He opted for the short version. "The ones who chased me off Mars. Convocation inquisitors."

"INQUISITORS?"

OK. That wasn't the part he'd expected her to protest. In fairness, she hadn't seen his map for this conversation and thus hadn't planned ahead of maximum incredulity. "Yeah. Wizards Snow and Slater. And it can't be a coincidence."

"We should inform someone. Like, NOW."

Eric drew a steadying sigh. "They're cagey. If I'm wrong, or if they're setting me up, I don't want the Phabian Ministry of Wizards thinking I'm unstable. I need to catch them and *then* tell someone."

Hecuba headed him off even before he moved toward the door, spreading her arms to bar his way. "No. You're not going out there alone."

"I can't let you come with me." This was cliché, but it had to be said for form's sake.

"Damn right I'm not going out there. I took basic self-defense. That's it. I wouldn't trust myself against a technologist with a blaster. The Ministry have their ssentuadi enforcers. We'll call *them* in for help."

"I can reason with them. They won't want a fight."

"How can you be sure?"

It was a great question. In lieu of a better plan, he went with honesty. "I'm not. But I'm not worried if they try. I bested them before. Then again, they know that too, so they probably prepared something new—an incantation, something from the vaults, maybe backup." Eric shook his head vigorously. "I'm no good at predictions. I just need to go find out if they're really here or I'm worrying over nothing. I won't go far. You wait here; I'll be back."

"Are you even listening to yourself?"

Eric paused. "No." He furrowed his brow. "Should I be? I think that's your part in the conversation."

"What if they double back on you? What if they want to use me as leverage?"

Egad. What an awful idea. Yet at the same time, it sounded plausible enough.

"Do you trust me?"

"Yes," Hecuba replied instantly. "But I think you're acting a little rash right now."

Stepping around her, Eric stood before the door, hands held up, fingers outstretched. He didn't form words, just direct images of the outcome. The ideas hurt, but it was a pain easily borne. Red runes sprang to life around the doorjamb, tracing an outline as more and more scribbled themselves into existence. They raced along the walls and ceiling, following edges and spilling into the bedroom and washroom. Eric even directed them around and into the closet.

When he finished, Hecuba's apartment was outlined in glowing, pulsating red glyphs.

Hecuba backed away a step. "What... what language is that even?"

Eric wasn't having that conversation right now. "You've never heard of it. But no one's getting in here until I get back."

She gulped. "And if you don't come back?"

"It's powered by my life force. If it fades before I get back, run."

Hecuba threw her arms around him. "Please be careful!"

Eric patted her back, careful to only touch where she was covered by silk.

"I'll try," was the best he could manage without lying. Then he stepped out into the night.

━━━

After the vivacious chaos of the dance festival, the Phabian night felt almost peaceful. Sure, all the visible "stars" in the sky were ion engines and running lights from thousands of ships. Sure, the pleasant aromas on the breeze were pumped out the exhaust vents of civic air filtration stations. But there was a calm, too. If not a shutdown, it was at least the planet taking a breath between bouts of manic productivity.

Jessie strolled barefoot across the open plaza between the function hall and a section of the refugee zone she'd yet to visit. Her hat hung behind her with the cord applying light pressure to her throat. The boots that had come with her costume she clutched in one hand by the tops, now two open chimneys of foot odor as they aired out.

"YOU DO NOT LIKE THE SHOE'AE?" her companion inquired, gesturing with an oversized finger. Grosstet ambled at her side, matching her pace when she knew his long gait would have easily outpaced her.

"Just a costume. Not really meant for daily wear."

"VERY IMPOLITE."

Jessie broke stride. Quickly, she switched to hopping as she tried to put the boots back on. "Sorry, I didn't mean any offense. I just—"

"NOT YOU. THEM. BAD FORM. DOES YOUR KIND WALK WITH NO SHOE'AE?"

"Usually not. But it's not a problem. We're not acclimated —that is, I mean—"

"WHAT IS 'ACCLIMATED'?" It was asked with idle curiosity yet, in that booming voice, sounded like a demand. He had the manner and demeanor of a statue that guarded a tomb by asking riddles.

This linguistic bullshit was the stuff Eric liked. Well, if she ended up getting an undergraduate teaching degree out of this assignment, so be it. "Um, acclimate means getting used to. Not all at once, but over time."

"AH. I WILL REMEMBER." Satisfied with the answer, Grosstet didn't follow up. After a moment of companionable silence, he began a new thought. "I THANK YOU FOR DANCING WITH ME. I COULD TELL MANY WERE SCARED. MANY LAAKU'AE MADE AN EXCUSE."

Oh, Jessie could well imagine. "Minor accidents are common when learning to dance. I think, with you, they worried there was no such thing as minor."

Grosstet trumpeted; she took it for a laugh. "MINOR IS SMALL, YES?" Jessie nodded. "I DO NOTHING MINOR.

IT IS NOT THE WAY FOR ALL MY PEOPLE. I AM MORE." He parted his mouth in a grin.

"I can only imagine how you'd be bragging if you knew more English," Jessie joked, then her face fell when she realized what she'd said aloud.

"WHAT IS BRAGGING?"

Her cheeks warmed, and she could only hope his skin was as thick metaphorically as it must have been biologically. "Uh, bragging is someone talking about how great they are."

"IS BRAGGING ALWAYS TRUE OR SOMETIMES UNTRUE?"

"It can be both."

Grosstet swung his head side to side, though not far enough to menace with his giant tusks. "SO MANY SMALL DETAIL'AE. YOUR LANGUAGE WILL TAKE LONG TO LEARN WELL. BUT I AM VERY GOOD AT LEARNING. THAT IS BRAGGING. THE TRUE KIND."

Jessie laughed. She had to wonder about the culture that embraced that kind of brazen self-awareness—or blithe unawareness—when speaking with a relative stranger.

They arrived at the custom-refitted apartment the laaku had set up for the ambassador. A giant hand scanner activated a four-meter-tall door. Grosstet stepped aside and bowed and, with a twirl of his trunk, indicated she precede him inside. "MY HOME FOR MY VISIT."

"Wow."

It was like stepping into a dollhouse, except Jessie was from a different toymaker that built her to a smaller scale. It looked like most of the apartments she'd seen during her brief time in the Phabian refugee program. But everything here was giant. The seat of the couch was chest high. She couldn't see onto the table without rising onto her toes. The interior doors stood open, just as large as the one to the outside.

That initial door slid shut behind them.

Ambassador Grosstet tapped a device he'd retrieved from his kitchen table. Jessie felt a buzz in the air. She spun, wondering whether that was a force field she sensed.

"IT IS FINE. THEY LISTEN. NOW THEY DO NOT LISTEN."

Holy fuck! He was running anti-surveillance tech? They knew so little of his people, their technology. What had Jessie gotten herself into? She tensed, wondering what her best and quickest escape option might be.

The haathee ambled over to his refrigerator, which appeared to have been an unmodified restaurant walk-in. "MAY I GIVE YOU A DRINK?" He lifted a barrel with a flip-out pour spout and hefted it to the countertop with one hand. With the other, he fetched a pair of keg-sized plasti-glass mugs from a cabinet.

When he poured, Jessie caught a whiff and one word came to mind. "Beer?"

Grosstet turned his head. "IS IT? I HAVE HEARD THE WORD. THE LAAKU'AE SAY THEY DO NOT HAVE IT. I MAKE THIS."

Jessie's mouth watered. Alien booze? When the alternatives were zero-alcohol laaku substitutes, import-controlled stuff brought in from human-controlled space at extortionate prices, and black-market stuff that might get her in trouble at work, haathee moonshine didn't sound like a bad idea. "Sure."

When Jessie received her drink, she could barely heft it. There had to have been six or eight liters of the amber liquid in there, and the handle was cumbersome to grip. "I'll never be able to drink all this."

"NOT IMPOLITE. DRINK OR NOT DRINK. I WILL MAKE MORE."

With her face hovering over the mug, she had to admit, it smelled great, like one of those mid-colony micro-breweries. With a grunt and some balancing, she tilted back and sloshed a mouthful. "Wow. This is great! What's in it?"

"I DO NOT KNOW ALL THE WORD'AE. I WILL SHOW SOON. I MUST DRESS. DRINK. I WILL RETURN SOON."

Wondering if she'd severely misinterpreted the haathee's meaning, Jessie took another swig. If there was an uncomfortable conversation to have when Grosstet came back from the bedroom, she wouldn't have to have it sober.

Across the Milky Way, there were connoisseurs with palates bordering on mystical. They could discern traces of minerals in the soil and herbs grown in proximity to the ingredients, determine minutiae of brewing techniques, and tell the difference in storage vessels that had contained a brew. All Jessie knew was that this haathee stuff was excellent. It was the type of beer too good—and yet all too easy—to get hammered on. On an upscale colony, a beer like this would have been served by a human with a handlebar mustache, suspenders, and a white dress shirt rolled to the elbows.

She was just feeling a light buzz settle in when the haathee returned.

Jessie blinked. Without any knowledge of the haathee customs for undergarments, she suspected that he wore nothing but a bathrobe. The robe itself was burgundy with gold embroidery and a cloth belt as thick as her arm, tied in an elaborate knot. Grosstet was barefoot and now had a distinctly floral aroma.

"AH. NOW, THE PLANT'AE THAT MAKE—" His next sound was a mix of trumpeting and verbal syllables she couldn't pick apart, clearly his own language. But his statement was accompanied by the presentation of a placemat-sized datapad. With a few finger gestures, he flipped the screen through a series of nature-documentary flatpics of crops, displaying both farmland and close-up views of each in turn.

Some kind of wheat.

A couple herbs.

Hops.

She was no horticulturist, but Jessie nodded. "Yeah. That's beer. I guess just about every species figures it out eventually." She gulped another mouthful, pausing to take a long breath through her nose before swallowing. It was time to head off possibly the most ill-advised come-on in the history of inter-species relationships. "Look, Ambassador Grosstet, I think you're fascinating, but—"

"STET. MY NAME IS—" He trumpeted again, but the oral noises that accompanied it combined to sort of sound like Grosstet. "I SAY GROSSTET TO MAKE EASY FOR SPECIES'AE WHO HAVE NO TRUNK. ALL SPECIES'AE HAVE NO TRUNK, I THINK." He parted his mouth in a grin at his own joke. "STET IS EASY AND YOU CAN SAY RIGHT."

"Smooth. Stet, we need to have a talk about—"

A chime sounded from the door.

Stet's eyes—easily his smallest facial feature—grew wide enough for Jessie to see the whites all around. "THEY ARE EARLY."

"Who's early?"

The haathee knelt and bracketed her with his tusks, putting his face close to hers. Somehow, clearly distressed, she didn't find his proximity threatening. He dropped his voice to barely human volume. "I need a favor."

"What kind of favor?"

"Hide." He paused as if searching his vocabulary. "Please."

"Are you in some kind of danger?" Jessie couldn't imagine

who'd be ringing the door chime on Phabian who might be looking to cause a creature this size harm. But she couldn't rule it out, either.

A tiny trumpet escaped Stet's trunk. "No. Hide. Stay hide. Then exit." He made a walking-fingers gesture common to all bipedal species. "I give a favor back."

Whatever this was about, Jessie had a job to do here. Offer her the choice of a million terras, and she'd still pick the favor.

Jessie tried to put down the mug, but Stet pushed it back into her hands. "TAKE. HIDE BEER TOO."

As she was ushered into the storage closet off the living area, Jessie mused that at least she wouldn't go thirsty. The closet door was even louvred so she could both breathe comfortably and see out a little bit. Once she was inside, in the gloom, Jessie settled in to spy.

Seriously, could this guy be making her job any easier tonight?

When Stet answered the door, Jessie gaped. Had she been out there in his living room, she couldn't have maintained a polite expression as she saw three stuunji dancers from the festival pile in. And while she hadn't been around too many of their kind and couldn't understand when they spoke their own language to the haathee ambassador, there was no mistaking the giggling—the deep, throaty, stuunji giggling.

The dancers had performed *Winter Becoming Springtime in the Valley Between Three Hills*, possibly the easiest of the dance-alongs that night. They'd changed out of their costumes but still wore the horn jewelry and face tints that went with the outfits.

They fawned over him. They tittered at his conversation. Then, in unison, the three of them turned their attention to the complicated knot tying Stet's robe closed.

Oy vey! Jessie suspected she'd gotten the ambassador's

intentions correct. But his amorous intentions hadn't been directed at her. The biological incompatibility had been blatant. But with stuunji? Jessie shuddered. She also couldn't bring herself to stare as the dancers tried their hands at alien sailor's knots.

Eyes acclimated to the low light slipping through the louvres. There wasn't much inside with her. Other than her beer, there was a tall contraption propped in the corner. In an effort to distract herself from whatever courtship ritual was getting demonstrated out in the living room, Jessie studied the example of haathee technology.

Her first impression was of a landscaping blow-jet with an extended nozzle and no evidence of plastic in the construction. But there was little chance of Stet doing any garden work planetside on Phabian.

Outside, the giggling and conversation grew louder, more excited. Jessie spared a glance just in time to see the ambassador naked from behind. One of the dancers let out a delighted whoop as he lifted her cradled deftly on his tusks. The other two, Stet lifted in one arm apiece, carrying them riding atop his biceps without a hint of effort or exertion.

Despite him turning around to head past the very closet in which Jessie hid, she couldn't look away. In the process she got a view of mating equipment that would haunt her the rest of her life. Jessie didn't blink.

Stuunji weren't delicate creatures. They could run four hundred kilos easily. Maybe these dancers were svelte by species standards, but Stet had to have been carrying more than a ton of thirsty stuunji while carrying on joking conversation.

Once the bedroom door closed behind them, Jessie carefully slid open the manual closet door. It was heavy but well within the limits of her strength.

In the light from the living room, she took another look at the garden blower.

In light of the sight she'd just witnessed, she realized what she was really looking at.

That giant thing was a handheld blaster. Adjusting her expectations, she could pick out the grip and trigger.

A squeal of amorous delight from the bedroom shocked Jessie from her awestruck immobility. Swallowing, she quietly slid the closet closed. Then, stepping carefully around the discarded bathrobe on the floor, she fled the apartment.

Eric rolled over and fell off a couch. The sudden impact of the floor startled him awake abruptly. Blinking and rubbing his eyes, he crawled back up to cushion height. He recognized the little hand-embroidered pillow; at a touch, he found it still warm from his head's recent rest upon it.

Hecuba had stitched it herself. That was her throw pillow. This was her apartment. Eric forced his eyes shut and focused.

Phabian.

Refugee district.

Off the run; recently *on* the run with Jessie.

What had happened last night?

Flying carpet races? No. That wasn't it.

Dragging Colou City below the newly breathable Sabian Ocean? No. He couldn't do that sort of thing out here.

Multi-xeno dance festival? No. Wait... Yes. That was part of it, but something nagged that he hadn't solved his mystery just yet.

Patience might have been a virtue, but simple mental flailing eventually took long enough that the dysphoria faded on its own.

"Snow and Slater," he said aloud. He'd been here, at Hecuba's apartment. They'd been silly and danced most of the way back from the festival. She'd been hot and sweaty, changed into a nightgown. Eric had felt the inquisitors—his personal nemeses—lurking nearby. Hours of searching hadn't yielded any clues. They must have realized he'd been alerted and taken better precautions.

He'd fallen asleep on the couch, crying on Hecuba's lap because he couldn't stop them harassing everyone in his life.

In retrospect, he'd been a bit of a mess. Mornings always filled him with fresh optimism. A night spent as an immortal overseer of a brain-sized universe was quite the confidence booster, it turned out.

"Hecuba?" he called out. The apartment was tiny. Even a thorough search was over in seconds. She wasn't home. However, this was not a new mystery. Her little kitchenette table held a bowl of dry cereal with a globe of cold milk suspended above it—a waiting breakfast that wouldn't get soggy if he overslept—and a handwritten note.

Just stopping by Kel+Cas's place before work.
See you soon.
XO Hecuba

He'd have to ask about the initials. Meanwhile, his mind concocted guesses.

Xenia Ophelia.

Xylestra Olloscyrene.

Xaxon Oscarella.

Eric had been the beneficiary of scientific naming conventions that resulted in bland, predictable guesses. With hereditary wizards, more exotic selections were common.

Flicking his fingers, Eric broke the charm that kept the milk at bay and let it splash into the bowl. In retrospect, lowering it slowly into the cereal might have made less of a mess, but Hecuba had a kitchen towel that made short work of the spray of milk and cornflakes.

A quick breakfast and a brisk walk later, and Eric was back to work. At least, he made it as far as the entrance to the factory.

"Wizard Doonah wants to see you immediately," one of the security guards—Bromek, according to his nametag—informed him as soon as he stepped inside.

"OK. Thanks." Eric waved, but Bromek and another guard nametagged Orneg hustled over to flank him. "Oh, it's one of *those* wants-to-see-mes?"

"Afraid so, Wizard Eric," Bromek confirmed.

Eric sighed and didn't get either of his escorts in trouble. In fairness, he had a long history of not ending up where he'd been told to go. But unless Phabian had way better spies than he'd been led to believe, none of his coworkers or employers should know that.

Doonah wasn't alone in his office.

"Hi, again," Eric greeted the pair of ssentuadi inquisitors bracketing the door as it shut behind him. And for his boss, a cheery "Good morning."

"Is it?" Doonah asked. "I wouldn't call it that."

"Phabian doesn't really get bad weather. Everyone looks healthy. War's still way back thataway." He hooked a thumb in the general direction of human-controlled space. "Why wouldn't it be a good morning?"

"That's a very good question. And rather than interfere with an official investigation, I'm going to ask that you accompany these two individuals and cooperate in whatever way they require." Doonah laced his fingers and fixed Eric's chin with a firm glare.

Enzio had explained it to him once. A wizard convinced of his own superiority wouldn't hesitate to look you right in the eye. It was a dominance display. Staring eye-adjacent like that was a cheat. It was an attempt to appear tough, and if the recipient wasn't willing to look straight back, it was easy to slip past as an actual stare-down.

Never look a strange wizard in the eye, Enzio had hammered into the kids, human and laaku alike, with the cheeky caveat that, *All wizards are strange.* Eventually, Enzio had quietly, aside from the rest, relaxed the requirement, just for him.

You're strange enough that you're the one doing them *a favor.*

Since Eric was looking straight at Doonah's eyes, this gave him all the information he needed to make a simple demand. "Tell me: is Hecuba OK?"

"For the time being, yes," Doonah replied after a hesitation.

"And Jessie?" Eric pressed. His window of deference might close soon; he ought to cover his bases.

"I have heard nothing to the contrary."

"Fine. Whatever. That's all that matters. Will this take long? Windows aren't going to turn themselves transparent without a little coaxing."

One of the ssentuadi inquisitors slithered up beside him. When Eric looked them in the eye, a glossy sheen protected them from his gaze. "You do not need to work today. Consssssider it a day off."

Eric cocked his head. Doonah nodded a confirmation.

With a shrug, Eric followed his inquisitor escorts.

Jessie extended a hand and helped Master Frabet to his feet. They'd both felt the rib crack with her final kick, so the taboo against helping a third-ring grandmaster of quadrijutsu stand didn't apply. Making the medics enter the sparring circle to tend to him would have been the greater disrespect.

Off the mat, forming a loose line of laaku bodies, spectators watched in measured disbelief. They were a mix of data-pushers who'd caught wind in the we'd-deny-its-existence-if-it-weren't-so-blatantly-obvious rumor mill, agents and analysts in the gymnasium for their own health benefits, and a few people with actual reason to be in attendance. Namely, those few were evaluating Jessie's Earth Navy service record.

Section 74 had its own way of doing things. Paranoid ways. Mildly condescending ways. Nominally, they treated her as an equal, but time and again, they undercut her, doubted her, subjected her to tests and training and protocols that would have been easy to opt her out of.

"You didn't have to follow through," Frabet muttered for her ears only as he winced with each step, hanging onto Jessie for support.

Hell yes, she did. Passing her close-quarters self-defense cert would have been forgettable. It would have left all the impression of a fart on a windy day. Half-carrying the agency's top trainer was a hedge against anyone downplaying her or second-guessing her qualifications. "You said not to hold back. Or did that only apply when you thought you'd win easily?"

"Your technique is still sloppy."

"And you telegraph your moves."

"Instinct will only get you so far."

Jessie held a hand up to her ear. "Sorry, couldn't make that out. Can you speak up?" she asked, knowing that even breathing had to be paining the quadrijutsu master. Was she being childish? Maybe. Did he deserve it? Fuck yeah.

The medic on hand helped Frabet to a seat on a hover stretcher and tended to him on the spot.

Futhrek met her on the way to the gym's shower facility. "You could have killed him."

Jessie paused at the door and resisted the temptation to duck inside, pretending he hadn't intended to glean an answer. "He could have certified me ten seconds into that test. I could have snapped his neck, but a couple broken ribs made sure everyone knew he lost."

"How much was the side action?" Futhrek asked snidely.

Rolling her eyes, Jessie stepped into the locker room rather than dignify the accusation with a reply. To her shock, Futhrek followed right along behind her. "Do you mind?"

"What?" the spymaster asked as if he wasn't in the wrong here. "It's a common enough joke around here. If you want the fast track to getting field certified, skip the shower."

"Seriously? I cleaned 100 on your piss-easy firing range. Timed on that obstacle course that's a *little* xenoist if you ask me. And I just rearranged the bones of your top self-defense instructor. You've got my service record. I'm not an impostor. If you're seriously going to make me take a flight test—"

"No flight test. I actually opted you out of that one."

Primed for an argument, Jessie deflated. "Thanks."

"But the psych eval is supposed to be a surprise when the subject is fatigued."

"You've gotta be shitting me."

Futhrek snapped his fingers twice. "C'mon. If you get down to your resting heart rate, they'll want you to run the obstacle course again."

Jessie couldn't tell if he was kidding or not. She hustled to follow as he left the locker room.

Eric sighed. "Yes, I know who that is. Don't tell me; he's missing too?"

The chamber was small and looked smaller. Curved, arcing walls gave the impression of being inside an egg, and the metallic walls were mirrored. Images duplicated ad infinitum, but the myriad identical ssentuadi, laaku, and Erics only reinforced just how little there was for the walls to work with.

The pair of ssentuadi rarely spoke, merely on hand in the hand-me-down Convocation tradition of doubling up on wizards on the theory that two heads were better than one—not that either of them *had* hands. By contrast, there was hardly a moment that passed without Special Agent Granek of Phabian Investigative Services filling the cramped space with his voice.

It wasn't that he was uncomfortable. The magically floaty stool seat was the only seat in the room, and they'd let him have it. Mostly, he was getting bored.

"Funny you should mention it. Yeah. Him too," Granek replied with such heavy sarcasm that one might think his voice couldn't hold the weight by itself.

"Really. You know, I'd heard so many glowing things about Phabian Investigative Services. But if this is how you guys go about solving missing persons cases, I gotta say: I'm not impressed."

Granek appeared nonplussed by the criticism. Yet, for all the accolades heaped on his organization, they were employing the same methods Eric had used when he'd lost track of Hecuba. "You were seen chatting in line for the dance festival."

"Yeah. It was fun hearing the differences between spoken in-tik and the translations from the science necklace. He was looking forward to taking holos of the dances."

"Are you aware that Mr. Chik-ta has a wife and hatchlings?"

"He mentioned them. Like, a bunch of times. I think it was

his first night out on his own since helping incubate them. The hatchlings. Not his wife. I didn't get the impression they had that kind of age difference."

"You were also seen entering the all-species washroom around the same time as Mr. Chik-ta."

Eric bristled. "You have people watching when I pee?" He revised his impression of PIS. They were kind of creepy.

"Why didn't you use the standard washroom? Why use the xeno-access facilities?"

Eric shrugged and glanced over at the ssentuadi inquisitor. "We're guests on your planet. Here, I'm the xeno."

"Did you speak to Mr. Chik-ta in the washroom?"

"I don't know the in-tik urination customs, but *my* people consider it rude. We exchanged the Nod of Companionable Silence. That was it."

"Are you aware that no one saw Mr. Chik-ta after that?"

"How could I possibly know that? I'd have to have talked to everyone."

"Or you might have seen what became of him in that all-species washroom..."

Oh. Oh, well, that changed the tenor of this whole conversation. Eric blinked several times, suddenly finding the countless reflections in the background distracting. "Wait. Is that why you're asking me about every missing persons case in the past two weeks? New wizard planetside; just blame him? I thought Phabian was more galactic than that."

"Why else did you think we were interviewing you about six sentients, all of whom were last seen in your presence?"

Eric paused. Did he owe this Granek an honest answer, or was this the point in the holo where he demanded a lawyer? As a refugee, was he even entitled to legal representation? Or was this one of those deals where his immigration status meant he had to play their game, their way?

And how would this affect Jessie?

Relenting, he huffed. "I thought you were a bunch of nincompoops who searched for missing people by just asking anyone who might have seen them. It was frankly starting to get on my nerves, and my estimation of Phabian's law enforcement system was dropping by the minute." When he sensed a rebuttal about to interrupt him, he raised a finger. "But that changes a little now that I realize you've been interviewing a prime suspect instead of just one of dozens of random innocent people. Not that I'm not innocent. To untangle that double negative before it causes confusion, I *am* innocent."

"Do you have any theories, then?"

Oy! What a question! Boy, did Eric have theories. His cheeks puffed as he let out a long breath. "I've considered the possibility that Astral Space is curtain at a theater the size of the universe. There's also a chance that everyone just set their calendars ahead five years just to mess with me and my sister. And—"

"About the disappearances."

"Oh. My number one theory is that you don't have any idea what happened and you have political pressure building to solve a case where you have no leads."

Granek scowled. Reviewing what he'd just said, Eric sympathized. "Please state, before the inquisitor, whether you had anything to do with the disappearances of Kenneth Sloan, Ovilak, Drascz Fyllis, Evander Days, Mindy Sedgwick, or Chik-ta."

"Nope," Eric replied easily. When neither Granek nor the ssentuadi wizards appeared satisfied, he elaborated. "I didn't hurt anyone, hide anyone, smuggle anyone, shrink anyone, turn anyone permanently invisible—or temporarily—unless, of course, one of them had disguised themselves as a slab of steel and snuck into the glassteel factory, in which case maybe I did by accident. Whatever or whoever caused these disappearances, I didn't do it or have any idea who might have." Perched atop the floating stool seat with his feet dangling, he folded his arms. "That good enough for you?"

Granek and his inquisitor friends exchanged a glance.

The special agent stepped aside and tapped something on his datapad. A section of the wall opened, revealing the door by which they'd all entered. Outside was a nondescript corridor in the Phabian Investigative Services Immigration and Refugee Processing Substation. Luckily, Eric remembered the way back if they decided to be assholes and hold a grudge for him not agreeing to be guilty as suspected.

"You may passss, Wizard Eric," the ssentuadi told him as they glided out of the way.

Eric hopped down from the stool. As he stepped outside to resume his freedom, he turned back. "Hey, if you do solve any of these cases, can you let me know? They were all nice people. I wouldn't mind seeing them again."

⌐⌐

The bustle of a busy office shut off like the tap of a switch as soon as the soundproof doors slid closed. The full-length glassteel hazed over and became privacy-screen translucent. A hum of surveillance blockers snapping on filled the silence as a ring of purple runes at chair rail height encircled the room with magical protection.

Around the conference table, laaku and a token ssentuadi found their seats and cushion, respectively. Datapads settled onto the glossy surface. Laaku hands tucked into baggy sleeves.

At the head of the table, Deputy Director Trevek of Japardi stood and addressed the team. "We are coming up on two weeks since the disappearances started. We have twenty-three witnesses, none of whom actually *saw* anything happen. And our lone suspect is a model citizen and political coup for the suits in Bantlek to have pillaged from the Human Civil War. Please tell me your polite, non-confrontational interview yielded any actionable clues."

Then the deputy director sat; he fixed a glare on Granek until the special agent stood to make his report. "I have just filed a full report on the interview with Eric Ramsey. In short, he professes ignorance. To elaborate, he recognized the names of all the disappeared and admitted to being at the sites where witness statements had placed them together. He gave general characterizations of innocuous, conflict-free interactions that give no hints of possible motives."

"Do you think there's any risk to the sister?" Trevek asked. He sat with his fingers laced atop the table and his other fingers laced below it, his walking gloves discarded on the floor.

Granek sat as Dr. Denlethi rose to field this one. "With the caveat that all traditional psychoanalysis breaks down when applied to wizards, our immigration interviews suggest that Jessica Ramsey is his primary social support. Separating the two of them forcibly might trigger resentment. We don't have a full profile, but I don't think the reaction would be positive."

"Do we trust his statements?"

This time, Issthiff coiled higher on his cushion. The ssentuadi had attended the interview as a lie detector. He hissed a polite greeting to the group. "Eric Ramsssssey did not appear to lie."

Trevek rapped his knuckles on the table. "Hold up. That's less definitive than your typical assessment. Care to elaborate?"

"Hard to exxxxplain. There are two typessss of truth. If the ssssusssspect liessss, the universssse will know. I am very ssssskilled at thissss. But there issss alsssso the lie that the ssssubject believessss. Harder, but I can ussse thissss method assss well."

"Are you telling me Eric Ramsey was lying but didn't know it?" That wasn't great news. A serial killer was always bad news, but one so broken inside that he didn't know he was doing it was even worse. "Is he covering his own tracks so well he doesn't even suspect himself?"

"Possssibly," Issthiff replied. "He may be erasssssing his own memoriessss. But that would not exxxxplain the universssse failing to catch the lie. But that issss not the problem. There issss neither lie nor truth when I hear him. You have machinessss that do thissss too."

Trevek nodded. It was common knowledge and completely legal, if not admissible at trial.

"Well, imagine hooking your deviccccce to a holovid. Or a parrot. Or a comm panel."

"What are you getting at? He lacks the mental faculties to lie? By all accounts, he was a middling university student, not a remedial education case."

"No, Deputy Director. The universsssse holdssss no opinionssss of Eric Ramssssey. A sssstrong enough wizard can lie behind iron-clad wardssss. He issss not that. He issss ssssimply not available to query. What do rockssss think of mussssic? Doessss wind have honor? Can the void of the Black Ocean know love?"

Granek piped up, "I think he's trying to describe a type-mismatch error kickback. Like trying to store an integer in a Boolean variable?"

"We all get it, Special Agent Granek," Trevek griped. "What I need is for someone to tell me whether Eric Ramsey is out there killing off a species-diverse cross-section of refugees."

"We could take him off the streets. See if the killings stop."

The suggestion came from a junior agent, just in this meeting as part of her professional development training.

Trevek chose not to take offense and instead use it as a teaching moment. "You might be able to make an argument for probable cause, based on a preponderance of circumstantial evidence. But we don't even know for certain whether we're investigating kidnappings or murders. And Bantlek is watching this one. I'm on comms with senators and cabinet ministers asking about our progress. They don't want to admit we might have a human wizard in our refugee program going rogue and murdering xenos under our protection. So, no. Until I get better than guesses and innuendo, I'm not placing Eric Ramsey in custody." To avoid the appearance he was browbeating a junior agent, he turned his attention back to Granek. "Anything to the girlfriend's claims?"

Granek shook his head. "Our moles on Earth don't have anything on two inquisitors working on Phabian. We haven't had any other reports of suspicious characters in the refugee zone. And he hadn't reported anything himself. We're just going on secondhand info. Firmly back-pocket stuff until I hear it somewhere else."

"We have alsssso heard nothing. But it issss possssible. Convocation wizardssss, we have too few their equal. Wizzzzard Eric would eventually be part of our defenssssessss against Earth sssspiessss."

Trevek stood. This meeting had been as fruitless as he'd feared coming in. Tonight's bout of political comms out of Bantlek would be as fun as an end-to-end gastric probe. "I want round-the-clock surveillance on our evasive wizard. And while we're at it, I want a protective detail on the girlfriend, too. We have all the personnel hours allocated to this that we need. For now, we keep vigilant. Dismissed."

⊂⊃

A crisp wind blew in from Boston Harbor, lending a chill to the open-air court being held that afternoon. Lunch had come and gone, a traditional clam chowder appropriate to the occasion. And Emperor Khosrau Blackstone drummed his fingers as a pair of Imperial Senators strode briskly away from their audience.

They'd wanted his backing for a measure to imperialize corporations who hadn't declared fully for Earth in the rebellion. He'd only had to ask whether Earth or Mars was making more money from the neutral megacorps and who had more to lose when Mars retaliated in kind. Idiots. They were lucky they did as they were told; otherwise, he'd have spent the evening appointing their replacements.

The Martians were treating this as a war of ships, and while that was true to a degree, wars were about money, ideals, public sentiment, and logistics. Surely, the GNN executives in New York Prime would report evenhandedly if the emperor provoked Mars into shutting down their Martian affiliates, arresting their reporters, and confiscating galactic-scale news-spewing technology.

Vincente cleared his throat. "Next is... *that* appointment."

Khosrau rolled his eyes. "Private audience."

"Understood." With a few subtle gestures, the imperial vizier cleared the courtyard—or rather, directed an efficient crew of palace guards to do so on his behalf.

As their last duty before shutting the doors behind them, the guards allowed the next petitioners to enter. The trio averaged over a century in age apiece. Each wore formal robes, no two alike. Each represented one of the venerable orders of Convocation wizards. They crossed the manicured lawn like they owned the place; in fairness, for the most part, they walked everywhere that way.

Khosrau leaned slightly over the arm of his raised throne. "Anyone search them?"

"As you commanded, Your Majesty."

Khosrau smirked, then greeted his petitioners. "That's far enough. You loudmouths can make yourselves heard from down there." He stopped them in their tracks before they reached the stone steps that ascended toward the throne. "I appreciate you all showing up together. Whatever your beef, I don't need to hear it three separate times."

Brutus Allemontero took a step forward, chin lifted. "On behalf of the Order of Hephaistos, I hereby declare no confidence in the throne."

"By the throne, you mean me?" Khosrau clarified for him. "Considering your constituency, I felt the need to ask."

"This isn't personal, Khosrau," Brutus declared. "It is the very notion of lone rule that is flawed, whoever embodies the office."

Khosrau circled a hand. "Let's speed this up. I assume you talked over your script beforehand. There's no one here to impress except this guy." He hooked a thumb at Vincente, who cowered slightly at the attention being drawn to him. "And he's hard to impress."

Alastair The Brown stepped up next. "On behalf of the Order of Gaia, I hereby declare no confidence in the throne."

"You can claim all you want that this isn't personal, but I won't buy it."

"I wouldn't insult the occasion by denying my antipathy for you," Alastair replied in that reedy, snide tone that he couldn't clean up if he ever tried.

"Fine. I won't plan on Mercury being ready for a vacation palace anytime soon. Next? Let's get this over with."

Pao Wenling took the fore. "On behalf of the Order of Morpheus and the Grand Council, I hereby declare no confidence in the throne."

"Oh, really?" Khosrau teased. "Really? How many of those votes did you coerce? How many on the Council told you what you wanted to hear because they were scared of you? But ask yourself, how many of those voters are really loyal to me?"

"It's over, Khosrau," Wenling declared. From a hidden pocket in her sleeve, she produced a purple gemstone the size of a chicken egg.

Brutus likewise slipped a slender rod from within his sleeve. With a sharp shake, it snapped to the length of a war staff, topped with a mummified hand that clutched a crystal sphere.

Alastair lifted his arms as embroidered runes across his robe glowed to life.

"Just to make sure I grasp your intent, you want me to choose either abdication or assassination."

Wenling brandished the gem. "If you give up willingly, I can transfer your mind to a creature. Nothing with magic affinity. Nothing especially long-lived. But you could exist beyond this afternoon."

"So, something along the lines of a standard newt or toad, I take it?"

"Something like that."

"He's stalling," Alastair butted in. "Relax your defenses or be struck down. You're no match for all three of us, and your lapdog won't make a whit of difference."

Khosrau affected a yawn. "No. He won't. But the rune circle under the topsoil you're standing on will."

"WHAT?"

Undeterred by the sudden outcry from the imperial traitors, Khosrau continued. "In keeping with the formalities we're observing, I hereby judge you guilty of treason, yadda, yadda..."

He felt the throes of magical attacks directed at him. A bolt of violet energy stopped at an unseen, cylindrical barrier. A gout of fire from Brutus's staff redirected straight to the grass, feeding the runes. When the fires had sketched a perfect pentagram, with the three esteemed wizards trapped inside, the flames flared a hundred feet into the sky. As flesh and fabric and arcane artifacts charred and burned, the last to go were Alastair's robes, protective runes finally failing long after the man inside had been reduced to a blackened skeleton.

When the flames died out, the harbor breeze blew smoke out into the city.

"Who've we got next?"

Vincente trembled. "Um. I took the liberty of keeping the remainder of your afternoon clear for... cleaning."

"Huh. I rather fancied it as an object lesson. Oh well. Do you at least have a Ramsey update for me?"

Khosrau's most trusted assistant nodded vigorously. "Yes. Of course. Still on Phabian. There's some legal entanglement brewing with a series of disappearances tied to Eric. They have suspicions, but nothing they'd be willing to violate their refugee protection laws over. There are rumors of our people planetside looking for him."

"Do we have anyone on Phabian?"

"No one qualified to involve themselves. No one official, at least. If we have inquisitors, they're either impostors, freelancers, or lost in the paperwork between assignments."

"Well, no proper wizard can live on Phabian forever. And when he's had enough, he'll bring Jessie with him."

"Um..."

"Really, Vince, you're not on the barbecue list. I pay you to speak your mind when no one's around. Spit it out." With the smoldering bodies still a dozen yards away and smelling up the place despite a favorable wind, it needed saying.

"If you don't mind unraveling a mystery, why Jessica? I understand the chronomancer. Even if he never works for us, simply preventing him from scrambling the timeline warrants keeping him close at hand. But why his sister?"

"Other than as a method to ensure Eric Ramsey's good conduct?" Vincente nodded. Khosrau rubbed his chin. "Fine. You've proven trustworthy. All other factors aside, she possesses a limited form of chronomancy herself."

Vincente recoiled in surprise. "She's a wizard?"

"No. Nothing that fancy. Plenty of non-wizards out there with a touch of magic. Oracles who can read tarot cards. Morpheans with uncanny skills at poker. Hell, I'd lump in star-drive mechanics. Liaisons are rife with semi-wizards. So are the culling classes at every university. Jessie Ramsey just happens to have something more Chronos than Delphi when it comes to seeing the future."

"I will reveal nothing." Vincente bowed formally.

Khosrau snorted. "You don't reveal my coffee preferences; I'm not worried. Just make sure I get a daily update from Earth Interstellar on the Ramseys. If nothing else, it'll keep them from forgetting how important this is to me, personally." He glanced at the corpses within the burnt pentagram. "Make sure someone comes by before this gets cleaned up and replanted."

━━━

Lorraine Van Kleese stormed out of the eight-floor lift of the Richelieus' downtown New Singapore villa. She wagged the datapad in her hand, jaw clenched, ready to unload her ire.

When she punched the door panel with her thumb hard enough that she worried about a potential broken bone, she winced but immediately screwed the scowl back onto her face before anyone saw weakness.

"WHAT IS THIS?" she demanded as she hurricaned into the room the instant the door released.

James Rucker blinked and looked away from the Silver League fight on the holovid. He fumbled for the remote and paused the feed—not shut it off, Lorraine noted. "What's what?"

Lorraine threw the datapad at him.

Once he'd shaken loose the injury to his hand in trying to catch it and reoriented the device to read right side up, James scowled. "Ramsey kids are on Phabian. Beautiful. Safe as on their mom's tits."

"And under investigation for a string of murders."

"They guilty?" James inquired with an air of professional curiosity.

"Who even knows? What matters is this got in front of Esper. Esper, who is doing four in-person media blabs a day. Esper, who can't afford the appearance of wanting the presidency to negotiate for the release of family friends. You got them off Mars to avoid this problem in our backyard. It's not that much of a relief if it enters our foreign policy agenda. We do *not* need to be on record with a position on this. And you know Esper; she's going to have an opinion."

"Despite your best efforts." James reached over and grabbed a half-empty beer bottle from the side table. "Look, keeping her on message is your department. What're you sore about?"

"Someone fed this to her. I need you to find out who."

"You think I put Tiffany on them?"

"I worry that *she* did."

James rubbed a hand over his face. "Fine. I'll find a job for Tiff. Something time consuming and distant."

"And if she refuses?"

"Something high paying. And what if it's not her?"

"I've got housekeeping to do. We're behind in the polls. I can use that to turn over some of the staff if I have to."

James hoisted his beer and flicked the holo-projector back on. "You do that."

Lorraine confiscated the remote and shut it off. "How about now?"

James wrestled it out of her grasp but didn't put the fight back on. "Look. I got money on this bout. Tiffany Bell isn't going to jump when I comm. I'll take care of it. And let's just be clear here: Esper already knows. You want to do something about this? If anyone brings up those spacer brats, have her pivot it to the refugee crisis and Earth's treatment of Martian and non-declared citizens. Free travel and right of return for Martians in League space."

There was a moment where Lorraine just blinked. "Was that... a policy suggestion?"

"Hey, I'm watching a fight here."

With that, Lorraine excused herself quietly from the suite, wondering whether Esper could be corralled into using the Ramsey situation as a boomerang to draw attention to Admiral Alphonze's lack of a solution to the exodus of humans from the core.

———

Hecuba liked tutti frutti ice cream. It was something of a revelation about her. The standard household food processor didn't make that flavor. Eric knew because Ozzy'd asked Mom for it every time they'd gotten a new one. As they exited a Swirly Girl shop near the refugee district, he commented to that effect.

"You haven't said much about your brother. What's he like?"

Eric took a lick of his strawberry ice cream as he considered an answer. "Well, he was my little brother. He was still figuring out what kind of person he wanted to be when I left for college. He's almost my age now. At this rate, he'll be older than me soon."

Hecuba tittered. "I don't think you need to worry about a fluke like that happening again."

Eric kept his eyes pointed elsewhere, pretending to admire the Kethlet skyline from underneath it. "Well, my point's more that I'm not sure I know what he's like. I know what he *used to* be like. But it doesn't seem fair to draw him with Wax-i-Rods."

"With what?"

This was a cultural disconnect Oxford hadn't prepared him for. He hadn't had deep-thought discussions about childhood with his classmates. "You know. Wax-i-Rods. Every color, but never look like real things."

Hecuba shook her head with an apologetic scowl.

"Kinda oily. Like scribbling with a candle. Little candles. Like birthday size."

They strolled at a leisurely pace as Hecuba struggled to relate. "Like chalk? I had colored chalks as a kid."

"Close enough. But it's better on paper and worse on permacrete. About as good on walls. If you eat some, it doesn't make your stomach as sick as chalk."

"You mean if a kid eats some."

"I said what I said."

She giggled. "Hey, you want to see a holo?"

Eric scanned the street on both sides, wondering where the theater was that prompted her non sequitur suggestion. There was none in sight. "Uh. Maybe? It would be late when it ended.

All recent things considered, maybe we shouldn't be out on the town after dark."

"It's never *that* dark here. And I'll have you with me." She slipped an arm around his. Eric adjusted his gait so that their feet didn't tangle. "Come on. It'll be fun."

Eric didn't even know what was showing. Then again, this was Phabian. Theoretically, everything was playing somewhere. And if it wasn't, they could find someplace willing to arrange a bespoke viewing experience. Doonah had stomped around the brushfire, but Eric seemed to be making a respectable income. With seniority over him, he assumed that Hecuba was compensated even better. Between the two of them, they could afford an evening's entertainment of their choosing.

"OK. Sure." Eric felt his stomach tugging on his intestines with the intent to practice macrame.

Hecuba gave Eric's non-ice-cream arm a squeeze. "Hey. Don't go tensing up. I'm sure that now they know you're onto them, those two 'friends' of yours will leave you alone."

It was cute how she enunciated her quotation marks so clearly. Eric knew that Snow and Slater weren't his friends. And he knew she knew that. Yet her logic was sound; the pair had discovered on Mars that they couldn't suppress his magic on their own. Even Phabian's massive resistance to magic wouldn't make much of a difference.

Eric took a long, deep breath. "You know what? You're right. I don't know what's good these days. You pick us something, and we'll have popcorn and Gummi Dotz for dinner."

It didn't take long for Hecuba to find them a theater and buy them tickets to see *New Year's Kiss*. Eric hadn't realized until the scene where Joanna LaFontaine's character, Ginny, had her date for New Year's Eve cancel on her last minute that he'd been jonesing for a Joanna LaFontaine holo. He'd whispered a quiet apology to Hecuba for being the one to start the crying domino effect. In the end, they left the theater with spent tear ducts and laughter in their hearts.

"Oh, I almost didn't forgive Brett for taking Alicia to the Kents' New Year's party when he'd already said yes to Ginny." Hecuba wiped a finger under an eye that still hadn't fully dried from the final, cathartic kissing scene.

Eric harrumphed. "You know, it still miffs me when the villain turns out to be a wizard with a love potion."

"It's cheap, but you can just overlook it."

"Just feels a little prejudicial. You never see holos where someone uses dark science to make someone fall in love."

Hecuba scoffed. "You just don't watch them. Trust me, they're out there."

It was the waning dusk when they broke out into the fresh air. Eric and Hecuba's bellies were full of barbecue chipotle popcorn and Frooti Explosion Gummi Dotz. They took a slow pace, letting other pedestrians pass them, allowing the questionable meal a chance to settle before angering it.

She was right. Maybe about the dark science holos, but definitely about needing this evening out. After all, the refugee zone was a little light on recreational activities. Much as they tried to be wizard-inclusive, Phabian specialized in digital entertainment games.

Not that holos weren't technological. Wizards, as a bloc, tended to give scientists a pass on one good idea or so per century.

"Shall we take a scenic route along the waterfront?" he suggested. There was plenty of night left. Eric wasn't eager to spend the rest of it alone.

Hecuba nudged him playfully. "So much for not wanting to go out after dark?"

They held hands and strolled Zethel River's edge, where street performers played and danced for tips and gave the impression of a year-round party. Jugglers, fire twirlers, acrobatic stackers, comedians, Eric gawked his way through the crowds. Had he not been tethered by the hand, he'd have been liable to lose track of Hecuba with so much to draw the eye.

"Oh, look!" Hecuba exclaimed, giving a tug for Eric to see where she was pointing.

A pair of laaku were flinging a disc across the river, its outer edge glowing with blinking lights that raced around the perimeter the opposite direction, coming to a near halt in an optical illusion that broke when the disc slowed mid-flight. But what Hecuba clearly meant for him to see was the ratatoret passenger riding the disc, luckily not spinning along with the outer ring. He wore a tiny helmet and may have been responsible for steering the disc's swerving path.

"Oh, shit!" Eric said under his breath.

Hecuba chuckled. "I'm sure he's fine."

"Not him. *Them*." He turned back, and Hecuba followed his gaze.

Snow.

Slater.

They weren't even in disguise. Both wore their own visages and plain wizardly daily wear with baggy sleeves. They were weaving their way through the loose crowd between performers, heading straight toward the pair.

"Wait a minute. Is that...?"

"Yeah."

"Crap!"

Eric tugged and Hecuba didn't hesitate to follow as he headed off in the opposite direction. "We've got to lose them."

"It's a public space. We can call the police."

"Best case, they'd authorize me to hurt them. I don't want

that."

They picked up their pace, struggling to maintain a grip on one another's hands as they navigated varying densities of crowd as the variety of acts differed in quality.

"That's noble and all, but they can't touch you here, legally. Let's stand our ground."

Eric bit back a hurtful comment. This wasn't her fight, and not because she was only tangentially involved. If it came to violence, he'd be doing the hurting people, not her. "That's not going to help anything."

"It'll put an end to this. Maybe it'll be messy, but you can't let them chase you all over the galaxy. Confront them. Prove they're real." Eric jerked to a halt. When the length of two arms ran out and Hecuba hadn't stopped, he let go of her hand. Her own grip wasn't enough to keep hold of him. When they parted, she quickly reversed course to come back for him. "What're you doing? Are you going to do it?"

"What did you mean, 'prove they're real'?"

Hecuba huffed an impatient sigh. "They're real. I believe you. What's the plan?"

This was one of those instances where wizards enjoyed a certain degree of social invisibility. Dressed clearly as their profession dictated, laaku and xeno pedestrians were going out of their way to ignore them. There was hover-wreck interesting that drew people like locusts, and there was wizard interesting, which caused scientific folks to pray for safe harbor.

"But you didn't believe me until you saw them for yourself."

Hecuba wouldn't look him in the eye. "You have to admit, it was a little far-fetched."

"Yeah. Convocation doesn't have the resources to go after a guy who misses five years and they want to know how so they can do it too and figure out a way to go backward maybe which

I tell anyone who'll listen isn't something I know how to do but try telling them that when they don't know how to do forward either."

"Eric, calm down."

"What do I have to be calm about? The fact that I have a whole planet promising I'm safe here and not only am I not safe, the person I trust third-most on the entire planet doesn't even believe me?"

"Third?"

Even in the midst of a tirade spiral, Eric couldn't help being as technically accurate as possible. "My friend Trebla lives here, too." Jessie went without saying, so he didn't mention her. While he might have had other acquaintances that might be on Phabian right now, the majority wouldn't rate higher than Hecuba for trustworthiness.

"What about us, Eric?"

A bucket of ice water ran down Eric's spine. He spun. "Hi, Wizard Slater. Fancy seeing you here."

Snow spoke from behind them. The two of them had been so preoccupied that Eric and Hecuba had allowed themselves to be surrounded. With a river to one side, it was a messy triangle, but there would be no getting past them without a fight or a swim.

Flying might have been possible, but that was merely thinking in three dimensions.

Eric spoke from the side of his mouth. "Do you trust me?"

"Trust you about what?" she whispered back from breath-on-the-earlobe distance.

Wizard Snow closed in slowly. "There's a place for you back home." For the inquisitor, Eric knew that meant Earth.

"A lot can be brushed over with a little cooperation," Slater added.

"Take my hand," Eric instructed softly, fumbling around

until Hecuba's fingers found his.

Step aside.

The universe didn't need much prodding. It was vanity, frankly, overexplaining to an omniscient, omnipresent entity that transcended consciousness.

Looks of shock, surprise, and outrage flashed across Snow's and Slater's faces with comical haste. They moved like a holovid on speed-skip. So did the crowd, the river current, the little ratatoret whizzing back and forth across the river. Pedestrians flowed past them, through them even. All the while, Snow and Slater milled around, argued, fretted, grew paranoid. Then, suddenly, they beat a hasty retreat.

Kethlet police on a routine patrol sauntered by at high speed.

The street festival broke up as pre-dawn brightened the eastern sky.

Long enough, it seemed.

Eric took a step forward, pulling Hecuba along with him. She clung to his hand with a murderous grip; his fingers tingled with lack of blood flow.

He looked all around. No one seemed shocked enough by their appearance to make a fuss about it. Either they'd been overlooked, or the wizardly invisibility rule was working in their favor. "Should be safe for now."

"Safe?" Hecuba released Eric's hand and snatched hers away. "What was that?"

Eric cleared his throat, indicating that she knew darn well and he wasn't feeling at liberty to confirm it aloud.

"No." She shook her head and backed away. "I can't have. Do you realize what you've done?"

Eric followed gingerly, not looking to get closer, just not having to continue the conversation at increasing volume as Hecuba retreated. "Yes. I found a non-violent solution."

"You made me complicit. I have to report this."

He patted the air. "You don't have to do anything. You're free to choose. Look around. Buildings didn't go dark. Hovers didn't rain from the sky. It was just a little bit and really safe."

Hecuba swung her head in violent denial. "You don't even know what that word means!"

When she fled, Eric let her go. His heart was too heavy to drag in pursuit.

⊏⊐

Jessie hunched over the flimsy folding table she'd picked up at the local Cheapo Depot, a micro-circuitry welder clenched in her teeth. The still-glowing tip of the welder warmed her cheek by proximity. Through the magnifying inset on her datagoggles, she maneuvered a pair of tweezers, every jitter of steady grip exaggerated to the verge of frustration. There was a reason that high-tech manufacturing was all done by machines.

After what felt like hours, she had the chip settled into place. Holding her breath, she retrieved the welder from her teeth and gingerly soldered it into the location detection circuit. Once it was secure, she activated the device. Indicator lights blinked a startup sequence before going obediently silent.

Letting out all the tension in her chest, Jessie gave a few puffs of non-conductive impact-resistant resin spray. It dried and hardened in under a minute, after which she snapped the access panel shut.

What she was left with was a slightly tapered, slightly ovoid cylinder nearly the length of her forearm. She slipped her left hand through it, and once it was in place, a soft whirr of an interior bladder inflating tightened the TeleJack onto her arm.

She gave a few test flexes before tapping the interface and adjusting the pressure. While she'd eventually settled on a women's model for the fit, the preset assumed someone with a less intense strength workout. The balance would take a few days to grow used to, but it hadn't been that long since she'd last worn one. For all she knew, her old one was in storage somewhere in an Earth Navy evidence locker. She gazed down.

"Hello, new friend."

A few minutes of setup, and she'd bio-attuned the device and linked a few key accounts scattered across the omni. Her modification might not have proofed her against all forms of digital invasion; it was at least enough that common criminals and underfunded government entities couldn't just stroll through her data.

Sleek and matte silver, it was a military-grade model, even without being plugged into a League Navy network. Blaster resistant and impact rated, with limited anti-jamming technology, she wouldn't have been allowed to purchase it yesterday. Now, along with the little Jodek-IX tucked in her shoulder holster, she was cleared for more than civilian ownership rights.

She slouched back in her chair.

Finally.

She almost felt like a soldier again.

Maybe her blaster was set to stun with an auto-revert if she left it switched to kill while unattended. Maybe her TeleJack didn't give real-time tactical locations of her squad or allow her to call for aerial fire support. Maybe her credit hadn't been able to cover the purchase of both a TeleJack and a higher-end set of datagoggles in the same month.

For now, it was enough normalcy to provide relief.

Her mission wasn't tactical. She wouldn't even be smart carrying this stuff to hang around with Stet. Elephants might have been notoriously afraid of mice. Luckily, so far, the haathee hadn't shown the ability to even notice a rat.

Just wearing it out for dinner would be a relief.

Tossing on a jacket to hide the blaster she wasn't supposed to be flaunting in public, Jessie laid ions.

————

When Jessie entered the coffee shop, she had expected to be the first to arrive. After all, all "Eric" and "early" had in common were two letters. Trebla tended to be either precisely on time or egregiously late, depending on whether he got caught up in some fascinating project. Yet as soon as she stepped through the doors to Queen Been, the pair greeted her with raised hands and beckoning gestures.

The whole place was old-Earth kitsch. Human-owned and franchised across half of what was once ARGO, the chain had an unmistakable aesthetic. Playing off the queen bee and coffee bean mashup, everything was black and yellow stripes, from the takeout cups to the waitstaff's uniforms. Unlike so many of the backwater locations she'd visited, this one had the staff outfitted with holographic wings and antennae instead of the cheap plastic or fabric versions.

"Took the liberty of ordering your coffee," Trebla said by way of greeting.

This meal was his treat. As such, it had been his choice of restaurant, seeing as it wasn't anyone's birthday. Considering that Queen Been wasn't exactly fine dining was a subtle yet unmistakable hint that money was stretching tight for their laaku cousin.

Jessie slid into the semicircular booth, boxing Trebla in between Ramsey siblings. "I'd ask if you remembered how I take it, but I know I'd get a snide answer."

"Some things never change."

"Yeah, but look at you." Jessie waved a hand up and down

to indicate all of him. "All... workforcey and shit."

Trebla shrugged with his upper palms upturned. "What can I say? Selling out makes a living."

A waitress on hoverskates slid to a halt in front of their table. In rapid succession, she plunked three striped cups down in front of the trio. "Apiary quadro, unsweetened, two shots of pollen; larva-size honeycomb latte with triple jelly; queen-size super sting with a single shot of honey. Careful, that one's got some zing."

Jessie lifted an eyebrow as she picked up her oversized beverage. "Thanks, but I grew up on this stuff." She pried off the lid with its sippy spout for taking on the go, then quaffed a slug of the stuff. Despite the lingo and the occasional use of honey-based sweeteners, it was just regular, strong coffee.

Eric stared into his before taking a sip of what amounted to liquid candy.

Trebla leered after the waitress as she departed.

"Seriously?" Jessie lowered her voice. "It's a baggy uni, a knee-length skirt, and she's a core 3 at best."

"That's Sheila. I've been here five times since I got to Kethlet. Figure I can dangle myself here two or three more times before I head home."

"You even talk to her?"

"Just ordering drinks."

"You're hopeless. And if you're calling this a meal, we better at least be able to order off the dinner menu."

"The Royal Start to A Buzzy Day," Eric read off his cup, holding it in front of his face. His voice was flat, lifeless.

"What's his deal?" Jessie demanded, hoping for Trebla's version. Eric had a glassy look in his eyes, and he was wearing a weird necklace of pink jewels—the cheap plastic kind given to kids to play dress-up.

"He said he'd rather not get into it twice. Presumably, now

that you're here, we can get enlightened."

They both fixed Eric with stares in a unison practiced by long hours growing up together in a small starship.

With melodrama written across his features, Eric heaved a sigh. Taking a sip of his coffee to steel himself, Eric launched into what, for him, was a brief explanation. "I had quite a day."

"This have something to do with Hecuba not being here after I told you to invite her along?"

Trebla swiveled his head to face Jessie. "Who's Hecuba?" Then back to Eric. "Is that the girl you were with at the dance festival?" Back to Jessie. "This guy got an actual girlfriend?"

"Not even a friend," Eric replied sullenly. He addressed the striped cup he clutched in both hands. "My fault, really. Always is."

"Have you talked to her about it?" Jessie prodded. If she were a betting woman—which she was—and someone was taking bets, she'd have laid a hundred of whatever the hell currency was floating around the galaxy these days that Hecuba had no idea she had been in a fight.

"She implied she'd be reporting me to the police."

So much for *that* bet. "Fuck me; what'd you say to her?"

"Ah, don't worry about the law," Trebla chimed in with that reassuring smarm they'd all picked up from the adults in their lives. "PIS is all over some new serial killer. No suspects. No bodies. No clues. They're calling them 'The Void.'" He made twinkly fingers to add mystery, break the tension, or whatever shitty psycho-nonsense he felt the situation needed. "Unless you vaporized her, no one's got time for complaints."

Jessie doubted that very much. She needed clarity on this, and pronto. "What happened?"

Eric's downcast gaze didn't show signs of breaking easily.

"Eeeeeric..." It was a tone of voice that Mom had honed and Jessie had learned to mimic. Her brother was conflict averse, and he had to understand that she wasn't a problem that was going to go away by being ignored. "This conversation doesn't get easier making us wait. We haven't seen Trebla in— well, it's been even longer since he's seen us. Let's not waste the whole evening in a sulk. OK?"

"I asked her to trust me."

"Uh huh..."

"And then I showed her a trick."

Jessie didn't dignify the evasion with so much as a grunt. If she'd been the wizard in the family, her eyes would have been boring two smoldering holes through Eric's forehead.

"I was... you know... that thing I'm not supposed to do or show anyone. Well..."

Trebla waggled an interposing finger. "Um, he's not talking about..."

"Yeah," Jessie deadpanned. "I think he is. What possessed you to—"

"It was them!" Eric blurted, drawing stares from nearby tables. Jessie hurriedly shushed him, and Eric lowered his voice. "You know. *Them.*"

"Slater and Snow?"

Eric's nod was both slight and frantic.

"Who are Slater and Snow?"

"Convo spooks," Jessie explained. "The ones who chased us off Mars. They shouldn't be able to operate on Phabian. I take it you didn't exactly shout for help. Wait. You... used the thing? To get away from them?"

Eric cowered.

Jessie gritted her teeth. "Eeeeriiiiic."

"I know. I know."

"I don't know," Trebla interjected. "What's going on?"

"Eric poofed ahead in time to escape his parole officers."

"Not really a poof. More like stepping off a moving

walkway at a starport to let people clear out of our way."

"He can do it on purpose?" Trebla asked incredulously. Then he turned to Eric. "You can do it on purpose? I thought you said it was an accident."

Their waitress jetted up to the table. "Everyone ready to order?"

Eric glanced up. "Cinnamon honey muffin, swarm fries, and hive sauce."

The ease at which Eric switched orbits and ignored her hearkened back to their childhood days on the *Mobius*. But the quickest way to answers was getting rid of the waitress. "Honeycomb press sandwich with cheddar and mustard, swarm fries, mead sauce."

"And you, sir?"

For the sake of the waitress, Jessie hoped she hadn't been planetside long enough to read laaku body language. Trebla laid on the flirting comically thick. "I like everything I see." He was, at the time, not making eye contact with her. "Care to recommend something?"

"Same thing I'm having," Jessie stated firmly.

The waitress nodded a cheerful, silent thanks in her direction. "All rightie. Back in a few." She skated off with a flapping of holographic wings.

"Aww. C'mon, Jess. I promise I'm gonna say something one of these days. Just have to work up to it."

"Focus. Eric, what happened to Hecuba? Is she OK?"

Eric nodded emphatically. A knot of relief untied itself. Last thing she needed was to go begging wizardly authorities for help retrieving someone stranded in some parallel timeline.

"Hey, I gotta ask." Trebla leaned in conspiratorially. "What's it like?"

Eric groaned. "You know I can't explain magic to a tech-weasel like you."

"No. I mean having a girlfriend."

Jessie slapped him upside the head. It was a reflex, something that was par for the course growing up together but which could result in an assault charge if Trebla wanted to be a putz about it. "Sorry."

"I didn't mean—"

"I don't know why you'd think I knew. I've never had a girlfriend, either."

She'd seen this coming. Part of her hoped that something would click in that spaghetti brain of her brother's. Nobody could live their entire life on shower thoughts and leftover notions from dreams. One day, Jessie hoped that Eric would find something to ground him. Family hadn't done the job. Neither had school. His only hobby had been magic, and it had taken over his whole way of thinking. "Eric. What are the chances she really went to the cops?"

"I dunno."

"You need to find out. You need to make up with her. Apologize. Promise never to do it again. Then, you know, *don't* do it again."

Nodding obediently, Eric leaned forward to stand. Jessie caught him by the wrist.

"After dinner."

Eric sat back down.

"If it makes you feel any better," Trebla added, "I still think there's about a 20 percent chance you two hid out for five years, and this whole time travel thing is a long con. Whatever it is you've got going on... I want in."

———

Trebla had offered to take them on a cityscape cruise, high enough that Phabian would look a little like Earth with all the glowy dots of light at night. When Eric demurred, explaining that he didn't feel like having a night out, they changed plans, and the two of them headed to Curve Circus instead. Jessie made a show of being concerned about leaving Eric on his own, but she needed to blow off steam. It wasn't fair dragging her down with him. A cheery smile and a few assurances, and she'd been off.

Though she wasn't probably allowed to admit it, Jessie had an important job now. Oh, she'd been unhappy her first few days on Phabian, working some data job. Then, one day, she'd just been happy. That meant his sister wasn't sitting at a desk all day anymore. Her complaints about work dried up; mysteriously, she hadn't given a reason why.

Someone was paying Jessie to be Jessie again.

That was great. But being Jessie was dangerous and stressful, and it required frequent releases of the latter.

Eric needed to be Eric again.

He couldn't be that with Hecuba afraid of him, and he couldn't be that with Snow and Slater constantly harassing him. The former would take time, finesse, and probably a few false starts. The latter he would deal with tonight.

There was a chance that if he hid, if he kept quiet, kept moving, kept from using magic, that he could avoid the pair for the rest of his life. If nothing else, they were older than him. Maybe if he just outlasted them, he could be a wizard in fifty, sixty, or eighty years.

No.

They needed to stop. He needed to stop them.

Unfortunately, he needed them to find him. Despite catching hints of them, he'd yet to find a way to track them.

Luckily, there was a surefire way to draw their attention to him.

Eric strode into the night, feet a centimeter off the ground.

The next day at work, Jessie heard a rumor that ruined her productivity. Not that she'd been a great analyst to that point, but this time Banlee made a point of chiding her for slacking off. Yet how could Jessie pore through scattered reports of Ambassador Grosstet's ship being sighted at various points along his journey to Phabian when the laaku had outsourced investigating a local magical anomaly to the ssentuadi?

Laaku wizards were a joke. Even just hanging out on the fringe within earshot of Enzio Stiles, she'd picked up on the general opinion of them within the Convocation. Phabian wasn't a factor, magically. But a smart alliance with the ssentuadi provided a more respectable, more formidable source of magical muscle.

If Eric wasn't careful, his old friends from Earth would be the least of his worries.

And frankly, Jessie was starting to worry about whether he was getting paranoid. Hecuba didn't know them. It could have been two older humans about the right builds and Eric's own hyperactive imagination. She *hated* doubting him, especially when he was so sincere about his problems. Psychiatrists wouldn't risk their psyches trying to treat wizards. The legal system wouldn't look kindly on his behavior if it came to light. At best, as a sister, all she could do was take matters into her own hands.

Eric had proved on Echo Niner that he could take care of himself. To a degree. He just wasn't equipped to operate within a giant societal machine. Oxford had been a cloistered little oasis, and he'd gotten himself ejected as incompatible.

Had Phabian been a mistake?

Maybe a quick stop, a little side work, and passage to the

borderlands would have been a better plan than the refugee system.

It wasn't too late if she had to pull the plug on this plan. Jessie's life plan was on triple letters by now. It had to be, despite losing count long ago. What was another hasty revision?

As soon as her duties allowed, and before she was due for more schmoozing of the haathee emissary, Jessie headed out to the site of the riverfront festival the other night.

A hover-taxi dropped her off, and Jessie scanned the area with a tactical eye.

Pedestrians. Workers off shift. Street food vendors. Then she spotted a local police cordon, beamed off with a holographic security perimeter. While the colored light wouldn't stop a curious bystander from entering the area, a squad of laaku patrol officers with stun batons patrolled to keep lookie-loos like her at bay.

Jessie hated being kept at bay.

With her TeleJack's map for reference, Jessie staked out a spot on the far side of the river with a clear view of the site. She couldn't understand ssentuadi anyway, but she could at least read the body language of the patrol officers. Two ssentuadi slithered around, conferring in hisses implied by the flicks of their tongues.

Ssentuadi were one species that gave Jessie the creeps. It was xenoist, but she didn't care. Humans had a natural aversion to snakes that she'd felt no duty to work on, personally. They'd been, at best, tentatively neutral with the Convocation, and Earth by extension, for most of Jessie's life. Few treaties had existed between their respective species. Travel between human and ssentuadi territory had been limited. The fact that the laaku had formed an alliance so quickly just spoke to what expert collaborators they had evolved to be.

"Come on. Give up. Write it off." There wasn't anyone lurking nearby. Muttering to herself didn't hurt anything.

A tingle from her TeleJack alerted Jessie to a new comm.

She glanced away from the investigation to check.

Get out of there. Limit exposure. Stay on task.

There was no signature. There didn't need to be. If someone besides Bernek had sent the message, they'd have been no less right. This was stupid, risky, and might taint both the probe into the magical disturbance Eric had caused and her own mission.

What was she going to do, anyway? This was about peace of mind if they found nothing, and forewarning if they tied this to Eric.

Tapping at her forearm, Jessie composed a reply to the throwaway omni account that had delivered the message.

Quash this. No good outcomes.

If someone wanted to vague-comm at her, they could take one in reply. If Bernek had the pull he implied, he could make this go away.

Sparing one last glance, willing the ssentuadi to give up in confusion and frustration, Jessie used an app to summon another hover-taxi.

Her own size eights wouldn't be a problem. She hoped that the Altair Star Lanes would figure out a way to whip up some size forty octuple-wide bowling shoes for Grosstet.

―

The first night had been a bust. Sore feet and zero annoying nanny-wizards prompted Eric to give up on his self-appointed task before the dawn rose in the east like an alarm clock. Nevertheless, he chose not to venture into work that morning nor to return to his apartment lest any nosy coworkers stop by to rouse him. Instead, Eric purchased tickets for three matinee holos, slept quietly in a back row, and went about his day.

Avoiding people he knew was simplicity itself.

First of all, there were only a scattering of people on Phabian who knew him, concentrated predominantly in the refugee district. Jessie, Hecuba, Doonah, the rest of the factory staff, Daisy, Jean-Michel, Fobrek, a few names Phabian Investigative Services claimed were missing, Ebli, Vor'clek, and of course Trebla; he hardly counted because he'd be with Jessie unless he was back home a quarter of a planet away.

Of course, if any of them wanted to follow him, that would drastically increase the chances of being discovered. Also, he was human on a planet where he was vastly in the minority, even more so than the last time he'd visited Phabian.

So, Eric Ramsey became Fenji of Orion, a laaku linguist who had returned to her ancestral homeworld when the Human Civil War had broken out. Her fur was a medium brown, average build, dressed in offworld style but nothing that didn't fit modern laaku sensibilities. She spoke Kejathi with the faintest hint of English, which made sense growing up on a human-dominant planet. And since he was looking to pass as laaku, Eric employed the increasingly popular native language almost exclusively.

Ironically, he sometimes had to switch to English when actual laaku didn't speak Kejathi.

His pocket money was holding up. Eric ordered grilled papaya for lunch from a pushcart, and his dinner was banana salad. He strolled the streets, magical senses pricked for signs of company.

It wasn't long after dark when he got his wish.

Maybe taking every lonely, dark alley had worked. Possibly, the inquisitors had just caught up with him at a poetic moment.

"Don't tell me you expected that disguise to fool us," Snow scolded. The voice came from behind him.

Eric hid his smirk before turning, hands upraised like he was being mugged. "Parley?"

"Haven't we all done this before?" Slater asked.

Snow stepped in to conduct their negotiations. "We're done playing nice. We have transportation. You can come with us, or we can start coming after your sister instead. You'd come to Earth to save her, wouldn't you?"

Eric cocked his head as he melted back into his own form. "Really? That again? You know I would. But I think the question you need to ask is: what would I be willing to do to you if we don't come to an agreement right here and now?"

The inquisitors exchanged a skeptical look.

In his chest, Eric's heart pounded a drumbeat. If this had been a Napoleonic regiment, it would have been the signal for an all-out retreat.

"We didn't think you had it in you," Snow replied slyly. He pulled a small book from his robes. "Your sister's been a bad influence."

Meanwhile, Slater slipped a ring onto her finger. Then another. And another. Different metals and gemstones, each looked arcane and ominous. "After last time, let's just say we came better prepared."

Breath coming quick, Eric pressed his thumb to his middle finger. "Try me."

What was he doing? He knew better! This was a horrible idea. But they weren't listening. Wouldn't reason with him.

What choice was there?

The first word out of Snow's mouth was Aramaic.

Eric snapped his fingers.

There was no second word.

Snow and Slater were gone.

Fenji of Orion walked out of the alley unmolested.

The next day, Eric came back to the same spot and waited. He had nearly finished his ice cream when two startled wizards appeared in front of him.

"What happened?" Slater demanded.

Snow still held the book open in his hand. He pointed to a spot on the ground. "You were just... And the lights. *When* are we?"

"This is tomorrow. I spent the day avoiding coworkers and lying to my sister. But for you, it's just gone."

"This is outrageous!" Slater exclaimed. When she took a menacing step forward, Eric raised his non-cone-holding hand and once more pressed his thumb to his middle finger. He raised his eyebrows in warning. Daring. Challenging.

Snow snarled and stormed toward Eric. "By what right do you—?"

Snap.

The same time the next night, Eric was leaning against the wall of one of the alley-adjacent buildings when Snow and Slater reappeared. "I want you to go home. Tell them I'm dead. Tell them you can't accomplish your mission. I don't care. Be done. I want this over."

"We can't."

Snow nodded. "This is the job. Quitting isn't an option. Next inquisitors would be after us."

"I'm worse than them." Eric swallowed. He'd tried to calm himself before the reappearance, but he was clenching every muscle in his gut as he tried to out-tough his inquisitors.

Snow's smile was hurtful. "No offense, but no one believes that."

Grimacing, Eric snapped.

This time, it was a week before they returned to Eric's time.

"March eighteenth," Eric informed them as soon as the

instantaneous disorientation passed. "I took a week this time."

"It's a delaying action," Snow protested. "You're not free of us. You can't keep this up forever."

Slater nodded, lips pursed. "You know you don't have it in you to kill us. Sooner or later, we'll bring you home. Where you belong."

"I sent a note to work, letting them know I quit. It was a formality, since I hadn't shown up and didn't plan to."

"It's not that easy for us," Snow explained. He gently slid the Aramaic text into his robe where he'd found it. Keeping his hands in plain view thereafter, he moved slowly. "Look. Maybe we can make you some assurances."

"A few lies from us could smooth out a lot of your problems when you get to Earth."

Eric looked from one to the other. Snow. Slater. They were wheedling. The threats had petered out. "I found out just this morning that Hecuba lost her job because they blamed *her* for me quitting. Her. She didn't do anything but panic when *you two* chased us."

"It's you she's afraid of."

"Well, I'm done," Eric stated, staring down the pair. Today, his hands didn't shake. His blood pounded in his ears looking at them, but his vision was clear. "I don't know how far I can send you into the future. But I managed five years, not even meaning to. Azrin will have evolved into pacifist vegetarians by the time you show back up."

He raised his hand. Pressed his thumb to his middle finger.

"NO! WAIT!" the wizards cried out in terror.

Slowly, Eric parted his fingers.

"We—we'll make something up," Snow promised. "Maybe you're the one lost in time."

Slater turned to her partner. "Or the ssentuadi took him in. We still have an agreement in place, don't we?"

"I don't care," Eric replied calmly. "Even in courier astral, it's a while to get back to Earth. You'll have time to think something up."

Snow gave a curt nod. "Fine." He shook his head. "I don't know what happened to you, Eric. But something changed. When you first sent us forward, I knew you wouldn't do anything drastic."

"You did this. Oh, and speaking of things you did, if you didn't kill those people who disappeared, I'd like you to send them home safely."

"But we didn't—" Slater began to protest but stopped when Eric lifted a hand.

"I don't want to hear your excuses. Either return them or don't. Let your conscience guide you; whatever passes for your conscience. I'm done with you being my problem."

With that, Eric turned and started the long walk back to the refugee district once again.

———

Jessie tugged the knot and checked her tie in the mirror. Not quite perfect, but for a manual job, she gave herself a pass. The dinner party was "traditional attire," a mandate that varied by species. Her alternative to the black-tie ensemble would have been an evening gown, and she doubted there was enough booze on Phabian for her to spend an entire dinner party on display like that.

Weeks of work were finally paying off. While she'd spent time hanging out with Grosstet and tutoring him in English with kid gloves, this was the first time she'd earned a spot on a guest list someone of her social standing had no business making.

She bared her teeth, then stuffed the business end of a

horseshoe-shaped tooth scrubber into her mouth. Lunch had included spinach salad, and the remnants had clung stubbornly. As the device hummed and resonated, Jessie shrugged out of her holster and slid it away in a dresser drawer beneath a stack of undergarments. Her dress shirt was short-sleeved, leaving her TeleJack exposed until the moment she donned her jacket. Billowy pants dragged on the floor, tripping her until she rolled them into a temporary cuff.

The device timed out. She rinsed and checked again. Sparkling clean teeth this time. Her apartment was replete with buzzy little devices purchased during her time on Phabian, but none of them did her conscience a damn bit of good.

Recriminations would come later. Not from Section 74, which seemed happy with her reports and progress, but from herself. Grosstet had fed her more intel about his people via longwinded stories in choppy, grade-school English than their people had been able to gather through advanced scans, surveillance, and contact from species he'd encountered along his journey. She'd converted stories into data, inferred technological capabilities, estimated his crew complement, sussed out the geopolitical landscape of his own Earth-like homeworld.

Jessie downed a deodorizer pill that would suppress sweat production for the next several hours. She'd have to monitor her body temperature for overheating, but the TeleJack could watch that for her. With several species attending who were more olfactorily aware than humans—notably the haathee ambassador himself—Jessie couldn't risk giving away a heightened state of stress.

Lastly, she stepped into a pair of ankle-high stiletto boots with 15 cm heels. She felt like a circus performer, but at least she'd been practicing walking in them the past few days so she wouldn't make an ass of herself among the muckity schmucks in attendance.

The walk over to the haathee embassy gave her a refresher course on balance and coordination that no amount of hand-to-hand combat training could fully prepare her for. By the time she arrived to be checked off a list by one of MIRP's people, she was hardly struggling anymore.

The laaku on security detail barely spared her a glance. "Name?"

"It's me, Eepok."

"*Name?*" He glared from beneath his overhanging brow. This wasn't the time for informality.

She played along. After all, it wasn't her job on the line. "Jessica Ramsey." A quick wave of a handheld weapons scanner, and she was allowed inside.

Grosstet's place had been done up for the occasion by someone who'd never seen a dinner party in this half of the galaxy. Or, more accurately, it had been someone who wanted to show off a new sensibility. Wall sconces held dyed sheaves of wheat. His ceiling was a dangling forest of bird feeders with tiny songbirds gorging themselves more than singing. His oversized furniture hadn't been replaced but rather refitted for the smaller stature of his guest list. Scaffolds and bleachers and temporary steps created a mezzanine level around tables and chairs, allowing the politically influential class on Phabian access to the buffet.

Jessie had been excepted from the potluck aspect. Good old Stet had polled her on appropriate items she could bring but, when informed that she didn't cook, quickly crossed her off the list of those expected to represent her species.

As soon as she was inside, within the privacy shield, two things happened. First, she intercepted a waiter and plucked a champagne glass from his tray; it wasn't champagne, but the non-alcoholic cider was sweetened to within a centimeter of its life and packed a little kick. Second, she could hear the evening's host regaling a captive audience with stories.

"...IT WAS VERY COLD. I HAD THE HELMET BUT NO SUIT. BOOT'AE GRAB TO THE HULL." He made fists with those gargantuan hands of his, miming out the story in case his language failed him. "I WALK. THE HOLE, I CLOSE IT." He aimed a finger like a welder, tracing the seam of a patch job. She'd heard this story already. "I GOT BACK IN THE SHIP. I WIN THE FIGHT."

While there were still some gaps in his background, Jessie had learned that he'd fought in an interstellar war against a species that looked like octopuses. While his role as narrator complicated separating fact from fiction, he'd been a decorated hero in the conflict.

This retelling resulted in some polite applause and congratulations from the mixed crowd of mostly laaku dignitaries. Other than a couple admirals, few of them seemed interested in the old war story. Oh, and the lone azrin in attendance. By the rapt gaze of admiration in those feline eyes, she'd have gladly taken the chance the stuunji refugee women had the other night.

Jessie threw back her drink, eyes watering and teeth aching from the sweetness overload. She wiped a sleeve across her eyes before making her way over to join the gaggle surrounding the haathee ambassador.

"Hi, Stet. Nice shindig." She saw the momentary confusion in those comparatively tiny eyes before clarifying, "Nice party."

"AH. YES. MANY FOOD'AE. MUSIC FROM MY HOME." With the din of conversation—one voice in particular —she'd barely noticed the background soundtrack, heavy on woodwind and percussion. "MAYBE A DANCE?"

"I'd skip the dancing with this crowd," Jessie advised,

keeping a smile for the benefit of the audience anyone with Stet invariably drew. "But maybe crank up the music a little. Let them get the vibe from your planet."

Jessie tried not to dumb down the vocabulary she used with him, and she knew he wasn't picking up everything she laid down. But this time, he gathered enough. With a few taps on a pocket datapad, the volume of the haathee orchestral piece rose to the point where people had to raise their voices to converse.

She nodded her approval.

"HAVE FOOD. BE CAREFUL. THERE IS MEAT."

Jessie chopped a scolding finger at Stet. "Omnivores. Remember?"

The wink she received in reply let her know that he had remembered. It was tough at times, reconciling the interstellar ambassador with the neophyte English speaker. Even the plouph had the sense to send expert English speakers as diplomats. But the haathee had no one else who'd even heard of humans a couple months ago. Hearing subtext out of a three-year-old's dictionary was dissonant; his reminder had been for the guest list at large, many of whom—like himself—were strict herbivores.

Again, it was rough when she only had his own word to go by, and his language skills left gaps. By his own tales, he repaired his own vessels, flew solo exploration missions before getting his own ship and crew, had performed stage plays, written books, served in elected office, and negotiated an armistice with a species that, from Stet's description, would have gone through Earth's forces like a Myllthog.

Jessie used a rickety plug-together handrail and climbed the stairs to the scaffold from which she could browse the foods on offer. As she was looking over the platters, trying to puzzle out what certain dishes were and who had made them, she spotted another of the few humans in attendance.

George Whethersby was a retired Earth Navy admiral who was now the Martian ambassador to LoIP. Though he wore an all-black suit like the other humans and laaku in attendance, Jessie could see the uniform like it was a second skin. Something in his manner, his carriage, his facial expressions told of a man who'd retired in name only.

At the end of the table, Jessie plunked a smoked salmon strip onto her plate—the azrin equivalent of lox—before turning the corner to continue around to the other side. That was when the admiral first acknowledged her.

"You don't belong here."

Jessie paid undeserved attention to ratatoret hors d'oeuvres before scooping a heap onto her plate. They were omnivorous but generally socially aware little creatures. They wouldn't have brought one of the few dishes that no other species short of a megalodog could stomach. But if she spent the second half of this party in the washroom bent over a toilet, they'd be her prime suspects.

"I'm a guest of the host."

"One of these days, you're going to slip up, and the laaku are going to sign off on my extradition request."

Jessie had suspected that there was a skirmish in the datascape over her and Eric. Bureaucrats would upload files at one another, and nothing would move in meatspace. This was the first time someone from outside her protective bubble had mentioned the matter.

A scoop of an indeterminate root vegetable mash slapped down onto Jessie's plate. She gritted her teeth to keep from raising her voice. "We're just having a nice meal here."

"You're on notice. Maybe you're a political exile from Earth, but on Mars, we want you for murder. The laaku are going to see things our way sooner or later."

It was hard to argue self-defense against a whole planet.

But to her way of thinking, Mars got what they were looking for. But there was no denying that the law-respecting laaku might eventually be persuaded to hand her over on a legitimate murder rap. Unlike Earth, the Martians didn't need to trump up a charge to make her a criminal.

Before Jessie could think of a diplomatic reply that wouldn't ruin the festivities, a trunk tapped Admiral Whethersby on the shoulder. The Martian ambassador nearly took a tusk in the face whirling to find Grosstet standing behind him, still taller despite the scaffold.

"THIS IS RUDE. YES?"

While he glowered at the admiral, Jessie knew the question was for her.

"You don't need to stick up for me."

"NO. THIS IS ONE. I AM SURE."

Jessie shook her head just a fraction, but emphatically. She *knew* the haathee understood the gesture; his people had the same conventions for yes and no.

"THIS IS AN ASSHOLE."

Jessie cringed. Oh, how she regretted teaching him that one, but many of their language lessons happened over beers. At the time, it had seemed like an essential part of both Earth language and culture. That night was a little fuzzy, and she didn't recall every detail of what she'd taught him.

Stet brewed some great beer.

"Listen here, sir. I don't know who's been coaching you on human language, but—"

"WE THROW ASSHOLE'AE RIGHT THE FUCK OUT. YES?"

Jessie coughed into her hand. "It's optional. Maybe now isn't the time..."

"*EEPOK*," Stet bellowed. Everyone nearby covered their ears or whatever passed for ears. He glanced back at Jessie as the door guard hustled in. "THIS IS A FIGURE OF SPEECH. YES? I DO NOT THROW HIM MYSELF?"

"You'd hurt him."

Admiral Whethersby was red faced and speechless in a glorious combination of embarrassment, outrage, and mortal terror.

"PLEASE THROW OUT THE RUDE ONE." To make himself perfectly clear, Stet hoisted the Martian ambassador to floor level and pointed straight down at the man's head with his trunk.

There was no violence. The ambassador accompanied the security laaku out without a fuss.

Haathee music played. All sounds of eating and conversation had petered out.

"STILL A PARTY. ONE ASSHOLE GONE. *ENJOY!*"

It was tentative at first. But the dinner party slowly swung back into gear. Imagine that. A dickhead diplomat started throwing his weight around and got some comeuppance. Even if it wasn't going to stop his extradition bullshit in the background, for the moment, it felt nice.

Jessie hung around until most of the guests had departed. Caterers buzzed around collecting dishes and removing decorations.

Stet caught her on the way back from the washroom— which was an adventure all its own. He dropped his voice so low she could almost have suspected no one else overheard him.

"Join me in the next room. We must talk."

———

The titanic door slid shut. Lingering clatters of the party cleanup all but vanished. Grosstet ambled over to a bed-sized ottoman to sit and patted the spot beside him for Jessie to do likewise. She climbed up and stood to hear why he'd invited her inside.

Stet's bedroom had an odor to it, a mixture of barnyard sweat, fragrant gifts from multiple species, and activities she tried to block from her thoughts. Instead, she focused on the worried expression the haathee displayed.

"What's going on?"

"THIS IS HARD TO SAY."

Well, as his unofficial English tutor, there was only one way to answer that. "Do your best. I'll help if you get stuck."

"NOT THE WORD'AE. THE—" He paused and held up a finger. Then, on his H-tech datapad, he tapped several commands. The air all around them buzzed. "AH. NO MORE LAAKU EAR'AE."

"I gotta get one of those," Jessie muttered, eyeing the device.

"I MUST WARN YOU. WE HAVE A SHARED PROBLEM. WE ARE BEING USED."

Jessie scowled. "Did your English just spontaneously improve?"

"SOME. I PRACTICE ALONE. TOO MANY LAAKU THINK I LEARN TOO FAST. I MUST HAVE STUDIED BEFORE. THEY ARE FOOL'AE."

"If you really want to practice, stop pluralizing things with 'ae.' It works for like five English words. Most just got plural with an S?"

"TRULY? I HAD THOUGHT THAT MERELY INFORMAL."

"Nope. Full disclosure, I thought it sounded quaint."

Stet wagged a finger. "QUAINT. THAT IS A EUPHEMISM. YOU MEAN YOU WERE LAUGHING AT ME WHEN I WAS TOO FAR TO HEAR."

"A little?" Jessie replied with a cringe.

Her embarrassment was short-lived. Stet burst out laughing. "I HAVE CHOSEN WELL. A JOKE WITH NO HARM." He tousled her hair with his trunk. "THAT IS WHY WE WILL SAVE OUR LIFE'AE—UM, LIFES."

"Lives. Don't worry, English is more exceptions than rules. And what kind of danger are you talking about?"

Thus far, their relationship had been that of a xeno exchange student and his host sister. They'd hung out, swapped stories, tried elements of one another's culture—a mostly one-way street, but she'd gleaned a little of the haathee culture in return. She'd only known him weeks, but Jessie had yet to get the impression he was paranoid.

In fact, this meeting was the first hint she'd seen of him viewing himself as anything less than a visiting deity on holiday among the tiny species.

"HUMANS ARE AT WAR WITH HUMANS."

"More common than you might think, historically."

"I HAVE PATCHED THE OMNI. I HAVE LOOKED MYSELF."

It had been a bone of contention even within Section 74 as to whether Ambassador Grosstet's omni access ought to be filtered through a counterintelligence throttle. Supposedly, the connection the Phabian Ministry of State had provided would only give limited cultural access—on the surface, to keep ARGO's old dirty laundry stuffed in the closet.

"Well, then you know that this isn't anything new or too unexpected. Overdue, probably. If the eyndar were still enough of a threat—"

A giant hand patted the air, forestalling her rambling. "YES. YES. BUT I KNOW SOME OF YOUR TRICKS. WE ARE GOING TO BE THE NEXT TRICK, AND IT WILL NOT WORK."

Jessie swallowed. "Stet... what did you overhear with those scanner-disk ears of yours?"

The haathee snickered. "NOT THE EARS. THE COMPUTERS. I DECODED LAAKU TRANSMISSIONS."

Shaking her head. "Don't trust anything you think you decoded. Phabian and Earth are in a computations race. Neither can get far enough ahead to crack the codes of the other. Well, that's not entirely true. Phabian's cracked a bunch of older systems before they get updated to the latest. Anything you cracked without a team and a bunch of—"

"WITH THIS." Stet waggled his datapad. "I DON'T KNOW HOW IT WORKS. BUT IT IS FASTER. MUCH FASTER. AND DO NOT THINK TO STEAL IT; IT IS MINE." He held it well out of Jessie's reach, but the smirk told her he was joking.

"Fine. What did the messages say?" She was willing to at least hear him out. If Section 74 got a report that Stet was proudly confident of breaking their encryption, they'd also want to know what he claimed to have discovered.

"YOU ARE GOING TO KILL ME."

Combat instincts took over. Jessie dove from the ottoman and rolled to her feet. "I what now?" Her heart pumped extra blood to her ears, thundering as she awaited a reply that might be among the last words she'd ever hear. Unarmed, she couldn't think of a way to fight the behemoth. Escape had to be the next move.

"I HOPE YOU WILL NOT, OF COURSE. BUT THEY WILL TELL YOU TO. NOT ASK. YOU DO NOT BELIEVE ME YET. HERE."

A holograph popped out of Stet's datapad. There was no proper image, just something akin to a voice-level readout.

"We are satisfied with the level of intel. Even if it's only the

one ship, the cross-share is worth it. Which way does your agent lean?" Jessie didn't recognize the laaku speaking.

The next voice was Bernek's. "Big-time fence sitter. Long run, I can pitch Martian amnesty and safety from Earth. From everything she tells me, he's Tedrek of Roosa among his people."

Stet paused. "I RESEARCHED. THE COMPARISON IS A HIGH COMPLIMENT."

"Good enough. Get her to plan it. Requisition anything required to make it look like Earth was responsible. Your budget is unlimited."

"If I can convince her to somehow involve a villa on the Zethel River, can I keep it afterward?"

The unknown laaku snickered. "You'll likely end up with my job when I make minister in the next election cycle. Take your win, but first... win it."

"Copy that."

"They didn't use names," Jessie pointed out.

"YOU ARE NOT STUPID. YOU KNOW WHO THEY TALK ABOUT. ME. YOU. THERE IS A STRATEGY. YOU WILL KILL ME, AND MY PEOPLE WILL JOIN YOUR WAR IN ANGER."

Jessie deflated. "A false-flag Pearl Harbor. And I get to be Gavrilo Princip of an escalating Milky Way War."

Her companion blinked several times. "I HAVE SO MANY THINGS TO LOOK UP."

With her spot on the ottoman still available, Jessie climbed back up to see what could be done about this. "First off, I have no intention of murdering you."

"UNWISE. YOU WOULD FAIL ANYWAY."

Oh, that was where this haathee needed an education. "No offense, big guy, but you're still a living creature. If I needed you dead, I'd dead you."

"KILL."

"Don't fucking correct my English, you pedantic trumpet!" They both chuckled. "This is serious."

"VERY."

"If they hit me up for this job, and I don't do it, they'll send someone else. Don't believe for a second these people don't have a backup plan."

"AND YOU WILL BE KILLED."

Jessie scoffed. "Don't tempt me into going along with them."

"YOU WILL BE KILLED IF YOU SUCCEED. ESPECIALLY, EVEN."

"Shit." She'd be a loose end. If Section 74 didn't arrange her death, someone from either Mars or Earth would be bound to come after her, and not just to rein in Eric or try her for some self-defense-adjacent murders.

"SHIT INDEED. AND THE PLAN WILL FAIL ANYWAY. MY PEOPLE WILL NOT JOIN THE HUMAN WAR."

"Not even when the mighty Grosstet is murdered by one side?"

The haathee hung his head, tusks resting on the floor. "They will never know."

"I don't see how any side in this would keep it a secret long. If nothing else, your crew would notice when you stopped sending—"

"I HAVE NO CREW. I AM ALONE."

"Alone?" She demanded. Stet nodded. "On that cruiser-sized ship?" Again, a nod of confirmation. "Having traveled the length of the Milky Way to get here?" A sigh through Stet's trunk that sounded like the last air being let out of a balloon.

"IT IS A LONG TALE. I WILL TELL IT, BUT NOT TONIGHT. THERE ARE MORE TRANSMISSIONS

YOU MUST HEAR. AND YOU MUST SLEEP WELL. TOMORROW THEY WILL ASK YOU TO KILL ME."

Jessie took a long breath. Sleeping well would be some neat trick after what she'd learned. Sleeping at all, for that matter. "Plan A has to be getting you off Phabian, pronto."

"NO."

"Don't even with that shit. There's only one of you. You can't fight them."

"WE WILL LEAVE PHABIAN. BUT NOT WITH THE PRONTO."

She narrowed her eyes and met one of his. "What've you got cooking?"

Stet spared a glance at the bedroom door. "A CURE FOR DRINKING TOO MUCH, BUT THAT IS NOT IMPORTANT. WE HAVE BUSINESS ON PHABIAN BEFORE WE LEAVE."

"You keep saying 'we.' But you just got done telling me you came to Phabian alone."

"I CAME HERE ALONE. PERHAPS I DO NOT HAVE TO LEAVE ALONE."

Eric took another sip of his coffee and shook his head when a laaku couple gestured an inquiry whether he was finished with the booth. Queen Been was hopping—buzzing would have been better but didn't fit Eric's impression of the atmosphere at that moment. But despite being alone, he had a second cup across from him.

He'd been there for nearly an hour.

Normally, he'd have left long ago. Squatting in prime-time morning real estate was rude, but he needed to risk the mild social offense. Just in case.

"How long have you been here?" Hecuba asked.

Eric stiffened. When he glanced up, he fought against the intrusive thought that she was a figment of his imagination. "Hi!" He gestured to the seat across from him. "A while. So you got my note?"

With a huff, Hecuba slid into the far side of the booth. "I got *all* your notes. I figured you'd never stop sending them unless I said it in person." She took a sniff of her cup. "Let me guess. Regular brew with soy milk, two sugars?"

Eric nodded. It was mostly two sugars—two sugars' worth of honey at least. "I just want you to know how sorry I am about scaring you."

"It's not about being sorry. I *believe* you're sorry. I get it."

He smiled tentatively. "OK..."

"What you don't understand is how dangerous you are."

"Not to you." He reached out.

Hecuba picked up her coffee and leaned back out of reach. She took a sip, wincing in anticipation. "This isn't tepid. Have you just been ordering replacements every few minutes?"

Eric hunched and didn't look straight at her.

"Right. Magic. Super easy. Especially for you, I bet. Did you even think about it? How maybe you fuzzled someone's datapad? Maybe some medical thingy keeping someone's kidneys alive? No. Of course not. Because why would you, when you got away with... with..." She glanced around the coffee shop. "Well, you know."

"It was better than the alternative."

"Really? *Really?*" She shook her head emphatically. "I don't buy it. We should have stood our ground, pointed them out, and screamed our lungs out for the proper authorities to deal with them."

"They might have hurt people. They might have already.

There've been those disappearances that everyone seems to know about but no one's talking about."

"Everyone's talking about them. Just not to you."

"It wasn't me."

"And how can I believe that? You *could*. I know you could. Doonah and them? They don't know what to make of you. Turned down a fast track to being Phabian's first terramancer or whatever you wanted to do. You scare the shit out of the ssentuadi."

"I do?"

"Dogs are afraid of snakes because they can't smell them. Those snakes get freaked out because, near as they can tell, you're not even a wizard."

"I never graduated."

Hecuba scowled. "When you worked for the planet, everyone overlooked your quirks. But now... let's just say I'm giving you more benefit of the doubt than most."

"You didn't turn me in. They'd have arrested me by now."

Hecuba didn't respond directly. "It's a little late now. I'd look half as guilty. I don't know what you expect from me after that little stunt, but we're over. No more notes. No more me and you. Got it?"

"Pardon?"

"What part of 'breakup' are you not hearing?" He noticed her eyes were wet.

Eric's brain turned sideways in his skull. "Wwwwww... what?"

An accusing finger jammed toward his face, making Eric cross his eyes to focus on the tip. "That. Right there. That's the problem."

Eric averted his eyes so he didn't peer up her sleeve. "I don't know what you mean. We were just... I mean, you were my first real work friend."

Leaving her barely touched coffee, Hecuba rose. "I thought you were cute. Shy. Not like the other wizards who could tie their shoes without touching them. Star-drivers are humble. Not Oxford alumni."

Standing seemed like the thing to do, so Eric stood. "I got kicked out."

"Yeah. Wonder why. You were thoughtful and sensitive and not pushy at all. But I was wrong; you're just not right in the head. You treat people like things."

"That's not fair." Eric was more befuddled than angry. This wasn't how people acted. Hecuba was the one broken here.

"Not disposable, like most pompous wizards. No, like we're a tea set so delicate you're afraid to break us. But the second things get hard, you brag about your juggling skills and throw us around."

"That's a mean analogy."

"Thanks. I spent a long time on it."

"So...?" These were new waters, and Eric wasn't much of a swimmer. He was more of a floaties-and-wading beachgoer.

She lowered her voice. "Look. I don't even *know* if you've got anything to do with that missing people stuff. But it looks bad, and I don't want to be involved."

"It's a very good frame job."

Hecuba huffed. "Oh, not the puppy dog eyes." She leaned in and gave him a quick, unexpected hug. "Take care of yourself. Don't try to find me again."

"Wait." He held up a finger, then shut his eyes. Much as he'd avoided the subject in the Village of Eternity, things had gone too far to try to salvage this friendship on his own.

An impromptu conference convened. Eric polled poets and lovers, men and women, humans and xenos. Uriela chimed in with her vast life experience.

But when Eric opened his eyes a couple seconds later, Hecuba was gone. A chill of panic froze him briefly, thinking maybe he'd wished her out of existence or ahead in time without meaning to.

Then he caught sight of her breezing out the door of Queen Been and out of his life.

Jessie got home from work to find Bernek sitting at her little Cheapo brand table. The lights had been off, but she knew a trick to adjust her eyes to the low light almost instantly, and she spotted him before setting foot inside.

"Amateur hour, Bernie?" she teased once the door had shut behind her and she turned on the lights. "Or do you have a remedial spycraft cert coming up that you need to practice for?"

"Your filtering up to snuff?" he asked brusquely. His manner was so uncharacteristically serious that she had to glance around the apartment to make sure it was just the two of them. This had the whole "we're onto you and you get to choose quick or painful" vibe, and she wasn't liking it. Methods of murdering Bernek most efficiently flashed through her head. "Quit thinking of ways to kill me."

"Habit." Jessie relaxed. He wouldn't joke about it if he thought she'd need to beat him to death with a folding chair or stab him in the throat with a multi-tool. "And you know I don't have access to anything that'd keep Section 74 out."

"Good enough." Bernek stood up and ambled to the sliding doors to Jessie's balcony. He peeked out the closed curtains. "It's time to move on to the next phase."

"Who's my next target?"

Bernek shook his head. "You're right. You've gotten all

you're liable to get out of the elephant man. But he's still got a role to play that you're going to play a key part in."

"Big lug might be a lot of things, but I don't know if he's the choice to broker a renewed ARGO alliance."

"We can't reunite with Earth until they put Mars back in their place."

"Fourth orbit not good enough?"

Bernek strolled the room, not making eye contact. "You know your own species' history."

"I'm no expert."

"You know the best way to drag allies into a war?"

"Pay them? Promise them territory? Marry off a kid or two? Lemme say, I caught sight of him naked, and I can't condone a political marriage in good conscience."

"Assassination." There. Bernek had said it. Jessie didn't need to dance around the word pretending she didn't know what the operative's orders had been.

Jessie puffed her lips with a sigh. "I know he could. Don't know if I've gotten close enough to convince him, though. Who would we even target?" Not that she wasn't being intentionally obtuse, but she briefly pondered the question as if she weren't. One of the Martian presidential candidates, trying to influence the election favorably toward reunification; not that she knew which candidate's death would make that work.

"We kill Ambassador Grosstet. What we've been able to glean from your intel and limited scanner data, the haathee taking Earth's side in the conflict would be decisive. If they want Earth to end the rebellion, they could share a few technological secrets and make short work of them. Given the sieve of Earth Navy Intelligence these days, we'd be likely to get copies of any shared data."

Wow. That level of confidence meant Section 74 had to have moles inside Earth Navy. Back-channel connections could benefit both sides if they were sanctioned. If not, Earth had problems almost as big as Mars.

"Glad to be of service."

"You're not done yet."

"I see."

Bernek cocked his head. "This going to be a problem?"

"No. Just a shame. He's not a bad guy. But better xenos have died to make Earth what it is today. What's the plan?"

"You're going to be involved heavily in the planning process. Your day-to-day changes only slightly. Focus on his schedule, his habits, his blind spots. And think about it the way a Martian operative would think of it. We'll provide whatever matériel and support to backstory you double-crossing *us* to kill him. If you don't get tabbed, great. If it comes to light, we'll have you stashed on a LoIP-aligned world—needle in a haystack."

"And you cooperate with the haathee crew to investigate the murder, maybe even contextualize it for them."

"Exactly."

Jessie nodded along, mind already turning over these new details.

"Problem?"

Jessie blinked, giving her full attention to Bernek. He needed to hear something decisive, something that would sell her being all in on this.

"Start looking into Martian-made high explosives."

⸻

Jessie had her datapad out, poring over the map of Kethlet's refugee district in three dimensions. So much of the space was devoted to simply housing the cast-off members of various non-laaku species. But mixed in, out of necessity, were the services and merchants that made housing livable. Restaurants, clothing stores, medical facilities, factories that supplied charity-grade jobs, museums, and a variety of refugee-owned businesses that gave a multi-world flavor to the architecture and signage.

Stet wasn't a creature of habit. Bon vivant was a better descriptor, and he'd spent his time on Phabian trying this, that, and the other experience provided by this entirely new sector of the galaxy to him. One might, if they were to believe him behind closed doors, think he was doing it with security in mind.

Well, since the big brain in that big body was in on the assassination plot from the ground floor, maybe she could convince him to take up a hobby. Maybe a class that met on a set schedule.

With the haathee ambassadorial apartment highlighted, Jessie scanned the area for appropriate activities.

Violin lessons? Probably more suited to a demonstration than learning the minuscule instrument.

Boxing? Fuck's sake, he'd kill someone.

Before Jessie could get any farther along in her selection process, there was a knock at her door. There was no pause, no waiting for her to reply. Without forewarning, a figure stepped through the door.

Instinct took over. Jessie drew her Jodek-IX. She aimed center-of-mass on the intruder, then took a fraction of a second to identify him.

"FUCK! Eric, do you know how close I came to—" Jessie cut herself off. Reflexes might have allowed her to get the drop on someone who'd stepped through a solid door without opening it, but that bought her the time to identify someone she loved before squeezing the trigger. It also gave her enough time to notice that Eric was sobbing.

For his part, her brother didn't even seem to register the

attempt on his life. He shambled forward, stretched out his arms, and wrapped Jessie in a hug.

Heedless of the incriminating display sitting face-up on the table on her datapad and having to hastily discard a weapon beside it, Jessie gathered in her little brother and held tight.

When his blubbering finally resolved itself into words, the first thing she understood was, "I did something horrible."

Jessie felt sick. Part of being Eric Ramsey's sister was committing to loving him before he managed to elaborate. Had he stepped on an endangered flower? Scared an infant? Shorted out the tech on a hoverbus full of people? Gotten their refugee status revoked on a technicality after a long, casual conversation with a bureaucrat?

Everything was on the table.

"It's all right. I'm here."

He took a shuddering breath. "I had—a real friend—except —I didn't. It wasn't—the time travel. She was never—a real friend. She was just—using me for—for—*sex.*"

"Oh." Well, emotional devastation had a limited radius of collateral damage. Unless there was a jilted lover revenge epilogue to this tale, Jessie didn't have to worry about Phabian Investigative Services breaking down her door.

Eric cried a while longer with no words between them.

Eventually, he calmed. "I thought she liked me."

"She did," Jessie assured him.

"Sure. But ulterior motives matter. She never asked what I wanted."

He might have been in the mental space for tough love; he might not have. Jessie could spare him this breakdown but couldn't stay up all night coddling him. Not with the stakes she was playing for. "She didn't think she needed to ask. It was obvious to everyone else."

Eric looked up, then, catching Jessie's Mom look, pulled

away. "Naw." Jessie nodded. "Really?" She nodded more emphatically. He emptied his soul with a sigh. "How come no one told me?" Using one baggy sleeve, he blew his nose.

"We all hoped you'd figure it out on your own. Or that you already had."

"Why not just tell me?" he pleaded.

"You can't live life with a chaperon. And what was that you were blabbering about time travel?"

With the air of a man that just didn't care anymore, Eric looked off into the distance. "Oh, I just zipped us forward a few hours until Snow and Slater gave up waiting for us to come back."

"WHAT! YOU TOOK HER WITH YOU!"

"It's fine. I came to an understanding with them. They'd stop harassing us, and I'd stop bouncing them forward into the future."

Jessie blinked. "You what now?"

"They were pretty stubborn. But I made it clear that I'd show them a future where azrin had gone vegan."

"You could do that?"

"I'd have tried. Really getting sick of those two."

Jessie managed a chuckle. She side-hugged her brother. "Hey, that's the spirit. You ever need bodies buried—"

"Nope," Eric cut in before she could finish the offer. "You're going to your grave owing me for that. Quit trying to get me to accept repayment." For the first time, Eric seemed aware enough of his surroundings to realize she was up to something. "We planning a heist?"

"Assassination."

"Aww. Not the haathee. He's great."

"You've met him?" she asked, genuinely curious.

"No, but he just exudes greatness. And he does silly dances without caring what other species think of him."

"He exudes all right. And don't worry. It's a phony assassination."

"For your new spy friends?"

It was Jessie's turn to stare incredulously.

"Oh, don't look so surprised. You got a boring job and you're happy about it. It's a cover. I... I guess I didn't say anything, either."

"Well... keep not saying anything." If nothing else, they were Ramseys. They'd stick together, keep their mouths shut, and get through whatever came their way. "Good chance that after this, I'm going to need to be off Phabian in a hurry."

Eric peered at the datapad as if he could read a map properly. "Need help?"

⸻

Jessie had wanted his help. Fine, maybe she had given him a Cheesi Bar and sat him on her little two-seat couch while she did the work, but she'd also promised she'd find a role for him to play. Part of him worried his sister had just said that to make him feel better—which, in fairness, it had—but a louder part insisted that what plan *wouldn't* benefit from the inclusion of a wizard?

It wasn't like Eric had another job to be doing.

They were going to leave Phabian. Whether Jessie's convoluted, politically tedious, potentially multi-treasonous plot succeeded or failed, this wasn't going to be a safe haven much longer.

Eric wished that bothered him more.

As he made his way home in the dead of night, he tried to remember all the people he'd miss.

He tried to be honest.

He tried to be fair and fair-minded.

Trebla.

It wasn't much of a list. All the other acquaintances he'd made would fade into obscurity, none having made an impression that could escape the yawning void of Hecuba's presence in his recollections of Phabian.

There wasn't even anyone else he felt a need to say goodbye to.

He was wandering. The same nagging need to move his feet that had kept him from accepting Jessie's offer to crash at her place now steered his feet through a zigzag of interstitial spaces between buildings that weren't all proper streets. Alleys, loading zones, courtyards, patios, if there was an out-of-the-way spot in the refugee district, Eric took it.

One of the cafes had a rear seating area tucked away in a little garden. It was cordoned off by decorative fencing and manicured hedges, but Eric wasn't so proper that he was above getting his clothes a little naturey climbing over one. He lost his balance going over as his pant leg snagged but caught himself on the edge of a wrought iron patio table.

Why had he felt such a rush to hop in here? He took a seat and caught his breath, winded from the minor ordeal.

Before his heart rate had finished slowing, a woman appeared out of nowhere, in a seated position, with no chair beneath her.

"Oof!"

Eric rubbed his eyes.

The woman was around his age, give or take time-skipping anomalies, with dark skin that set off brilliant pink eyes that were clearly the work of science. She wore a white crop top, stretch leggings, and sporty sneakers. Her nails and lip tinter matched her eyes. For some reason, she struck Eric as familiar.

"You all right?" he asked, reaching a hand to help her to her feet.

She clasped wrists with him. "Cheeky li'l bastard, poppin' off with the chair while I got my eyes shut."

"I didn't do anything to the chair," Eric assured her.

"Wot?" She looked all around. "Fuck did all the people get off to?"

Eric slowly narrowed his eyes. He tilted his head to match an angle. "Is your name... Mindy Sedgwick?"

"Presuming it din't change the past five minutes, yeah. Wait now. Is that what you're on about? Mind games, is it? You messing with me head?" She reached out a hand toward the hedges. "How'd you manage it? Screen or something?"

"No." Eric stood and backed up a step. "This isn't happening. What day is it?"

"Thursday night, mate. What're you on about?"

"It's not. It's Wednesday. The 16th. Of March."

"The fuck it is." Mindy dug out her datapad. When nothing showed up on the screen, she slapped it against her thigh a couple times. "Shite little bastard. On with ya." She turned her attention back to Eric. "Wager yours'd tell me it's whatever bloody day you like."

"I don't own a datapad."

"Sure, mate. Wizard. Right. C'mon now. Game's up. Gag wasn't funny, but you're twisting a rock now."

A lump formed in Eric's throat, and he swallowed it down. "This isn't a game. But I don't know what's going on. I think you lost nearly three weeks."

"Naw."

"Yah," Eric replied in kind. "There's been a proper hubbub. Police are involved."

"So, you din't actually *have* a plan to get me off this monkey-run rock?"

"I don't even remember—"

Mindy waved a hand in front of Eric's face as he froze mid-sentence. "Hullo? You still with me, mate? If'n you don't have transport, I'm gonna hafta ion outta here."

"Wait. Bear with me one minute."

Before she could object, Eric shut his eyes.

A campsite had sprung up where Eric appeared within the Village of Eternity. Tent, campfire, recreational vehicles, all the trappings were present, plus the inclusion of stacked bookshelves and a wingback sitting chair. Other than that, everything in the entryway was just as he'd left it.

He didn't have to summon Uriela. She was perched cross-legged in the huge, comfy-looking chair, nose deep in a tome.

"OK. I have a weird question for you."

"All your questions are weird, Eric. But yes, I have the memory you sequestered." She reached into a pocket and pulled out a yellow gemstone, offering it on an upturned palm.

Eric approached slowly. This was his mind. He was, best he could tell, perfectly safe here. Still, people ran around loose and had agency and plans and goals and hobbies of their own. "That was weirdly specific and accurate."

"It'll all make sense when you take back the memory."

"Have you been waiting long?" He was in no rush, considering the temporal shear between the Village and the physical world. Eric edged closer, hoping for this to make sense before he connected something to his mind.

"Couple months. Didn't want to be tardy, and there was no telling when you might decide to pop in once Mindy showed up."

"So, you know Mindy."

"*You* know Mindy. I just work here."

"OK, but then how do I—"

Uriela lobbed him the gem. "Just take it. You're asking things you already know."

The gem tumbled in slow motion, facets gleaming in sunlight that came from no sun. Eric caught it, and instantly, he realized what had been going on.

"Oh, dear."

"I told you it was a bad idea. I said my piece. Kept the gem secret until the time you picked. Rest is up to you."

Eric nodded frantically. "I have to get moving!"

"Come on. Follow me."

Mindy didn't hesitate, immediately falling into step half a pace behind Eric. "Bit of a nap done for ya, eh?"

"Just had to gather my thoughts," Eric replied, striding confidently through the deserted back streets of the refugee district in the dead of night.

Mindy had to jog to keep up now. She caught up and held her datapad out for him to see. "Lookie that. Fuck me if'n you din't pull it off, ya mad goblin."

Eric looked her up and down. She looked very much like the picture the police had of her. "Would you mind being someone else for a bit?"

"Seeing as how you's able to toss me more'n a fortnight up the calendar, how's about someone rich and famous?"

"Would you settle for blending in and not being recognized?"

Mindy paused for a few jogging paces. "Long as I'm done up nice. I s'pose."

Eric lifted a hand. Like raising the curtain on a play, the scene was set, and a new actress emerged.

"Oi! Where'd my knockers get off to?"

"What's less obvious than a guy?" Mindy was now a businesslike human in his mid-thirties with sideswept hair and a sailing-ship jawline.

"I look like a ghost." A few paces later, she added. "And that best not be what I'm thinking it is knocking 'round like a bell clapper in me trousers."

"Focus," Eric scolded, possibly the first time in his life he'd been on the dishing-out end of that particular reminder. "Nothing makes sense right now, and it's not going to for a while. Just pretend this is a roller coaster and the bar just clicked and the car just started climbing the starting hill."

"Whelp, either I'm dreaming or this mess ain't nothing I'm sorting on me own. Lead on, guv."

Eric pulled up short at the loading dock entrance behind the refugee quarter function hall. "Wait here."

Doors were a suggestion. Locks cowered before him. Alarms didn't know what to say. Eric raced through a food storage area and the deserted kitchen before emerging into a side hallway with an all-species washroom. When he realized he was early, he made use of a toilet.

A terrified squawk from the adjacent stall startled Eric out of his shoes. Hurriedly finishing his business, Eric scrambled out and found Chik-ta panicking. None of what he said was being translated by the ubiquitous vocal emitter all in-tik wore out in the galaxy.

"It's OK. I'm here. I'm here. Slow down. I can't understand you talking that fast."

The flapping of wings died down. Chik-ta's heaving chest steadied. "*I felt it. My time was ended.*"

"All time went a little weird for you. This is fifteen days after you disappeared. The plan is working. Kind of. Come on. We're on a tight schedule."

Chik-ta was too disoriented to object when Eric took him

by the claws and led the way out of the washroom. With any luck, the translator was just acclimating to life in the future. If he'd fuzzled it permanently, Eric promised himself he'd act as translator until they could find him another.

"Who's he?" Mindy demanded, voice incongruously unchanged. "We getting all omnicultural or something?"

Chik-ta answered with a string of flustered vulgarity.

"He's Chik-ta, and he says it's nice to meet you." When Chik-ta protested, Eric backpedaled. "Well, not exactly. I paraphrased."

"How many more's we got in on this dodgy adventure, anyway?"

"Disguises," Eric said to himself, ignoring the question. "Chik-ta, mind being a human for a little while?"

The in-tik's objections held surprising merit.

"OK. Good point. Laaku it is." With a snap of his fingers, Eric was now accompanied by one human and one laaku woman dressed in mechanic's dungarees. "No. I'd never really thought about it. I suppose I'd feel weird with feathers if the situation was reversed."

Over the course of the next hour, Eric's little band of time-stashed victims of a fictitious serial killer grew to six.

He retrieved Drascz Fyllis from an alley between two waste reclaim chutes. Azrin ruffians had just disposed of several of her paintings, and she'd been considering going in after them, knowing it was certain death.

Evander Days reappeared under a bridge spanning the Zethel River. Eric had to distract the participants in an illicit purchase to extract him without anyone noticing.

They found Ovilak in the confessional of the little One Church outpost in the district. He'd gone in seeking answers to questions the other vish kinah couldn't answer for him, but Eric had proposed an alternative.

Uom'pe had not been on the Phabian Investigative Services' scanners. She'd sat placidly atop an apartment building within view of Eric's window. Originally, he'd raced over to convince her not to take the fall that would have shattered her shell into a million pieces. But she'd been sitting on rooftops for decades, she claimed, and had yet to tumble. She simply didn't have anyone else in her life. The two of them had talked until sharing a sunrise before Eric jettisoned her into the future and lopped off his own memory of the whole incident.

Kenneth Sloan, the last name on the police missing persons list, now lived in the Village of Eternity. He'd been a tech liaison and, given his options, preferred the magical life of existing in a bespoke universe over what he'd called Eric's "crazy alternative."

The troupe traipsed back to Eric's apartment incognito. Mindy scouted ahead, since there was little more mundane and less prone to scrutiny than a moderately well-dressed, well-groomed human strolling the refugee district at night.

When the coast was clear, Eric herded everyone inside and warded the door. It being a wizard-oriented building, that fact was nothing unusual. The gentle hum of protective magic allowed Eric a well-deserved sigh of relief.

With a wave of his hand, he dismissed all the disguises. "OK. This is what everyone really looks like. I know it was a bit of a waterslide getting here, but you can take some time to get to know one another."

Drascz sniffed the air, whiskers twitching. "We are not alone here. Someone—*two* someones—is in the next room."

"That's what you smell?" Mindy demanded. "Not the bloody chocolate chip cookies?"

Eric wasn't really paying attention to the smells, but now

that she mentioned it, his apartment didn't usually smell like freshly baked snacks.

Two ratatoret skittered out of Eric's bedroom. "Ah-there-you-are-We-were-beginning-to-get-worried-that-something-might-have-gone-wrong-with-your-plan-Glad-to-see-that-you-were-merely-delayed—"

"We-decided-to-prepare-cookies-as-the-cultural-touchstone-of-your-people-I-hope-that-they-came-out-tasty-The-dough-was-certainly-delicious-but-the-makeshift-equipment-had-never-been-used-for-baking-so-we-couldn't-be-sure—"

"However-given-the-small-batch-size-mandated-by-the-limits-of-our-workspace-we-added-a-smaller-cookie-to-each-as-a-quality-assurance-sample-and-they-have-been-repeatedly-meeting-with-our-approval."

Eric knelt. "Um, everyone, this is Makket." He held his hands out to indicate the ratatoret in the apron. "And this is his wife, Tippitak."

"I think your time magic sped them up permanently," Evander observed dryly.

Eric ignored the mildly xenoist comment. "Thanks for keeping this plan a secret from me. Don't know if I could have, if things were switched." He held out two knuckles and received fist bumps from Makket and Tippitak in return. "No one's looking for them that hasn't been for a long time. I'd be subletting my apartment to them if not for the fact I'm not charging anything."

"Is. This. Everyone?" Uom'pe asked.

Eric huffed. "For now, yes. We'll move some things around, work out shifts. Get some sleep and lay low until it's time for the escape. Once *that* part gets into swing, we'll hopefully have two more members with bigger parts to play in getting us all off Phabian."

Nancy Weston was a pseudonym, and everyone knew it. A few of the members of the Red Rising knew one another on the outside by their real names, but those were kept a tight secret in general. Every link in their chain was a weakness. Every fact was on a need-to-know basis.

Jessie was dressed like a worker at the Lunar Reclamation Project factory that employed many of the human refugees. She wore an open denim jacket over her coveralls. A blonde wig was pulled into a messy ponytail. The warehouse they used for their meeting stocked bootleg beer and had its own firing range.

From a purely tactical standpoint, Jessie had judged these idiots as a minimal risk to planetary security. That was her primary criterion for choosing them from among the scattering of similar organizations on Section 74's scanners. Free Mars was mainly political, a sort of advocacy group that was more handshakes than blasters. Little Green Men consisted mainly of college students in the Phabian post-secondary education system. Bleed It Blue was frankly terrifying; Section 74 was just dotting i's and crossing t's before they rounded up and arrested the lot of them. They were heavily armed and wouldn't likely surrender without a fight.

And so it was that Jessie found herself setting down a liter-glass, savoring the off-brand aftertaste before taking up her blaster. Downrange, black silhouettes were safety-sign stick figures of a human, radiating a bull's-eye out from just off-center of the chest.

Five shots. That was the practice set these guys ran. It was a sporting cluster. That was the first red flag that they weren't a serious paramilitary group. Jessie took two breaths between shots, pretending to concentrate as she aimed.

XENO'S PARAGON / 187

"Not bad, rookie," Neddie said to her as he took custody of the blaster back. "Got all five on flesh. Better than a lot of first-timers."

Jessie offered a lopsided smile. "I've held a blaster before." What the dipshit rangemaster didn't realize was that Jessie hadn't been aiming at the bull's-eye. Her shots had been clavicle, throat, dick, kneecap, and liver. She could have disarmed someone with the first shot. The second would have been a messy, spiteful kill shot. Third was designed for a quick castration. The fourth would have ended a chase. A liver shot wouldn't have been fatal with anything resembling modern medical care.

But all Neddie saw was five shots that missed center of mass.

This was the first meeting where they'd trusted her with a weapon. It was an improvement. Most of the night was spent bitching. Mars. Earth. The war. Phabian not taking sides. Phabian ditching ARGO. Phabian starting their own version of ARGO without Mars. Frankly, for a bunch of guests on the damn planet, the members of Red Rising had a lot of beefs with their hosts. It was tempting to tell them off, to go back to Mars if the Martians would have them back.

That was the guilty little secret. Most of the rabble-rousers had reasons why they wouldn't or couldn't go back. Criminal records. Child support. Military desertion. The members were tight-lipped on their own personal excuses. Jessie imagined that most of it could be summarized as Loud Cowardice. Whether it was not wanting to fight Earth or simply avoiding the consequences of their own actions, none of them would have set foot on Mars if someone bought them first-class tickets on TransGalactica.

Section 74 had enough info on these fuckers and their ilk that Jessie knew the buzzwords. She had a dictionary of the lingo, a list of talking points, and an attitude that sold both. Neddie and his cronies were buying.

The beer wasn't on par with Grosstet's brewing master craft, but it was strong. Jessie played it up and acted way drunker than she felt. She talked more freely, admitting little details of her cover story's life. A loner. A few misdemeanors. Skipped out on parole when the war made refugee status on Phabian a viable alternative. Violent temper. Big talker. Everyone was meant to think she was an all-bark blowhard.

At the end of the night, Jessie knew she was on camera. Her comings and goings with Red Rising were part of the after-story.

Several blocks away, Jessie hailed a hovercab.

Bernek was in the back seat. The pilot gave a little salute to acknowledge that he was with Section 74, too.

"How'd it go?"

Jessie blew a long breath, causing Bernek to wave a hand in front of his nose at the smell. "I think I made an impression. They won't forget me. You secure the explosives?"

"We'll make sure they fall into someone's lap."

"Soon. We've got a window here. I just need to be on-site with them. People need to see me recognizing them. Familiar with them. Having ideas. None of these schmucks will do a damn thing. But they'll *love* having it in their sticky little hands. I've just got to be the loosest cannon."

Bernek snorted. "Good thing you're a brilliant actress."

Point taken. Jessie knew she was no threat to win a cannon-tightening contest. "Look. We've got the ball. Clear shot to the goal, hoop, net, or zone of your sport of choice. It's not the putzes from Red Rising I'm worried about. That fucking elephant is the wild card here. He gets bored of daily sonic massages, we're sidelined until some other fad catches his fancy."

"We need to get him a gift card to the place or something?" Bernek joked.

"Ha. Ha. You think anyone charges him for anything? He gets comped. He's free advertising. I plan to make some lewd suggestions for alternate uses for those pulse guns."

Berknek cringed. All four hands tightened into fists. "Eugh. Those things can practically break bones."

"His main complaint is they don't get the deep knots in his muscles. Fortunately, he's also got literally zero shame or modesty. Even if he gives up on the massages, that'll get him to go back at least once more. If they kick him out, the route still works. But it'll be our last chance before more stakeouts to establish a new routine. If they're game... well, at least he'll die happy."

The laaku snickered as the hovercab swooped through the city. "Shit like this is why I don't miss fieldwork."

When they dropped Jessie off at her apartment, wig, coveralls, and jacket tucked discreetly in a backpack, she only ducked in long enough to ditch her disguise.

There wouldn't be a lot of full nights' sleep until she was off Phabian.

———

Eric was waiting by the door when Jessie rang the chime.

"Hi, come in, I've got to tell you something."

Jessie hesitated just long enough to check both ways down the hallway outside Eric's apartment before stepping inside. She waited a breath longer for the door to slide shut behind her before asking, "Does this have anything to do with the million ssentuadi inquisitors slithering all over the refugee zone?"

"It's more like a dozen. And maybe. Probably. I mean, there's a chance it doesn't. A small chance."

She took him by the shoulders. "Eric. You're spinning out."

"Sorry."

"This is me checking in on you. Are. You. OK?"

He smiled. It was a relief to be able to answer this one. "Yes! I'm not crazy or a murderer or a menace. I had a plan, and I hid it from myself. But now everything makes sense."

Still holding him by the shoulders, Jessie bulldozed him toward the couch. "Sit. Slow down. Explain." Just as they both parked on Eric's two-seater, she sniffed the air. "That doesn't smell like takeout. Have you been cooking?"

"No. And that plays into my larger point." He could already tell by her expression that he was running out of time for a large revelation if he wanted to avoid another outburst of scolding. "I have a few people hiding out here."

"Hiding out? Like fugitives?"

"Mostly no. A couple yesses with a caveat. Mostly it's the people who the police think are missing."

Jessie's eyes widened as her jaw went slack. "ERIC!"

"C'mon out, everyone. It's OK."

"It is most certainly *not* OK. Do you realize the problems this poses? We're not in a situation to—um, hi?"

The whole crew appeared from the bedroom, where they'd crammed themselves when Makket had spotted her from his lookout post.

Eric rushed through the introductions, keeping Jessie from interrupting with a chewing out he knew damn well he deserved. "And we're all doing just fine here. I knew deep down we couldn't stay on Phabian long. I was going to stage a runaway of my own, but it sounds like you've got something great in the works, so I don't see why we can't combine our efforts and get everyone off Phabian together."

Jessie said nothing. She blinked periodically. Her gaze swept the nervous, fidgeting assembly of volunteer stowaways.

"Um. If you can't take us all, I'll figure out a backup plan."

"No," Jessie replied instantly. She shut her eyes and let out a long, weary breath. "No, I'll figure out a way to make this work. How long would it take you all to get six blocks without drawing undue attention?"

Eric shrugged. "If we're leaving anyway, there's no big reason not to just use magic."

Jessie pinched the bridge of her nose between thumb and forefinger. "Do any of you have practical experience in tactical situations?"

Mindy inclined her head. "Yeah. A bit. I was stuck in with the rebels on Meyang. Light on rules, but tactics? Yeah. We had 'em."

"Fine. You're in charge."

Makket cleared his throat, sounding like a motorized shaving razor. "Excuse-me-but-if-you're-looking-for-someone-to-lead-a-covert-rendezvous-safely-across-approximately-one-and-a-half-kilometers-of-police-patrolled-open-ground-might-I-volunteer-my-non-military-expertise-on-the-matter?"

Jessie pointed. "Who's that? I didn't see any ratatoret on the police lists."

"Makket. He and his wife are wanted smugglers unrelated to the police thing."

"How long you been on the run?"

"While-we-didn't-start-keeping-track-as-it-wasn't-obvious-at-the-time-that-we'd-be-using-the-length-of-our-evasion-of-legal-repercussions-as-the-centerpiece-of-a-criminal-resume—"

"Just estimate."

Eric wrung his hands. As long as *someone* besides him was in charge, that would be great.

"Slightly-more-than-four-years." It was the shortest sentence Makket had spoken since Eric had met him.

Tippitak waved a hand for attention, then added,

"Clarifying-the-point-my-all-too-modest-husband-is-trying-to-make-we-have-been-living-and-smuggling-on-Phabian-for-that-time-We-did-not-just-recently-become-stranded-on-this-planet-Our-primary-offworld-contact-was-arrested-a-month-ago-and-we've-been-evading-active-searches-since-being-identified-by-name-to-Phabian-Investigative-Services."

Jessie turned to Mindy with a shrug. "Play nice. But these two are the ones who need to run this operation."

Evander spoke up. "I don't mind sharing a ride off Phabian with them, but I'm not taking orders from—"

Jessie had her blaster in the man's face. "I'd back that sentence up, pronto. You wanna be xenoist. Fine. But you jeopardize this operation, I bag you. We copa?"

Evander nodded mutely.

Jessie holstered her weapon, and Eric breathed a sigh of relief. "Look, this isn't a game. You're all getting this chance because of him. This whole plan flops if anything happens to me. And if I don't have Eric with me, none of you fuckers are setting foot off this planet. Eric, you'll have to watch out for those inquisitors. If they get close, give the smugglers a heads-up to arrange a scramble. I'll figure out how to find you."

Eric nodded along. He could sense her wrapping up. But he couldn't let her go with that heavy of a worry burdening her intricate and dangerous plans. "Don't worry about the inquisitors. We should be safe here for another week or so."

Jessie gave him a Mom scowl.

He replied with a tight-lipped, innocent smile.

"Stay put. Don't draw attention. Be ready when I signal you."

After receiving Eric's fervent assurances, murmured along with by his whole team, Jessie departed.

"She seems stable," Drascz grumbled.

Mindy shrugged. "I like her. She single?"

Eric watched the door, worried about his sister already. Without looking back, he answered, "Perpetually."

⊏▭⊐

The rooftop of Grosstet's embassy apartment building was hopping. Today was one of the rare occasions where he was opening up the shuttle. Jessie was present as his liaison, overseeing the maneuvering of a monstrous hover-cart laden with nutrient canisters. The food processor to make use of them was already parked and ready to be hauled inside. Every laborer had a security clearance. Every bean counter worked for Section 74. The officials were window dressing.

"SUCH FUSS. SO SIMPLE A TRADE. MY PEOPLE WILL FIND GREAT FUN IN TRYING THE NEW FOOD'AE," Grosstet confided in Jessie but at a volume that guaranteed no one failed to overhear.

Once the hover-cart was in position, Grosstet activated a loading ramp from his datapad. For some reason, damn near every spacefaring species came up with a similar fold-down design. Once the ramp touched down, all the laaku practically fell over themselves leaning and angling for a more advantageous view inside.

"SHOO," Grosstet told the workers manning the hover-cart, flicking his trunk in their direction. "WE DID NOT BARTER FOR A TOUR." He took custody and guided the canisters up the ramp himself. Pointing to Jessie, he ordered her, "YOU, BRING THAT ONE."

Jessie recoiled in feigned shock. "Me?"

"THE DEVICE IS SIMPLE. JUST PUSH."

Asshole. She was half tempted to go through with the assassination if he was going to be like that about it. But his condescension was part of the act. He couldn't treat her *too* differently without making the laaku suspicious. Plus, her assignment had been to get close to him. This was, in essence, justifying her work up to this point.

Dutifully, Jessie guided the food processor up the ramp.

"WE WILL RETURN SOON," Grosstet called down, then retracted the ramp with Jessie inside.

"I'll be fine," Jessie shouted down lest anyone worry that this might be a kidnapping in progress.

Grosstet activated a haathee-sized door at the back of the shuttle's cargo compartment and strode off. "FOLLOW ME."

Jessie chased after him at a jog. "We're going to have a slight problem."

"WILL THE PROBLEM PREVENT THIS TRIP?" he asked without slowing.

They passed a few rows of chairs meant for Grosstet's people before reaching a two-seater cockpit that was open to the passengers. "No, but you need to know sooner rather than later." Grosstet settled into the right-side chair, and Jessie made an obstacle-course climb into the other.

Haathee engines had an unfamiliar, resonant hum, hallmark of a technology she didn't comprehend. The frequency rose until Grosstet waved a hand through a holographic field, launching them off the rooftop. "AH. SPACE. MY OLD FRIEND."

"You a spacer at heart?"

"SPACER? ONE WHO GOES TO SPACE?"

"One who lives there. Born and raised there. Either or both, really. I'm one."

"YES. THAT IS ME. I HAVE MORE TIME IN SPACE THAN YOUR WHOLE LIFE."

Jessie smirked. "I'm not that old."

"IF YOU BECOME OLD, IT WILL NOT BE

ENOUGH, I THINK. NOW, TELL ME THIS PROBLEM."

"My brother is part of the plan. That much hasn't changed. But he... acquired some new friends that all need to leave Phabian too. A couple more humans, an azrin, vish kinah, tesud, couple ratatoret..."

"AHH, WE BECOME THE SHIP OF—" And he made a trumpeting noise too complex to mimic with human vocal cords.

"What's—?" And Jessie tried to copy the noise, fully aware of her abysmal failure.

The shuttle was smooth as wet ice as it sliced through the Phabian atmosphere headed for orbit. No hint of vibration gave clues about speed, acceleration, or weather on the other side of the hull. This was the part of the trip that should have had the comm panel barking automated systems messages, instructing pilots of approved exit vectors and orbital approvals, stuff she shunted off to text readouts to spare her ears. It didn't appear that Grosstet was aware of anyone official even trying to contact him about his vector.

"THAT WAS A HORRID ATTEMPT. SPARE YOUR TINY LUNGS AND STUBBY NOSE AND LEAVE THE TRUMPETING TO THE TRUNKS. THAT 'S' TRICK IS QUITE HELPFUL. MUCH EASIER TO SAY."

"Well, what's that thing I can't say?"

"WE WILL CALL HIM BEBEMOO TO MAKE IT EASY. BEBEMOO WAS A WATER EXPLORER. HE DISCOVERED THE THIN-MIDDLE CONTINENT. RETURNED WITH MANY ANIMALS."

"What'd he do with them?" Jessie asked, dreading the answer. The haathee was so perpetually genial that reading him was next to impossible. "Your people aren't carnivores, so..."

Grosstet turned and fixed her with a grave and solemn stare. "HE TOOK THEM ONTO HIS LAND AND BUILT THEM HOUSES. EACH UNIQUE TO THE CREATURE. LITTLE ONES FOR LITTLE ANIMALS. TALL ONES FOR FLYING ANIMALS. CUT PONDS FOR FISH."

"We call that a zoo."

Grosstet shook his head emphatically, waving those tusks with unintentional menace. "NO. I HAVE SEEN A ZOO. HE MADE A TOWN. HE MADE CLOTHES. STREETS. SIGNS. HE TRIED TO TEACH THEM WORDS. BEBEMOO WAS QUITE NOT GOOD IN THE MIND."

"So, about Eric's friends...?"

"NO. TOO MUCH A RISK. I KNOW YOU A LITTLE. YOU EARN A BROTHER. BROTHER DOES NOT EARN MORE."

Jessie gritted her teeth in frustration because she more than half agreed with the haathee. Eric had taken an already delicate operation and thrown a box of spare parts into the machinery. But she also knew the challenge of getting Eric to go back on a promise he'd made to someone out of the goodness of his heart.

This called for yet another change to the plan.

She'd already reached Plan D before settling on an explosion and frame job of Martian extremists to get out of becoming Section 74's patsy. Now, Plan E was out the airlock, and she was scrambling to salvage an F.

Much as she knew the urgency of coming up with a way to separate Eric from his coterie, Grosstet's ship was growing in her view. A gentle, deep blue giant lazed amid a security escort of Phabian Navy ships that kept curious souls at a safe distance. The glassteel dome Jessie had seen on newsfeeds and intelligence reports was hidden as they approached from the underside.

Grosstet fiddled with his control console. A portal in the underbelly irised open as a series of curved, triangular sections retracted. Jessie's heart raced with the prospect of being the first human to gaze upon the wonders hidden inside.

The shuttle rose through the opening with vast stretches of space to spare. Inside, darkness.

Below them, the aperture reversed and contracted shut.

Lights snapped on.

Morning sunlight had been reproduced with such fidelity that Jessie could practically hear birdsong. But that was where the sense of wonder ended.

Utilitarian and cluttered beyond belief, the cavernous hangar stretched in all directions around the central entrance. It was a circular kilometer of a junkyard.

"What the hell happened here?"

Grosstet shrugged as he set down the shuttle not far from the opening. "I NO LONGER HAVE A CREW, AND I LIKE COLLECTING THINGS BETTER THAN CLEANING."

Her host was already bustling, wrangling the food processor down the ramp as soon as it opened. Jessie joined in, powering up the hover-cart with the slurry and following to see where they were headed.

"Would you even notice eight more people on a ship this size?"

"I AM ONLY MOSTLY SURE MY CREW IS ALL GONE. THAT IS NOT THE ARGUMENT THAT WILL CHANGE MY THOUGHTS."

Jessie couldn't resist. She had to know. "What happened to your crew, if you don't mind me asking?"

"MIND? AN IDIOM?"

"If answering doesn't offend you. Was there ever even a crew on this ship?"

Grosstet ignored her for a time. He'd dug a cable and toolbox from amid the rubble of devices and parts whose functions she could only infer from her own AGRO-centric experience. It took several minutes of fiddling and bits of laser welding before Grosstet's cable developed a plug compatible with the food processor.

Seeing indicator lights wink on, Jessie quickly ran through a standard startup for a restaurant-grade device. Apparently, it wasn't too picky about its power source because, soon after, it was prompting for Jessie's order.

"HAH! EASY AS YOUR HUMAN PASTRIES!"

"Let me guess. There wasn't room on the ship for you, your ego, and anyone else?"

"EGO?"

"You can't tell me no one taught you that one. Ego: a person's opinion of themselves."

The haathee made a show of checking the cable and tracing it to its origin at a port in the floor. He casually brushed aside a hundred kilos worth of metal debris of questionable functionality to keep the cable's path clear. "NONE THOUGHT WE COULD MAKE IT THIS FAR. THEY WENT HOME."

"Mutiny?"

"IF THAT MEANS 'DID I STEAL THE SHIP?', NO. IT IS MINE."

"It means the crew steals the ship from its captain."

Grosstet threw back his head, laughing. "YOU HUMANS. SO MUCH THE TRICKS. THIS IS WHY I NEED YOU. NO HAATHEE CREW WOULD STEAL A SHIP. THE CAPTAIN WOULD QUIT."

"Did you quit?"

"I DID NOT HAVE TO. THERE WAS ROOM ON MY OTHER SHIPS."

"You had a fleet?"

"IF THREE IS A FLEET, YES."

Jessie hadn't stopped running through the setup of the device, answering a lot of queries with defaults, denying its every request to access the omni, and refusing all but the most essential customizations. "OK. Gonna need you to stay over there a minute."

"SO YOU MAY DO SOMETHING SNEAKY?"

"To *undo* something sneaky. I couldn't risk someone noticing me smuggling a data crystal along."

This was a cheeky little test as much as anything. Grosstet hadn't shown the first inkling of modesty in front of her, but she'd made sure he was aware of the general human and laaku opinions on the subject. Using the bulk of the food processor to shield her, Jessie drew her blaster and popped the power pack.

Let the randy giant think she was fishing it out of her underwear—or worse. She pried the power pack open, revealing a hidden compartment. It wasn't the sort of modification that would have helped her in a prolonged firefight. But the lost power capacity allowed something the size of a data crystal to ride along without undue scrutiny.

"All clear," she announced once she'd holstered the weapon again. Jessie emerged, shrugging and fidgeting like she'd just adjusted her clothing.

"THIS PLAN DISTURBS ME."

Jessie plugged the data crystal into the food processor and loaded the profile it carried. "Well, just be thankful you're a celebrity. You can find actors and politicians from a bunch of species."

"BUT IT CAN BE ANYTHING ELSE. WHY THIS FAKING?"

Jessie took a deep breath and steeled herself. Then she hit START. The food processor started humming, and somewhere inside, it began printing a gruesome meal. "Because planetside azrin get all these weird repressed hunting instincts. This is how some of them deal with it."

"BUT—" Grosstet pointed as he leaned back from the display.

"Look, I don't really get it, either. It's a carnivore thing. And it *is* illegal on Phabian. Technically, we'll be guilty of replication of sentient meat and surrogate murder."

Jessie fidgeted as the machine worked. She prayed that it didn't malfunction midway through. The two of them might have gotten it aboard and running, but they didn't have time for troubleshooting. Meanwhile, Grosstet left her to run errands elsewhere in the ship.

By the time he returned with a scanner-proof crate large enough to haul his own doppelganger back to the surface, Jessie had settled on Plan Q.

Eric needed to barely make it to the shuttle. There would be an unavoidable rush. Jessie would make the call to take off without the rest. It couldn't be Grosstet making the call, or Eric might cause trouble. Her, he'd forgive.

"I DO NOT ENVY YOU PLACING THIS."

"Gotta look like you blew up. They'll figure it out quick enough, but only after they switch from security mode to investigative mode. Rapid response is going to be trying to pick me up, not figure out if you really died."

"HOW WILL YOU DO IT?"

Jessie had worked out a discreet series of transportation services that would whisk in and out the area around Grosstet's embassy apartment and the massage parlor. She'd paid bribes, made threats, and lied her ass off at every turn to set everything in motion.

Then a twist occurred to her.

It wasn't Plan R. According to one of Dad's corny old jokes,

lens insets behind her shaders. The mission was timed to the second. From her TeleJack, she was receiving real-time surveillance on the alley behind Grosstet's massage parlor. If she hadn't scrubbed the tech herself, she'd have been paranoid that Section 74 was watching her watch, but they knew that PIS would be investigating. If anything on Jessie's person didn't look like a homemade job, a store purchase, or something she could have picked up from Red Rising, it could skew the investigation in directions that wouldn't fit the narrative.

If this *had* been a straight-up counterintelligence job, Jessie could have killed Grosstet from that monstrosity of a space station orbiting Phabian as a new moon. All it would have taken was a detonator with a stronger transmitter. But to look amateur, she'd want to trigger it from visual range.

To make sure.

Because bombs weren't real over the omni.

Jessie shook away the doubts.

This plan was solid.

She'd burned bridges with Earth by accident and Mars because she couldn't risk trusting them. Her ties with Phabian, while relatively new, would explode as surely as the bomb meant to sever any ties between the haathee and Earth.

Cameras could see her now.

No cap or shaders would hide her identity from real scrutiny. However this turned out, everyone would know it was her.

The timer counted down. Fractions melted away as the seconds blinked past. She didn't adjust her pace; everything was going so perfectly it gave her chills.

Muscle Machines Massage Market, the place that had been using Grosstet as an advertising ploy, loomed ahead. Jessie veered down an adjoining street. Down one alley. Line up with another. She gained a vantage on the door he'd be coming out.

Now, to wait.

━━━━━

Grosstet sighed as he pulled on his clothes. If he was going to be herding tiny sentient creatures, why not take the massage staff and some of their equipment? Of course, he'd made enough concessions already. Once free of this death trap of a planet, he could explore the pleasures this section of the galaxy had to offer.

"THANK YOU. SEE YOU TOMORROW." It was a lie, but a needed one. Jessie had been clear that he had to act as if he expected to be alive and living on Phabian tomorrow.

Uumik, head of his massage team, blew a sigh and waved with a lower hand. "We'll be waiting." He could tell they worked hard and that, in some way, he was improving their business by associating with them. The commercial dealings of these little creatures still made little sense to him.

Despite the fact he'd been exiting out the rear of the establishment for many days, the throngs of curious laaku had yet to camp there to glimpse him upon his departure. He couldn't help wondering whether Jessie had arranged that, too.

As soon as he was alone in the narrow street behind the building, Grosstet adjusted his belt. Everything below it was tender and sore, but nothing compared to what might happen if his shield emitter wasn't powered up properly. While he trusted Jessie to a degree, there was an amount of personal safety he simply wasn't going to leave in the hands of a human.

New to Grosstet's wardrobe was a Harvest Week hat that he'd retrieved from the ship. It was horrifically out of season, and he felt disrespectful to his people wearing it as a distraction, but it made the goggles he'd brought along with it less prominent. The laaku would just assume his change in attire was cultural, not that the goggles were to protect his eyes in case his other precautions didn't stop him getting hit with the blast.

He'd seen the technical specifications. Once converted to units he knew, he was confident that even taking the full blast, he'd only be badly wounded. These fragile creatures had grown so accustomed to killing one another that they consistently underestimated him. Half the assassination plans he'd seen thrown around among Jessie's coworkers would simply have failed to kill him, even had they worked as designed.

The alley was too short.

For the first time since conceiving this plan, Grosstet was having second thoughts.

One hundred nineteen years, and it could all end in an explosion he had helped to plan. An ignoble end to a noble life, redeemed only insomuch as no haathee would likely ever learn the details.

He saw the line up ahead, spilled on the ground. Subtle. Just a quick-food mess, but it ended in a sharp line impossible to draw freehand with condiments. He spotted the doorway. Grosstet danced a little, creating an excuse to swing his arms and trunk.

Grosstet brushed against a large, scanner-proof crate that was impossible to see. Invisible. Left by Jessie's younger sibling, an oddity among his own kind so obvious that even an outsider couldn't help but notice.

One pace more.

The blast blanked Grosstet's senses for an instant.

Stumbling, ears ringing, he stuck the end of his trunk inside his shirt to avoid breathing in the dust that now concealed him. He trod on a wet mess that he tried not to think of as, at some level, himself. He felt his way to the doorway that was his next step of the plan. Ducking through, he found himself in darkness.

His goggles glowed.

The interior of the structure resolved in green-scale. Seconds later, it inferred color and shifted to extrapolation mode.

Before going a step farther, he pulled out a bio-disintegrator, triple-checked the settings, then proceeded to clean off all residue from the blast. Maybe these laaku were clever, but they'd need to be a combination of clever and quick that he'd yet to bear witness to in the time he'd known them if they were going to catch him.

Grosstet had studied the architectural layout. The building matched in person. None of this was going to be comfortable or pleasant, but he found the floor hatch and pried it up with his fingers. Then he struggled to fit through an opening that may have been comfortably wide enough for even large humans.

Twisting. Wriggling. Squeezing. Angling his head to maneuver. Oh, vanity, thy name is Large, Glorious Tusks. Many career spacers cut theirs off or kept them shortened for just these types of tight-space navigations.

Once through, he reached up with his trunk and pulled the floor panel back into place.

He'd left a trail of scuffed footprints and microscopic DNA traces, no doubt, but given the dust and debris in the air, it wouldn't be immediately apparent.

The tunnels were structural necessities, even for haathee buildings. Fluids. Energy. What-have-you. Struts. Supports. Architectural flotsam. None of it was meant to be spacious, and Grosstet was reduced to crawling on hands and knees.

He hoped the ruse worked as Jessie promised, because otherwise, he was going to be rumpled and filthy for no good reason.

The blast was a shot of adrenaline through Jessie's veins. She relaxed her thumb on the trigger and moved her feet. This was performative now. Section 74 had made sure static security feeds would have her in their crosshairs at this point. Emergency response would be site-based first, seeking to treat the wounded. With any luck, they'd find no one to treat. Next would be a police cordon, keeping the public at bay as they worked in parallel to spread out and blanket the area looking for suspects. Section 74 had planned around that, arranging Jessie a route that would get clear of the expanding radius of control before it could encircle her.

Then there would be a forensic investigation. Section 74 hadn't done shit about that because, in their version, that pile of meat splattered across the alley behind Muscle Machines Massage Market was really Ambassador Grosstet, emissary of the haathee people.

Swift, sure strides steered Jessie along her appointed route. Blind spots were scattered along the route, one of which was meant to allow Jessie to divest herself of the detonator, keeping the authorities occupied actually investigating, metering the pace of the unraveling so that it didn't gift wrap itself suspiciously.

When Jessie passed the appointed waste reclaim, she tucked the detonator into her pocket instead.

In the next blind spot, she popped the access panel on a civic light post and retrieved a cloth bundle. She unwrapped it, slipping on the gloves and tucking away the black-market blaster she'd concealed earlier.

By the time she emerged, on camera once more, she had her gloved hands tucked into her pockets and was back on the Section 74 plan.

"Time?"

"Own a fucking chrono, why not?" Mindy snapped. It was a fair criticism. As much as the plan relied on chrononomy, Eric had never fully trusted the devices. Computers got hacked on the regular. Could scientists control time by tinkering with clocks? The timepieces seemed more like weaponry than tools.

"We-are-close-enough-to-the-appointed-meeting-time-that-we-should-start-making-our—"

Makket's instructions ceased abruptly when someone knocked at the door.

It was a familiar knock. A special knock. A conciliatory knock by someone who greatly preferred the electronic chime.

Eric silently shushed everyone, even though they'd all shut up instantly, and shooed them into the bedroom when they were already scurrying for cover.

He answered the door. "Hi!" The smile on his face was phony and scared and loud.

Trebla inclined his head casually. "Yo, sparkly-boy. Just wanted to swing by and say goodbye. Got a comm this morning cutting my vacay short."

"Oh..." Eric's face fell. He hadn't even planned on bidding his friend farewell. Trebla was just supposed to understand after the fact. They had the kind of understanding where that would have been forgivable. "Everything OK at work?"

Trebla shrugged. "Oh, it's great." It didn't sound great, but Eric didn't contradict him. "It's not like we aren't years from a new gen of quantum processor, but office politics. Grants. Shit you wouldn't care about."

"I care."

Trebla chuckled through a weary sigh. "Yeah. I know, bud. Corporate science is just a bit more of a slog than they make it look like in the holos. Anyway, got a tram to catch if I don't want to get knocked on my performance review. Been great seeing—"

"Wanna come with us?" Eric blurted.

Trebla blinked. "With you? You and Jessie blowing ions already?" He snickered, shaking his head. "Can't you just try to fit in for a *little while*?"

"Fitting in is for people who gave up," Eric told him, quoting a younger Trebla years back.

"Yeah, but—"

"Section 74 is real they're going to kill Jessie she works for them and they're making her a patsy for killing the haathee ambassador who's actually a really great guy and his ship doesn't have other people on it and has more tech than a million Phabians and if you come with us you'll probably never have to file a report or have a performance review ever again and frankly I miss having you around and I think this could end up being the most fun adventure you could ever hope for."

"ERIC!" several voices cried out from the bedroom.

"Who the hell are—?"

"They're friends. New friends, not lifelong friends like you. Forget the goodbye. Come with us."

Evander stepped forward. "You can't just—"

Eric whirled on him. "I can anything." He turned back to Trebla. "If you don't want to come, I can make you forget you stopped by. You won't get in any trouble. But you're not a planetsider. You're a spacer. Like me."

"Mom will kill me."

Eric grinned. "She'll only kill you if you're in. So, you're in?"

Trebla shut his eyes. He took one deep breath. Then he opened them again. "Yeah. Fuck it. One life. One big adventure. Right? I feel like this huge weight just lifted off my—"

Mindy shouldered past them. "Sort your feels later. We got to sod off and meet up, else we're all fucked."

With a wave of his hands that blew out every light in the building, Eric's entourage transformed. Moments later, a work crew of laaku in Phabian Power Services uniforms exited the building, grumbling about how letting wizards live around so many tech devices was a recipe for overtime.

Jessie knew the route. She'd studied it. Memorized it. Amended it...

This was one of the blind spots. A planned malfunction and a delayed work order combined for a stretch of side streets where Jessie was not only among the few pedestrians but completely in the clear from official surveillance. Anyone sane was heeding the omni blasts from Phabian Investigative Services warning civilians to remain indoors and allow them to control the situation.

Anyone with a sleek, black hover with jet-tinted windows could slide in and out with one fugitive, and hardly anyone would even notice.

On cue, Section 74's evacuation hover glided to a blazing halt just a few meters from her.

A rear door opened. A laaku held it open and motioned frantically with a lower hand for her to hurry.

Jessie climbed in, trying not to make eye contact.

The door slammed shut.

"We've got a problem." She pointed out the windshield, past the pilot, drawing the attention of both him and the agent who'd held the door.

"What kind of—"

Two quick squeezes. Both of them convulsed. The maximum stun setting was overkill for an adult laaku, and neither of the Section 74 agents was particularly large.

Leaning past, Jessie tapped with gloved fingers. The hover's console was *highly* skeptical of her inputs, requiring a manufacturing test override code before it would accept that, yes, this was a perfectly fine plan. She set a timer. Before hitting START, she ditched her hat and wig, retrieved an athletic training mask that simulated high altitude oxygen levels—a feature she'd disabled, leaving it merely a mask for her lower face—and stripped out of her coveralls. She hesitated to part with her blaster, but this wasn't a plan she could shoot her way out of if it went wrong.

Jessie tapped the start, and before the ten seconds expired, she closed the door with her outside the hover.

The vehicle rocketed off. Soon, it would arrive back at the secret Section 74 headquarters and miss the entrance while still accelerating.

Fitting her new persona, Jessie jogged away from the scene. Wearing a TeleJack, sports bra, shader lenses, the mask, and some leggings she'd worn under her coveralls, she had the physique to convincingly pull off the exercise nut who'd ignore civic warnings to get her run in. She'd even opted out of the work boots of her approved cover to wear sneakers that worked for both identities.

As she headed through another of the blind zones in Phabian's patchwork security coverage of the refugee zone, she waited for someone to find her.

She just hoped it was the right someone.

———

"What was that?" Trebla demanded. His voice had changed the least of all of them. As a honey-furred laaku woman with light brown eyes, he and Eric were twinsies. It was a private joke, since this was the appearance of one of Trebla's first crushes growing up. She'd been a teacher at one of the schools they'd ended up in briefly during an extended planetside stay.

"Explosion," Eric replied, keeping his response clipped. He and Trebla were supporting Uom'pe between them, with the tesud's lower hands only touching down every few paces. While they were all disguised in laaku bodies, the tesud had trouble conceiving of a walking pace faster than that of her natural form. "Good sign. Plan working."

"Hey!" someone on the street shouted to them. "My whole building is out!"

"Right then," Mindy called back, voice different but still sounding very human. "Soon's we got off break, we'll be right on it."

"How-can. You-people-speak. Bleh. With-these-slow. Mouths-that-stumble? Bleh. I'm-tired-and. Winded-already."

One of the laaku squawked awkwardly. Eric struggled to make sense of the noises.

"He said. Talk less. More running."

Calling what they were doing running might have been an exaggeration. More like phys ed class laps, where no one wants to be there, and the speed is set by whatever will stop the teacher from yelling.

The whole district looked bigger from laaku height. Feet with fingers required a little more thought to coordinate. Just looking like a laaku didn't grant a lifetime's experience operating four fully dexterous limbs. It reminded Eric of his first time wearing flip-flops, paranoid both about losing the minimalist footwear and tripping over them.

"How much farther?" Drascz demanded. Since she'd

seemed self-conscious about being perceived as prey, Eric had given her the burliest of the disguises and an intimidating scar across her laaku face.

"Just over. There." Eric pointed, then needed to renew his grip on Uom'pe. Only a couple blocks left.

The more Eric thought about it, the easier his part of this whole plan seemed. All he had to do was transform fewer than a dozen fugitives into other species or appearances and walk a few blocks. Sure, not everyone could do the same, but he could never have done Jessie's or Grosstet's part in the plan. This was a piece of cake.

Karma eavesdropped on those silent conversations.

"Sssstop. Who are you? There issss no work crew authorizzzzed in thissss area."

"Shit," Trebla said under his breath.

Eric calmly set Uom'pe down. She wasn't infirm, just slow. He took the lead as spokesman for the group. "There are outages in the area. We undo things like that. We're workers. Workers who undo outages."

The ssentuadi wore an inquisitor's uniform, which basically amounted to a torso-size leg warmer, the way Eric figured it. He tried not to stare as he sought to figure out how the garments didn't slide up or down during routine wear.

"You sssseem ssstrange." The ssentuadi flicked the air with their tongue, muttering in the sibilant native language of their species about everything tasting like magic around here lately.

Eric softly hissed an agreement, trying to gain trust through commiseration.

That perked the ssentuadi up immediately. "It'ssss you!"

"Crap."

Eric snapped his fingers. The ssentuadi vanished.

"What did you do to him?" Trebla demanded, aghast.

"Not now. Sometime later, when things calm down."

Trebla grabbed Eric before he could hoist one of Uom'pe's arms up over his shoulder to set out again. "No. I need you to tell me you didn't just vaporize that guy. What. Did. You. DO?"

"Thought cha knew this blighter. 'Not now' 's just what happened. Sometime later's when that scaly narco's gonna pop back up."

"I wasn't too specific. I was in a hurry. I'd have taken the time to put him on my calendar if I knew I was going to have to explain this much."

"LOOK!" Makket shouted.

Sharp eyes were often more a function of attention, Jessie had always told him, since they had roughly equivalent eyesight, medically speaking, and she always noticed things he didn't. With everyone using standard laaku eyes, the ratatoret had been the one watching the skies as they ran and blundered into inquisitors.

Silver and misshapen, the haathee version of a hover gleamed as it dove toward them. Eric flung out his hands for the group to halt.

Pedestrians, already scarce, scattered at the sight.

It was time.

Eric let go of the magic surrounding him and his fellow evacuees, just in case Jessie or Grosstet wouldn't recognize the large grouping of laaku in energy company uniforms.

The shuttle looked ready to crash when it slowed deftly to perch on the plaza paving stones. Eric relaxed his cringe and quickly waved as the ramp lowered and Jessie pinwheeled an arm to usher them all inside.

Despite being last, it was the fastest Uom'pe had moved since Eric met her.

They were airborne before the ramp closed. Gravity aboard the shuttle was exemplary, giving no hint of acceleration as the ground fell away beneath them. Everyone shuffled into the open passenger compartment, but Eric's progress was halted by a hug that should have been less surprising than it turned out to be.

"Idiot," Jessie whispered in his ear.

Eric knew what she meant. They weren't supposed to drop the disguises until everyone was aboard. It should have looked like a group of locals were part of a conspiracy. "I was worried about magicking inside the ship."

"Grosstet said it was plenty rugged."

All well for *him* to say. For all Eric knew, haathee wizards were like stuunji, firm but gentle and highly predictable. He wasn't willing to risk their escape on *his* magic being tame enough to safely use without harming a strange ship. Especially not since he'd been a one-man tech outage since this whole stressful endeavor had started. A water pipe had burst under the plaza a suspiciously short time after that inquisitor got to see his own future.

"JESSICA! I REQUIRE YOUR AID!"

The panic in Jessie's eyes told the story before she said a word. "Strap in. This can't be good."

With that, she raced toward the cockpit.

━━━

Jessie dodged around Eric's gaggle of misfits as they tried to figure out how to use cargo strapping and rock-climbing rope purchased from a sporting goods store to secure themselves to the giant seats. Ideally, she would have helped them navigate the oversized furniture, but Grosstet pleading for help had a note of panic that she couldn't ignore. She vaulted up to the copilot's seat as soon as humanly possible.

"What's our status?"

Grosstet pointed to a console whose haathee script and inscrutable interface clarified nothing. "WE ARE THE OBJECT OF ANGER. MANY COMMS. TOO MANY FOR ME." The haathee tapped something, and laaku voices flooded in.

"*Unregistered vessel, return to the surface immediately...*"

"*...violation of orbital control edict 447.8.62—*"

"*...subject to fines and impoundment—*"

"*...charged with theft of advanced technology—*"

"Enough," Jessie snapped. "What can you do? You said this thing was fast."

"FAST, YES. MANY, NO. TOO MANY AND SOME ALREADY AHEAD OF US. AND THEY ARE SHOOTING NOW."

Jessie felt nothing, but among the bizarre and inexplicable indicators in the haathee's arsenal of holographic dashboard displays, it was easy to pick out the shield diagram and the repeated flashes of impacts against their shuttle's defenses. "How long can we hold out?"

It wasn't *that* far to the main vessel, not at the rate this thing was traveling. But Grosstet hadn't been fucking around when he said they were already ahead of him. No straight-line path was going to get them to Grosstet's flagship without a collision; maybe not even a dozen collisions. The haathee explorer swerved and veered like the shuttle was an atmospheric racer. But outnumbered and without a contingency plan for this level of resistance, it was only a matter of time until disaster.

"LONGER IF YOU FLY."

"ME?" Jessie shouted in disbelief. Grosstet swiped a hand through his controls, and the holographic zone he'd been twiddling his fingers within slid over to Jessie's side of the cockpit. "I can barely reach! I have no idea how to fly this thing!"

"IT IS EASY. AND YOU CANNOT DO MY PART."

Jessie shoved her hands into the translucent holograph. Instantly, the ship lurched forward with a burst of acceleration that caused oncoming Phabian security vessels to scatter. She felt tiny vibrations when they took hits from incoming blaster fire.

In the absence of training, Jessie hoped for it to interpret her zooming and twisting motions.

A clatter from the corner tore her attention from their pursuit for a fraction of a second. Grosstet hoisted a device she'd seen in the closet of his ambassadorial quarters. So heavy she could barely have toppled it, the haathee grabbed it in one hand and rested it on a shoulder as he headed toward the cargo hold. "What are you doing!?"

"THE SHIP IS UNARMED. I AM NOT."

Jessie's breath quickened.

This was a mistake.

Her new xeno buddy was a madman.

She'd gambled her life and Eric's and several strangers'—and Trebla's for reasons she hoped to live long enough to get answers about—on a ludicrous plan that was unraveling with every twist.

Plan T: Eric could do some funny stuff with gravity. If they all leapt from the shuttle and stayed together, he might be able to land them with a feather's touch instead of bursting like blood balloons on impact.

Plan U: Figure out how to halt the shuttle. Surrender. Accept some consequences.

Plan V: Blaze of glory.

Wind howled behind them as the cargo ramp opened.

Twisting in her seat, she watched the haathee take up a wide stance and aim the giant blaster tilted sideways, tusks angled out of the way so he could sight down the barrel. The shots made a noise like wind chimes. Its payload wasn't plasma but something crystalline and sparkling like distant starlight.

A patrol ship exploded.

Two more shots. One miss; another ship gone.

Jessie redoubled her efforts to learn the controls. Holy fuck! A Typhoon didn't pack enough firepower to core out a shielded patrol ship in one salvo. And Grosstet was a deadeye shot with it, too.

Eyes scanning the dashboard, she figured out what the haathee used for a tactical readout. Ship after ship behind them flashed and disappeared. The ones ahead scattered.

The constant nonsense chatter on voice comm cut through Jessie's attention.

"...*stand down, Exxek Squadron... disengage...*"

"...*Roger that, control...*"

"...*word in from Bantlek... escort and monitor only...*"

These weren't open comms. Jessie was listening in on the law enforcement response. This had gotten political. Someone must have realized they weren't joyriders or thieves, and high-ranking government officials were worried that Phabian might be picking a fight they weren't looking for.

The blockading ships scattered.

A clear path opened up.

If this was a trap, so be it.

Plan S was back on track.

"Grosstet! Get back up here! We're winning! Take over flying before I get us killed!"

The shuttle settled down into Grosstet's enormous hangar. Rather than park it right at the floor aperture or near the food processor they'd assembled the last time here, they ended up near one of the walls, obscured from the entrance by mountains of scrap metal and flotsam from a culture she didn't comprehend.

Jessie's absence at the rendezvous hadn't gone unnoticed. Her TeleJack was clogged with comms from anonymous IDs demanding she contact them. No doubt, a majority were Bernek of Fenzel. It was hard getting around the fact she'd just murdered the two agents who'd come to pick her up—barring medical and hover-safety miracles that she supposed weren't out of the question on Phabian. Self-defense was a tough argument to sell, both because it was the state trying to mop up their human loose end and because, technically, the stun blasts had gotten her clear of immediate threat.

Jessie's training hadn't really emphasized a "stun and hope the legal system works" philosophy.

Grosstet led the way, stopping only to offer Uom'pe a lift, carrying the elder tesud gingerly, using one forearm as a bench.

Abandoning the shuttle, they entered a spherical chamber with glass walls showing tubes running off in all directions. The floor beneath their feet was clearly some sort of conveyor, but it didn't align with anything. That changed when Grosstet fiddled with a control panel too high up for Jessie to see what inputs he'd made.

The whole ship rotated around them. One of the tubes lined up with them, and everything stopped. A gust of wind blew past as the floor whisked away with them all. They flushed down the tunnel as sporadic lights blurred into streaky lines. Seconds later, they stopped. Another spherical chamber remained still, and the ship spun again.

"Wondrous." This was the first word spoken by a vish kinah who Jessie barely recalled from Eric's apartment.

"Three-dimensional internal transport system," Trebla

confirmed. "Independent localized gravity control. Like magic controlled with scientific precision."

"How are you even involved in this?" Jessie demanded. There were going to be enough questions from the family once things all cooled down without also having to explain to Aunt Shoni how they'd inadvertently kidnapped Trebla.

"Eric invited me."

Jessie lowered her voice to a private growl. "Bullshit. You didn't ditch a prestigious job to risk your life. Eric might buy that, but I'm a more discerning shopper." They glared at one another until Trebla broke. Beneath them, the floor shifted directions twice more.

"Fine. I had some side business. Call it an investment."

"Syndicates."

"Not that sordid. Venture capitalists. Private project."

"Corporate espionage."

Trebla huffed. "They were closing in from both sides. This vacation was the first time in months I hadn't been afraid for my life."

Jessie scoffed. "You picked the wrong escape pod, cuz."

"BLOODY BRILLIANT!" Mindy exclaimed. Jessie broke her attention away from her wayward cousin just in time to witness the bridge of the haathee vessel. It looked remarkably similar to many Earth Navy capital ships, except it was scaled twofold. Everything gleamed as if it was the only part of the ship the haathee explorer maintained with any diligence.

Grosstet was already marching over to the captain's chair, where he settled in like a king on his throne. He tapped with his trunk at one of the ubiquitous holographic control panels. "PLEASE REMAIN QUIET. ALL OF YOU EXCEPT JESSIE. JESSICA, STAND BY MY KNEE."

It wasn't the most dignified of positions, essentially looking like an ottoman for a single foot, waiting to be crushed when he discovered her unsuited to the job. The others scrambled for cover, which was available at any of the duty stations.

With a few twitches of a surprisingly dexterous trunk, holographic haathee officers appeared and populated the command crew. "PLAY THE GAME."

"What game are you—?"

Another holograph appeared, this time of a laaku in a Phabian Navy admiral's uniform. She was gray-furred with just enough brown peeking through to suggest she didn't dye it. "Ambassador Grosstet, explain yourself."

"I WAS WARNED OF A PLOT TO KILL ME. GAINING MY SAFETY WAS A PRIORITY BEFORE INFORMING ANYONE WHO MAY HAVE BEEN A PART OF THE PLOT."

"Ambassador, please let me assure you, the League of Independent Planets bears you no ill intent. If there was a plot in place, it was clearly the work of rogue elements. If *that one* is the source of your information, please be aware that Jessica Judith Ramsey is a criminal involved with Martian rebel extremists."

"SHE IS NOT. I DISCOVERED THE PLOT. SHE AIDED MY ESCAPE. I ALSO SEE THE SHIPS YOU ARE BRINGING TO HERD ME LIKE PACK CARNIVORES."

The admiral seemed nonplussed. "We will escort you while you remain in League space."

"That won't be necessary," Jessie chimed in.

"Jessica Judith Ramsey is wanted for questioning in an active murder investigation. We will not let your ship out of our sights while she is aboard."

Grosstet looked down as if studying her, weighing her heart like that Egyptian god whose name she could never remember from Uncle Enzio's old stories. "IF I GIVE HER TO YOU, I MAY GO?"

"Yes."

Jessie tensed. This hadn't been part of her planned contingencies.

Grosstet laughed. "PREDATORS. ALL ALIKE. SEPARATE THE HERD TO KILL ONE BY ONE. MAYBE YOU CAN TAKE JESSICA BY FORCE. MAYBE YOU CANNOT. BUT YOU MAY NOT TAKE HER WITHOUT IT." Grosstet flicked his trunk, and the admiral's image vanished.

"Thanks."

"IT WAS THE ONLY THING TO DO."

What a culture he must have come from, where protecting one another was second nature. Where they'd learned deceit from their enemies. Where they picked sides and stuck together with reckless confidence.

Unless that was just Grosstet. Hard to say, only having met one of his kind.

"Can we ditch them? How deep can this thing get in the astral?"

"ASTRAL. I KEEP HEARING THIS. BUT NO ONE HAS EXPLAINED IT WELL."

Eric emerged from his hiding place beneath a one-tusked haathee holograph who went about his imaginary duties oblivious to the happenings on the bridge. He cleared his throat. "Allow me to sum it up."

Though Jessie had a layman's understanding of astral travel, Eric expounded and stretched his metaphors on a medieval rack. But Grosstet nodded along.

"WE HAVE NOTHING LIKE THAT."

"What?" Jessie demanded.

"Hold up," Mindy interrupted. "We on a boat with no paddle?"

Jessie didn't let the interruption knock her out of orbit. "How'd you cross the galaxy?"

"REAL SPACE, THE WAY ERIC SAYS IT. WE ARE FAST, BUT NOT AS FAST AS HE DESCRIBES ASTRAL."

"Shit. You're telling me we're slower than your average intrasystem rental hover?"

"IT WOULD SEEM SO."

"They all still following us?"

"YES. WE NEED A WAY TO FLEE THEM. WE DO NOT HAVE SUPPLIES FOR ALL TIME."

"Kill a few," Evander suggested. "You have them outgunned. Use that."

"We'd be at war with the Legion of Independent Planets. Earth and Mars will already hate us."

The azrin, Drascz spoke up. "There are regions beyond. We could flee all known species."

"Fucking coward," Mindy shot back.

The in-tik squawked. Eric translated. "He wants to be let off if we're leaving League space."

This was getting out of hand. Phabian Navy was going to float along at what they hoped was a safe distance, dropping into astral with impunity to both evade them and keep contact at once.

"Eric. Can you move a ship this big into astral space?"

Eric shrugged. "Don't see why not."

Jessie pointed to her brother, speaking directly to Grosstet, ignoring the squabbles. "What if Eric can do the astral travel himself? No machine. Just a wizard."

"That's bloody daft!"

"Is-that-an-advisable-course-of-action-Eric-seems-like-a-nice-enough-wizard-but-to-place-us-in-his-hands-when-he-has-repeatedly-shown-a-limited-understanding-of-the-side-effects-of—"

"*SQUAWK!*"

"Let's all be reasonable here. We can negotiate with Phabian Navy. A show of force, combined with—"

"I. Believe. In. You." Uom'pe laid a hand on Eric's cheek. "YOU CAN DO THIS?"

Eric nodded. "Yeah. There's a lot of science in here, but I don't think there's enough to stop me." He shot a quick glare a Trebla, a reminder that he was the most advanced scientist aboard. Jessie didn't know if their childhood bowling games carried any weight these days, but their laaku cousin *used* to be able to interfere with his magic.

"Go on and ask him how many wizards ain't never been heard from, trying it."

"DO I NEED TO ASK?"

"No," Eric replied. "It's a lot. But I won't kill us."

"Cheeky fucking promise. Knows he won't be 'live to get 'is told-ya-sos if'n he—"

"Stuff it," Jessie snapped. "Eric. I trust you. If we want to get away from the law—and whatever political shitstorm is brewing out there—we need to go astral."

"How deep?"

Jessie cringed at the question because not only had she known it was coming, but she didn't have a real answer. "Deeper than they can give chase."

"OK. I'll err on the low side."

"I AM VERY CURIOUS TO SEE HOW THIS WOR—R—R—R—RKS."

Jessie felt like she'd been flushed down a high-suction waste reclaim. People screamed in several of their native languages. A trumpet sounded from the haathee. Every technological system aboard went dead.

When everyone's stomachs had settled back into place, a still silence pervaded. The only illumination was a pale red glow that emanated from outside the ship.

"Welcome to astral space."

Grosstet crept toward the forward window of his vessel. "YOU SAID IT WOULD BE GRAY."

"It gets colorful down deep. If you look close, there are still little gray swirlies." He pointed, not that the aim of a finger was any help.

"That's black," Jessie countered.

"Charcoal."

"THE MAGIC HAS DAMAGED THE SHIP. HOW DO WE REPAIR IT? IF WE MUST FIGHT, WE ARE HELPLESS."

"It'll come to its senses on its own," Eric assured everyone. "If it comes back at all. Sometimes things don't. But that's the exception. Usually, only big magic or really incompetent wizards ruin things permanently."

In the ominous red, the other passengers exchanged worried looks.

"But don't worry. We're down so deep, no one will ever find us."

****

Ready for more *Black Ocean: Passage of Time?*
Grab Mission 4, Time and Punishment

BACK MATTER

BOOKS BY J. S. MORIN

Black Ocean

Black Ocean is a vivid 26th century story universe where science and magic coexist—sort of.

Black Ocean: Galaxy Outlaws

Black Ocean: Galaxy Outlaws is a fast-paced fantasy space opera series about the small crew of the *Mobius* trying to squeeze out a living. If you love fantasy and sci-fi, and still lament over the cancellation of *Firefly*, *Black Ocean: Galaxy Outlaws* is the series for you.

Read about the *Black Ocean: Galaxy Outlaws* series and discover where to buy at: galaxyoutlawsmissions.com

Black Ocean: Astral Prime

Co-written with author M.A. Larkin, *Black Ocean: Astral Prime* hearkens back to location-based space sci-fi classics like *Babylon 5* and *Star Trek: Deep Space Nine*. *Astral Prime* builds on the rich *Black Ocean* universe, introducing a colorful cast of characters for new and returning readers alike. Come along for the ride as a minor outpost in the middle of nowhere becomes a key point of interstellar conflict.

Read about the *Black Ocean: Astral Prime* series and discover where to buy at: astralprimemissions.com

Black Ocean: Mercy for Hire

Black Ocean: Mercy for Hire follows the exploits of a pair of do-gooder bounty hunters who care more about saving the day than securing a payday. The series builds on the rich *Black Ocean* universe, centering on a couple of fan-favorites and introducing a colorful cast for new and returning readers alike. Fans of vigilante justice and heroes who exemplify the word will love this series.

Read about *Black Ocean: Mercy for Hire* and discover where to buy at: mercyforhiremissions.com

Black Ocean: Mirth & Mayhem

Black Ocean: Mirth & Mayhem delves into the origins of two vagabonds making their living among the stars. Mort is a wizard coming to grips with a life on the run and estrangement from the comforts and respect he had on Earth. Brad is an impressionable youth, too clever for his—or anyone's—good. And Chuck Ramsey is the mold that Brad's trying to break out of, which is harder than he could ever have dreamed.

Read about *Black Ocean: Mirth & Mayhem* and discover where to buy at: mirthandmayhemmissions.com

Black Ocean: Passage of Time

The year was 2586. A few minutes later, it was 2591. Caught up in a time travel snafu, Eric and Jessie Ramsey become fugitives from the people who want answers as to how they did it—and where their loyalties lie in the galactic war that broke out in their absence.

Read about *Black Ocean: Passage of Time* and discover where to buy at: passageoftimemissions.com

Twinborn Chronicles

The *Twinborn Chronicles* is an epic fantasy saga based on the possibility that our dreams offer us a glimpse into the life of another – another who can get the same glimpse into our world. Read about the *Twinborn Chronicles* and discover where to buy at: twinbornchronicles.com

Twinborn Chronicles: Awakening

Experience the journey of mundane scribe Kyrus Hinterdale who discovers what it means to be Twinborn—and the dangers of getting caught using magic in a world that thinks it exists only in children's stories.

Twinborn Chronicles: War of 3 Worlds

Then continue on into the world of Korr, where the Mad Tinker and his daughter try to save the humans from the oppressive race of Kuduks. When their war spills over into both Tellurak and Veydrus, what alliances will they need to forge to make sure the right side wins?

Project Transhuman

Project Transhuman brings genetic engineering into a post-apocalyptic Earth, 1000 years aliens obliterated all life.

These days, even the humans are built by robots.

Charlie7 is the oldest robot alive. He's seen everything from the fall of mankind at the hands of alien invaders to the rebuilding of a living world from the algae up. But what he hasn't seen in over a thousand years is a healthy, intelligent human. When Eve stumbles into his life, the old robot finally has something worth coming out of retirement for: someone to protect.

Read about all of the *Project Transhuman* books and discover where to buy at: projecttranshuman.com

Sins of Angels

Co-written with author M.A. Larkin, *Sins of Angels* is an epic space opera series set 3000 years after the fall of Earth. With the scope of *Dune* and the adventurous spirit of *Indiana Jones*, it delivers a conflict that spans galaxies and rests on the spirit of brave researcher Professor Rachel Jordan. Follow the complete saga, and watch as the fate of our species hangs in the balance.

Read about *Sins of Angels* and discover where to buy at: sinsofangelsbooks.com

Shadowblood Heir

Shadowblood Heir explores what would happen if the writer of your favorite epic fantasy TV show died before the show ended—and the show was responsible. If you wonder what it would be like if an epic fantasy world invaded our world, this urban fantasy story might give you that glimpse.

Read about *Shadowblood Heir* and discover where to buy at: shadowbloodheir.com

EMAIL INSIDERS

You made it to the end! Maybe you're just persistent, but hopefully that means you enjoyed the book. But this is just the end of one story. If you'd like reading my books, there are always more on the way!

Perks of being an Email Insider include:

- Notification of book releases (often with discounts)
- Inside track on beta reading
- Advance review copies (ARCs)
- Access to Inside Exclusive bonus extras and giveaways
- Best of my blog about fantasy, science fiction, and the art of worldbuilding

Sign up for the my Email Insiders list at: jsmorin.com/updates

ABOUT THE AUTHOR

I am a creator of worlds and a destroyer of words. As a fantasy writer, my works range from traditional epics to futuristic fantasy with starships. I have worked as an unpaid Little League pitcher, a cashier, a student library aide, a factory grunt, a cubicle drone, and an engineer—there is some overlap in the last two.

Through it all, though, I was always a storyteller. Eventually I started writing books based on the stray stories in my head, and people kept telling me to write more of them. Now, that's all I do for a living.

I enjoy strategy, worldbuilding, and the fantasy author's privilege to make up words. I am a gamer, a joker, and a thinker of sideways thoughts. But I don't dance, can't sing, and my best artistic efforts fall short of your average notebook doodle. When you read my books, you are seeing me at my best.

My ultimate goal is to be both clever and right at the same time. I have it on good authority that I have yet to achieve it.

Connect with me online
jsmorin.com